AVENUE CARS

CHRIS SPECK

Copyright © 2023 Chris Speck
Flat City Press
Hull 2023
All rights reserved.
Front cover by Syd Young

ISBN-13: 978-1-7393308-1-1

'You got to look after yourself first, fool. How else you gonna look after anyone else?'
BA Baracus - The A Team

CHAPTER ONE
Bev

The sign on the front of Avenue Cars was last painted properly in 1992 when Our Dave took over the business. He bought good quality paint from Derek at Chanterlands Ave Hardware shop down the road, and did a proper job, that's why the sign still looks good more than twenty years later. Unlike the last owner, Our Dave knows that businesses and relationships require upkeep. A few months ago, he cleaned and painted the windows inside and out, and refitted the wire mesh across the glass at the front of his taxi office. There's no need for a new sign, people like the old one. This is Chanterlands Avenue, Hull. People like things the way they have always been.

You'd like Our Dave. Most people do, that's why he's Our Dave. If you need a hand with something and he's got time, he'll help, especially if it's a woodwork job. In Steve's Cycles next door, the counter is rock solid with a clever hatch that flips up. All the pews in the Catholic Church of St Vincent De Paul on Queens Road are fixed and will last for at least the next fifty years, you can lean on the steady false walls between the tanning rooms at Ultra Smile, and the sign above Dundee Street chip shop doesn't fall off when it's windy. Before Our Dave ran the taxi office here, he was a joiner out of the council and before that he served as an apprentice fitting ships and trawlers on Hessle Road. Our Dave knows that doing the job properly will make your life easier. He might be sixty or he might be sixty-five, or fifty-eight, but he's slim, with strong arms, big hands and a bald head, a light grey beard and a smile for anyone. He listens as well as he talks, wears shirts with the sleeves rolled up and spends less time than you would have thought at his allotment for the amount of food it produces.

Our Dave opens the front door of the taxi office and the little shiny bell above jingles. It's early Friday afternoon. There aren't a lot of customers these days. He holds it open and a woman with a dark green headscarf walks in behind him. There are benches of solid wood around the outside of the waiting office and a locked door, beside is a square mesh where customers can tell the receptionist where they're going. A woman with bleached blonde hair and black eyeliner looks out from behind it.

"Let us in," says Our Dave.

"Why don't you come in the back way like you normally do?" asks the blonde. Nobody uses the front door anymore, for the taxi business is not what it used to be. Our Dave has only got three drivers including himself, four with the woman who follows behind him. There are hardly any walk-ins and all his jobs come from the council. It's a miracle that he's still open.

"I just wanted to show Dilva here the front door."

There's the sound of a bolt sliding across, and then the yale key turning in the double lock, it opens and the white-haired blonde looks up at Dave from inside. This is Bev. She is five foot one but fierce for her size, slim and with big blue eyes that have crows' feet because she is just into her fifties. She's wearing an off the shoulder summer blouse that shows the top of her shoulders and cocks her head at the woman with the green headscarf who follows Our Dave into the office.

"Who's this?" she asks. Our Dave turns and smiles at her from his six foot two. He has a light tan from spending so much time on his allotment behind Newland Ave.

"She's going to be a new driver." Bev narrows her eyes and looks the woman up and down. She has brown skin with high cheekbones and smooth mahogany eyes. The green headscarf is not tight to her head and only just covers her long black hair.

"She'll not be taking over any of my runs," snaps Bev. Dave holds up his hand as if to stop her.

"This is Dilva, she's a Kurdish lass. She'll be doing a few new trips that I've got lined up, starting next week." The

Kurdish woman looks at Bev with a fixed, neutral stare and Bev glares back. Like two big cats in the jungle, neither can work out if the other is a friend, but neither will give way for the time being.

"We'll I don't like her, Dave, she can stay out of my way." It's unnecessarily rude. This is Bev all over. She comes from a long line of Hull women who, at least in public, are unable to show any emotion except strength or sarcasm.

"You've not been asked to like her," says Our Dave, he knows Bev is worried more than angry, and will be nervous of someone new. Dilva steps through the door behind and into Avenue Cars. It's dim and a bit run down with an odd collection of shabby seats, an old armchair in the corner, and the smell of damp masked by air freshener. Our Dave turns round in front of her.

"Here we are," he says.

Across Hull and East Yorkshire there are a range of special children who for many reasons attend schools far away from where they live. They need taxis to get them there. Some of the kids are too wild, some are too disabled, the council foots the bill and Our Dave makes sure that he has the lowest tender for the job. That's how he survives. Bev is the perfect driver for the kids who are too troublesome to go to a normal school - those who survive abuse and come from breaking and broken backgrounds because, she is almost the same as they are. The blonde woman moves into the little galley kitchen just behind the driver's office as Dave steps in. Another woman with short black hair stands up to present herself. She has a big toothy smile and kind eyes as she holds out her hand to shake.

"This is Liz," says Dave. "I know it's a lot to take in," he adds. It's not really. This is the second of Our Dave's daytime drivers, Liz, from Newcastle originally but the accent has gone to leave clean middle English.

"Pleased to meet you," she says as Dilva shakes her hand.

Liz is nearly as tall as Our Dave and she is almost the complete opposite of Bev, friendly, emotionally aware and warm, at least in public.

"Marhaba," adds Liz. It's a Muslim greeting. Liz has used it before on her trips around the UK and on her gap year from university in the nineties when she went to Morocco.

"Thank you," says Dilva. Her English is heavy with accent.

"Liz here drives the big taxi for the disabled kids," says Our Dave. Just like Bev knows how to handle the wayward, Liz has infinite patience with those who, for one reason or another, walk or move in a different way. Back in Newcastle, Liz spent her childhood looking after her mother in a wheelchair, without issues, a woman who taught her humility, grace, manners, how to love books, and how to smile through it all.

"Listen up then, you two," says Our Dave. "Dilva here has her UK driving licence and she's been in Hull for two years, so she knows where everything is. She'll be taking some of the foreign kids to school and back, you know, there's kids from Iran, Iraq and whatnot and Dilva can speak their language."

"Can't she speak for herself?" asks Bev, now standing at the door of the galley kitchen with a mug in her hand.

"Her English is a bit shit," answers Our Dave.

"Well, what's she been playing at, for two years?" asks Bev. It's not that simple, Bev knows this. She is being cruel. Dilva eyes her from under the dark green headscarf, she could easily strike back at this woman with something, but she'll wait. She needs this job, just like they all do. Sometimes you can say more with less.

"I'm just here to drive and get paid." Dilva's accent has strong r sounds but her energy is good, she means what she says as she fixes Bev with her mahogany eyes. It's a good answer, a shrinking feeble response would have made Bev hate her. These two are more the same than either may think.

"We're all here for the money, love," says Bev. Dilva holds her level stare.

5

"I need to speak to you in the back," says Our Dave and he nods to Bev. He indicates to the galley kitchen where she stands. She backs off and he follows her into the little room to the backdoor almost, where they can't be heard. As soon as they are out of earshot, Bev begins:

"She'll not last, none of them do." She isn't discriminating against Dilva for who she is or where she's from, it's just that she's a new driver, and some of Our Dave's choices are poor. He likes to give people a chance. "She'll cock it up as soon as it gets rough," continues Bev. "Has she got kids?"

"Yeah, two."

"Little kids?"

"Aye. She's married."

"The first time one of them has a bad cough, she'll call in with some sob story, you'll see."

"I'm not here to talk about Dilva, Bev, she's my problem."

"She'll be my problem though, if anything goes wrong. I'll have to do twice the work when she screws it up." This is not true. Our Dave is never further than a phone call and ten minutes' drive from the allotments behind Newland Avenue or his house down the road.

"I need a favour," he asks. If it were anyone else, Bev would say no, straight away, without thought, but this is Our Dave. It was Our Dave who gave Bev a chance many years ago when she was not as strong as she is now. He gave her a chance when nobody else would. "I need you to do the last drop off for me."

"I can't," she answers. "I've got Chloe." This is Bev's daughter.

"She's eighteen, Bev. I need to see a man about a dog. You'll be finished by half four, and back home for your tea at five." Bev huffs.

"Just this once then," she says. She owes Dave. "Where will you be?"

"Like I told you, I need to see a man about a dog."

6

"I hope it's another woman," she says.

"My Hazel would throttle me."

Once upon a time the taxi business lived on things called Friday and Saturday night. Thursday could be ok too. Sunday was a belter if there was a bank holiday after it. The long bars that used to be rammed in the eighties and nineties are not gone, just empty. There are still lines of punters at taxi ranks and still fights, and people staggering along the city streets but it's not like it used to be. Taxi driving has changed too. Back in those days there were offices all over the city, 721721, 334334, Borough Cars, Humber Cabs and more, but now they're all gone, swallowed up by technology on a mobile phone that does not need a taxi office anymore, and automated computer systems that can organise pickups and payments. Avenue Cars has changed. Once the bottom really fell out of the business, Our Dave dropped all the cars from after 6 o'clock so he could focus on the council stuff and now, the only drivers he has left are the girls from the dayshift. Our Dave will be swallowed up by the big companies as well in time to come.

Bev makes Dave's last run of the day. It's up to the special school, the one where they send kids that other places exclude. She turns at a school sign and drives her big, sleek white Mercedes through the gates that have been unlocked now it's time to go home. Ordinarily they are padlocked shut, not just so the kids can't get out, but so that others can't get in. It doesn't look much like a school with a green, trendy sign above the door that reads 'The Zone', but this is the place for kids who can't behave at all. The young people here swear, spit, fight, throw chairs, poo themselves, smash windows, stab each other with pencils and everything else you can think of. Kids like this are very useful in the wrong hands, with a few bags of gear and a new mobile phone, any forward-thinking dealer can turn them into a money-making unit, that's why

Avenue Cars picks them up from right outside and drops them home with their families. Whatever you might think, these teens don't all come from broken or poor homes. Like this one - there's a blond kid in a blazer with his shirt untucked. This is James Boyce, not Jim or Jimmy or Jay, but James. The arrogant snarl comes from his father who inherited a fortune from the trawler businesses his family ran until the eighties. He lives in a mansion in the suburbs where the front drives are bigger than most people's whole houses. He walks out into the empty car park. Bev's met him before and he's got an attitude. She pushes the button and her window slides down.

"Taxi for James?" she asks. He gives a half snarl from his spotty face.

"Where the fuck's Our Dave?" he asks.

"Shagging your mam," she answers. There's really no reply to this, so the lad opens the back door and gets in. Bev has driven a taxi for the last 14 years, there is nothing you can say to her that she does not have a quick reply for, so it's unwise to take her on verbally. Those who are foolish think it makes her heartless, but this is not true, you can hurt Bev easily, but you will never see the damage done. She drives the Mercedes up and out of the gates and onto the main road, out of Anlaby towards the north of town where this rich kid lives. He's quiet. He's been picked up by Bev before and there is a sense of comradery with her, he gets the feeling that she is as much, if not more, of a nutter than he is, and so there's nothing to prove - he's among his kind.

"How was today?" asks Bev.

"It was shit," says the kid.

"Teachers are all arseholes," says Bev and means it. James nods. "They always have been. That's why they do their job. Imagine wanting power over kids?" There was a time when Bev trained to be a teaching assistant and so, she can say this with the certainty of experience.

The car moves on through the traffic of the late afternoon,

most going the other way into town. They drive past the semis, where the houses have leafy front gardens with unnecessarily big cars parked outside, carved ornate front doors and statues standing guard on stone walls. Bev brings the car to a halt outside a very large white house with a double garage next to it, and a monkey puzzle tree stretching into the sky. This is Packman Lane, Kirkella, opposite the golf club, and while it is not nearly the most expensive house in the East Riding, its grandeur is impressive. Bev looks through the windscreen at the two bay trees in marble pots flanking the front door and wrinkles her nose in disgust at how much money the family must have. She turns back to this kid, James, who is sitting there looking out the window.

"This is it," says Bev. "You're home."

"Can we just drive around a bit?" he asks.

"No," she answers.

"I don't wanna go back in there."

"That's not my problem," says Bev. "I'm at work."

"My mum's left. This time for good," he says. If Bev had shown him a crumb of compassion, he would not be telling her this. "It's my dad. He can't cook. He's a tosser and he shouts at me."

"Shout back," says Bev.

"I do."

"You're going to have to get out and face up to it. You can't sit here all day."

"I'm not getting out," says James. Bev unclips her seatbelt and turns around. She has had this kind of passenger before, the one who needs someone to talk to. As a new and inexperienced driver, she used to listen, but not these days. She's not a trained therapist.

"How does Our Dave usually get you out?"

"He drives me round a bit."

"That's not it," she says. The kid looks out the window at his house that is supposed to make him feel proud.

9

"He talks to me."

"What about?"

"He tells me about his allotment." Bev frowns.

"I'm not Our Dave," she answers, "but I am his friend. Now, if you want him to pick you up next week, then you'll have to get out of this car, and sharp. If you don't, I'll ask him to let me pick you up every day for the next month. How would you like that?" Her voice is not nasty. In Bev, there is someone you can reckon with, if she is ever cruel then it is usually because she is being honest. She could give this lad a little talk about how lucky he is to live in a big house with a rich father, but that's all shit, and he won't be able to see it anyway.

James gets out with his face looking like it's just been slapped. Bev winds down the window to shout at him as he walks up his drive.

"See you Monday," she calls. He responds by giving her the middle finger.

In times past, Bev lived in the leafy suburbs like this, on Tranby Avenue, Hessle, with her husband and daughter, Chloe, when she was a baby. It wasn't quite as swanky but they had a big, three bedroomed semi with posh neighbours and a front garden. Her husband ran a factory making electrical parts. It was all very civilized. Bev was doing a teaching assistant course at the college and volunteering at the primary school. She was going to help there, once she got qualified, but things did not play out. Her husband kept at the spliffs and the vodka of a weekend. He wasn't a bad man, but once out of his mind he was something different altogether. He pushed her down the stairs and held her against the wall, then threw her into the kitchen sink. She blamed herself because that was what her dad was like. When it all got too much, Bev moved back to the poorer part of town where the folk are friendlier and they call the police if they hear you screaming in the back garden at night.

She turns the corner at the bottom of the hill and drives, smooth and slow past the big houses. On the right-hand side there's a big pub with whitewashed stone walls and standing just on the street outside is a man in a dark suit waving Bev's car down like she's a normal taxi. She doesn't have to stop because legally, she's not allowed to pick him up. He's in the way and frantic, so she slows to a halt next to him and winds down the passenger side window. He looks in with a red face.

"Can you take me to Brough station?" he asks. He has short hair and a crisp white shirt under a grey suit jacket, Bev can instantly smell the whiff of his perfume and notices the silver cufflinks as he holds his hand to his face in worry. "I need to get there as quickly as possible to get my train."

"I'm not a black cab, mate," she says. "I can't pick you up."

"No, but I mean, I'm in distress, a taxi has to pick someone up if they're in distress." Bev shakes her head.

"I can't do it, have you tried another company?"

"I won't make it there in time. I'm in a pickle and it's vital that I get on that train to London." He leans into the window and flares his nostrils. "I'll give you fifty quid," he whispers.

"A hundred," says Bev.

"I don't have that much cash."

"You can pay by card."

"I need to be there before four forty-five."

"Get in."

She turns the Mercedes around in the car park behind the pub and makes a quick job of it. The man in the grey suit with the short hair has put his briefcase in the back and buckles up his seatbelt. He looks at his watch. They will make it if she drives well.

"The money is for you to get me there in time," he says in a matter-of-fact way. "This will be the most expensive taxi I've ever taken."

"I'm breaking the law," says Bev. "I could lose my licence and my job. I'm still doing you a favour." Bev is not greedy, but if a man is willing to pay fifty quid without thinking, he is willing to pay a hundred.

She takes off up the way she came, once more past the golf course and the big houses towards the new roundabout and the flat, open fields. She drives quickly because she wants this job done and the man out of her car as soon as possible. She won't get stopped by the police of course, but if she did, then it would not be good for her, or Our Dave. She glances at the man in the suit in the passenger seat, experience tells her to check out who she is riding with. He smells of mid-range aftershave and his suit trousers are pressed, his fingernails are rounded and clipped, and his skin is lightly tanned. His hands rest calmly on his lap and he checks his watch often. It's expensive but not flashy. This is a man who is professional at whatever he does, the clothes are functional rather than posh and designed to make him fit in to whatever corporate world he comes from.

There's just one thing.

The second knuckle on his right hand is much bigger than the others, like it has been broken, and Bev only notices this because she has seen the same injury before on one of the night drivers who was a boxer in his spare time. His wrists are strong and wiry. She turns her head and sees that he is wearing dark glasses and notices that his neck is squat and toned. The car speeds down the new tarmac, out of the city and across pretty, swaying fields of long grass and corn in the late afternoon summer sun. She looks at the digital clock on the dashboard.

"We'll make it there in time." The speedo climbs. He does not respond but keeps his eyes firmly on the road in front of them, then checks his watch.

"Could you slow down a little?" he asks.

"I thought you wanted to get there?"

12

"Yes, but in one piece." The man in the grey suit is suddenly level and not as frantic as he seemed five minutes previous. From his jacket pocket he pulls out a pair of blue surgeons' gloves, new, and he proceeds, as Bev levels the car out at 70, to put them on.

"What are you doing?" she asks. He snaps one of the gloves over his wrist and begins on the second, working his fingers into the plastic. Bev's hands grip the wheel tight. Perhaps he never believed he would pay her that hundred quid. He does not answer. The deserted road is smooth and the car makes barely any noise as it keeps a steady pace towards Brough some three miles away. The man's voice is calm and measured.

"As you turn round this next corner, you'll see a lay-by on the right. I want you to pull into it."

"You what?" she asks. It's the standard expression of confusion in this city even though his orders are clear and steady. She's not sure how to respond. "Are you off your head?" He does not turn to look at her but keeps on staring at the road in front of them through his dark glasses. She feels fear suddenly in her neck and it rushes up into her face. There is something very cold about this man who sits next to her in the passenger seat, like this has been planned already, like the reason he looked at his watch was to make sure they would be where they had to be at a certain time.

There's the electricity of danger in the air and she gets an iron taste in her mouth. Bev has felt this before, many times, it is the crackle of the world around her before something terrible happens. She felt it as the doctor cleared his throat before he told her about her sister's cancer, it was in the look in her father's eyes that Christmas Eve, in the grunt of the drunk who was about to hold her up against the wall of the toilets in a central Hull pub. She felt it just before her ex-husband dragged her along the kitchen floor to the back door. Bev knows this feeling. Just like all those times before, Bev does not crumple or break – she doesn't know how.

"I haven't got any money," she says, "and I'm in my fifties, I'm like a dried-up prune." The words are as she has learned, make humour to fight the terror, as if to ward off the evil. The man next to her does not alter his expression. "I've had two kids and if I don't dye my hair every three weeks it goes grey. Are you gonna kidnap me?" Again, the man does not change his position. The hands, now in blue surgical gloves rest on his lap. "I'll stop and you can take the car right now," she says. "You can have my wallet and my phone as well. What do you want with me?" The last sentence is the only honest part of anything she has said. She is fifty-one and not at all past it, she dyes her hair every two weeks.

"Keep your eyes on the road please, Miss" he says. A rash of fear creeps up her neck, over her jawline and into her cheeks, it is the red burning of pure terror. Her heart quickens. She glances once more at the man in the passenger seat next to her. He has not moved.

"What do you want with me?" she repeats. There is no answer. Outside the Mercedes wheels grip the new tarmac, she sees the lay-by up ahead. Bev applies the brake and shifts down a gear as she indicates left as ordered. Her palms are hot. "Like I said, I've got nothing," she repeats. "I won't go with you, I'll fight and kick, and there are people who know where I am, and they'll look for me too." She turns in, and still the man does not respond to her but keeps the same, terrible countenance looking dead ahead. She regrets her greed.

This is a quiet country lane that connects one roundabout to another and then onto the big main road out of Hull towards Leeds.

"This will be a lot easier on you if you cooperate," says the man. He unclips his belt with one of his hands in a blue surgeon's glove. His movements are smooth and unhurried.

Bev grips the wheel, and the eyeliner makes her frightened blue eyes seem bigger. She senses the world around her;

outside the deserted lay-by, the swallows dipping low over the cornfields, the rush of the traffic on the main road some half a mile off, the dark glasses of the man she picked up in Kirkella who lied and said he needed to get a train at four forty-five.

This is the moment, again. Bev did not let the doctor finish telling her that her sister was going to die, and she did not let her father beat her that Christmas Eve in 1983 and, in the toilets of Hull Cheese, she smashed a pint pot onto the man's head. After her ex-husband had dragged her across the new tiles on the kitchen floor, she knocked him out with a fire extinguisher.

She's not going to let this happen.

In a well-practiced motion, she grabs the gear stick and slips it into reverse, hits the accelerator and the white Mercedes lurches backwards. The man in the surgical gloves with the grey suit reaches out to her, but the speed of the car throws him forward and his temple slams against the shiny dashboard with a dull, empty thud. Lines of blood vessels under his skull rupture with the impact and, as she hits the brake and the wheels skid below them, he falls back into the seat, unconscious, or dead. Bev switches gears and the car bursts forward out into the empty country road. In her rear-view mirror, she sees the lay-by as it fades into the distance. She glances down at the body of the man in the grey suit, his glasses have fallen off and he is slumped against the white leather seat. Bev's heart is pounding hard as she expects him to lurch up, but his eyes are open as he stares at her, blank and dumb.

She drives over the new tarmac between the cornfields towards the little town of Brough, and the Mercedes engine hums. Bev's hands are tight on the steering wheel. She pushes the man in the grey suit down by his face and he slips into the footwell onto his knees like he's a soft toy, his eyes look upward blankly on a head that lolls back and then forward. She's not one for going to pieces in a situation isn't Bev but there's a driveway on the right where she has dropped Chloe off before at the scout base. She parks the Merc in the corner of the gravel car park, picks up the phone and scrolls down her list of contacts till she gets to the only person who can help.

Our Dave.

It's twenty minutes later. Bev waits in the car in the traffic at the railway crossing. The barriers are down and she is stuck behind a single decker bus. She must be patient; Our Dave has explained that she has to drive back to the office as calm as you like. She needs a wee. Her mouth is dry and her hands shiver on the wheel. One of her legs jiggles up and down in worry. The man who got into her car at Kirkella saying he had a train to catch is dead, and she covered him with a blanket out of the boot before she hit town. If she sees a police car, Bev thinks she might have an actual heart attack. The drive here has been slow and full of traffic, cyclists and red lights, temporary cones and daft drivers. Her stomach grumbles under her.

The train rattles by and the barriers lift, she follows the bus and then turns left past the graveyard and into Chanterlands Avenue. She passes Steve's cycles opposite Dundee Street chip shop which has a queue outside because it is Friday, then turns left and then left again into the car park behind Avenue Cars. She parks next to the red van with a rusted side and presses the brake button before she gets out. It's still light, about six o'clock.

At the back door leaning on the windowsill is Our Dave. He walks towards her and his face is serious.

"Are you ok, Bev?" he asks. She looks pale and her lips are pencil thin against her grey face as he approaches. She makes her way to the boot of the car and waits for Our Dave to come closer. Her mouth is almost too dry to speak.

"I've killed a man," she says. "He hit his head on the

16

dashboard and he's in the front seat." Our Dave does not respond straight away. He examines her face and her eyes, sees how she is shaking slightly in her pale off the shoulder summer top. He glances to the car and then behind to make sure nobody has heard even though the little car park is deserted.

"Did anyone see?" he asks.

"No," she says. She just wants this ordeal over with and she has nowhere else to go but Our Dave. "I didn't want the police involved," she says. "You know what would happen to a woman with my record. They'd say I killed him."

"Did you kill him?" he asks.

"It was an accident, and it was self-defense." Our Dave nods. "Will you help me, Our Dave?" she asks. He nods again.

"You'll have to give me the keys," he says. She passes him the black fob that will allow him to start the car.

"What will you do?"

"I'll think of something," says Our Dave. She steps back as he walks past her and opens the driver's door then gets in. He starts the ignition, backs the white Mercedes up and turns it round in the little car park.

Our Dave gives her a wave through the window as he drives through the gates, and then, he is gone. Just like that. Bev looks at the car park around her and sees the weeds growing under the big red van with the wheels replaced by bricks, she hears the beeps from the traffic along Chanterlands Ave and the squawking of the crows in the trees behind her. She puts her hand to her face and gently shudders.

She ought not to worry too much.

Our Dave has done this sort of thing before.

It's first light on Chanterlands Ave and the dawn is just breaking in the pale sky. It's Saturday. Few souls are awake this early. A battered dog-fox trots out of the bushes from the cemetery. He crouches low against the wall with his almond shaped eyes orange as he inspects the still street ahead. Above him is the red 'Ansdell's' brewery advert, it was whitewashed over in the seventies but it's been painted back on now because people like the nostalgia. The dog-fox keeps low as he goes round the corner and moves north down Chants Ave. He scurries past Wharncliffe Street and the mobility shop, stops at Dundee Street chip shop to smell the ground – there are sometimes chip wrappers here. It has been a good night on the cemetery, but now it's time for the dog-fox to slink back to his hole down the tenfoot on Newstead Street. He has a big scar down his nose – like this road, the dog-fox has seen better days but he is still up for the game. Chanterlands Ave is much like any other main street in any other northern English town. The houses were built before cars were a thing so parking is dreadful. There's a supermarket where items are too expensive, one where they are ridiculously expensive and another where the food is just about to go out of date so it's cheap. There's a pub - people stand out the front to smoke, takeaway shops of all styles, hairdressers a plenty, a closed down off-licence, a florist, a butcher and zebras crossings where cars don't always stop. From the cemetery at one end, you travel a mile or so to a blue iron railway bridge next to the petrol garage with the automatic car wash and a rookery in the tall trees opposite. There's a pushbike shop at one end where you can buy a decent cycle for seventy quid and a pushbike shop at the other end where you can buy a road bike for seven grand. The chippie near the railway bridge is good but at Dundee Fisheries, a queue forms before it opens at five on a Friday afternoon.

The dog-fox sniffs the air as the morning sun shines down on his sleek fur. He bounces up the ten foot and into the bushes, then through into someone's overgrown garden. He'll not be back out till the evening.

The street is waking up.

Lee Harrison sits at the desk at the end of his bed already and sharpens one of his pencils. He's halfway through his latest novel and he writes best in the mornings before the kids wake up. His head goes down and he begins to work, three sentences in, he is already lost in a world where airships fill the sky. On Westbourne Ave, Jess and her daughter, Robyn, tap the glass of the fish tank they scrubbed clean the day before, they have a new axolotl and her name is Pebbles – they are awake early because Pebbles is still on her back in the tank and looks like she is dead. In Steve's Cycles, Steve himself is in the back with a bike up on the stand and the TV blaring, it's a seventies gangster film with Michael Caine, he works on a derailleur that lesser bike mechanics would throw away. The pigeons under the iron bridge at one end coo beside the rivets, Derek of Chants DIY sweeps up the shavings from his wood turner. Mr Heron, who lives opposite the library, has put his shoes on already and is about to get his coat when his wife comes down in her dressing gown with a mild look of anger. He has the onset of dementia, yesterday he packed his suitcase to go on holiday. At the butcher's next to the supermarket, Jonny parks up his wagon. He was at the wholesalers at four o'clock this morning. Yesterday his teenage daughter told him she was about to go vegan. He thought about her arguments the whole journey.

The buildings here are as varied as the people. There's an avenue off one side with five bedroomed houses where university lecturers and their artist husbands tend to big gardens; and across the same street, on another avenue are two up two down terraces crammed with big families struggling to get by. You can get a tattoo done about halfway down, but Lisa won't do it if she thinks it will look shit, and near the garage you can get a tattoo that will look shit however hard Chris tries. You can buy a wedding dress and find somewhere to live. At the medical centre you can have your tonsils looked at. You can borrow a book from the library, or just sit in one of the chairs to keep warm. You can learn to sing, get a massage, get a taxi, have your computer fixed. You can buy slimming pills from Sandra at the tanning studio, get a prescription opposite, there's a post office, a pet shop and at the counselling studio at the bottom, Kim will listen to your problems in the morning and her sister, Kate, runs yoga from four till eight in the big waiting room.

This is Chants Ave.

The dog-fox slinks down into his hole under an overgrown conifer and wraps his long tail around him as he goes to sleep. No one will bother him here. This is a Christmas Tree that Archie Lamplugh planted in the garden five years ago rather than trying to cram it into his recycling bin. It's got out of hand all these years later at ten foot tall. The dog-fox will be safe under the wide and dark branches because nothing exciting happens on Chanterlands Avenue.

Nothing but the everyday.

CHAPTER TWO
Liz

It's Saturday morning. This is Liz, the tall bohemian lass who drives for Our Dave. She parks her light blue Berlingo van behind Avenue Cars, checks her phone from her handbag and then gets out. It's sunny and she smiles as she puts on her dark glasses. Liz is in a good mood because she's at work. She's wearing her denim dungarees and has a white boho headband in her dark hair.

Twenty minutes previous, she was at her childminder's house on Beverley Road, where she dropped her son Joel and until then, she had been morose and distracted. He is partly the reason she works for Our Dave at Avenue Cars, and in some ways, her son is the reason for everything she has done since he was born.

Seven years ago, Liz had a partner, a blond lad with a wide chest and good teeth who taught at the university, and they were happy. They rented a flat in one of the big houses on Princes Avenue with the high ceilings and damp problems, and their neighbours were artists and environmentalists like they were. Liz rode her bike to her teaching assistant job in the suburbs and all was well, until she fell pregnant with their son who was to be Joel. It's a delicate matter. They did not notice there was anything different about him for at least eight months and then, the blond lad with his well-kept teeth took a job in London. It wasn't as simple as that of course. A man like him would never leave because there was something wrong with his son, but the job was too good to miss, an academic opportunity too great not to go for. When Joel was nine months old the doctor told Liz, in the medical centre off the roundabout on Westbourne Ave, that he would most likely never walk and never learn, he would need care all his life and may never speak either. Liz was numb. The blond man said he would visit of course, and help with money too, if she needed it. He calls rarely and has not been up here for a long time. It's a year or more since Liz has heard from him. Joel is now eight.

Liz opens the back door to Avenue Cars and steps inside out of the sunshine, she takes off her dark glasses as she passes through the little kitchen. There is Our Dave, behind his laptop and it seems out of place to see him with such a machine. He looks up and smiles.

"Thanks for coming in," he says as he sits back from the screen. He looks pale in the darkness of the taxi office. Liz smiles because that's what she always does, especially when Joel is being looked after by someone else. She has come into the office an hour before to sign some papers.

"I'm happy to help. You look tired. Was it a busy night?" Liz can read how people feel through their faces and is not afraid to ask. She won't have any idea what Our Dave actually had to do last night.

"Kind of," says Our Dave. This is not a taxi office like it used to be. There is no late-night shift anymore, but Dave was busy doing an unpleasant job which he will not tell Liz about. "Hazel was up with a nasty cough." This is his long-standing wife, who Our Dave mentions whenever he can, and who Liz has never met.

"You have to look after yourself at your age," says Liz as she sits down opposite. Dave slides two documents over the table at her and she turns them right way up and reads down the page. It's a contract from the council, much the same as the ones that Avenue Cars has for the kids they ship across the city on a daily basis. Liz takes in the details.

"It's a new bit of business," explains Our Dave. "It came in yesterday and I wanted you to read it before I told them yes or no. It's your cab we'll have to use, if you take the job. They need you there this morning if you can do it."

"He's disabled," she confirms.

"He'll need a cab big enough for his chair." Liz nods. She has the special taxi already, a Berlingo she uses for the kids with wheelchairs. She needs it for her Joel anyway.

"Looks fine to me," she says.

"It's Saturday mornings, Liz. I thought you might like some time with your lad. I wasn't sure you'd want to work." Our Dave's eyes are earnest as he examines the tall woman who sits in front of him. Liz does not require time to think.

"I need the money, Our Dave," she says. Saturday is the worst day for Liz. She has nothing to do but look after Joel. She can take him to the park, the cinema, to visit friends, out to the beach up at Hornsea or swimming in Albert Ave baths, but the time is long and lonely with him. It makes her feel guilty that she hates it. Liz is used to political discussion and poetry, music and cooking, and the boy she has produced coos at flashing lights and dribbles his ice cream down his bib. Dave rubs the front of his bald head with his hands that are big from a lifetime of sawing through bits of wood and screwing in nails.

"Are you sure?"

"Yes," says Liz.

"If you look in the document it says he's difficult."

"I'm difficult," says Liz as she smiles. This is not true at all. At least to the outside world, Liz is the least difficult woman you could hope to meet.

"You're to take him out to see his brother, a pickup from Greenwood Ave to Withernsea." Greenwood Ave is the North Hull Estate where the houses are squeezed in like sardines in a can, Withernsea is on the moody coast of the North Sea, windswept, treeless, and lonely on grey days.

"Why a Saturday and not any other day of the week?" she asks.

"I dunno, maybe it's the only time his brother can see him" says Our Dave. "It's worth a few quid." Liz nods. It's a long drive from the North Hull Estate to Withernsea down busy main roads with lots of traffic lights. Each trip will take her a while.

"I'll do it, Our Dave. I need the money." She doesn't need the money at all. He nods.

"It'll be every Saturday till Christmas." That's more than four months away. "I'll sort the paperwork then, and you can pick him up today." She stands and gives her big toothy smile. Our Dave looks up at her and wrinkles his brow as he does.

"You don't have to take this job, Liz. We can turn it down. It won't affect the business and, if you're struggling, I'm here."

"I need to stand on my own two feet, Our Dave. I need to do this for me and my Joel."

"He'll be ready now. I'll telephone him."

"Great," once again she gives a big, beaming smile. Our Dave watches her walk back through the office and out the back door to the little car park. He rubs his big carpenter's hand across his face. There's something not quite right with her and he can't work it out. He will though, in time, and if he can find out what it is, he'll fix it. Our Dave can fix anything.

Liz drives out of Chants Ave and to the address on the letter that Dave gave her, it's Greenwood Ave and is not too far. It has a reputation for being a tough part of town, with roaming gangs of kids on pushbikes, drugs and run-down boxing clubs, pubs full of piss heads and little terraced houses. Swap the word tough for poor and this is a better definition.

Liz's Berlingo cab is a big roomy affair with high ceilings, the seats from the back have been removed and this is where Joel will usually sit. Two ramps come down from the boot, and you can push a wheelchair up so it locks in place when it's inside. Liz has got good at it. The taxi was expensive, but without it she wouldn't be able to take Joel anywhere.

When she gets to Endike Lane, she pulls up opposite a line of maisonette bungalows for the elderly, she's dropped people here before. She checks the address again, gets out of her car and walks to the front door of number seven where she rings the bell. There's no immediate answer, but she can wait, she's being paid so she has all the patience in the world. She looks up and then down Endike Lane, and when the door opens, she smiles at a man in a wheelchair. He has a square head and a grimace under thin combed over hair and big eighties style glasses. He's in his early fifties or older. Liz has read from the notes that he has MS. She can see it in his legs that are bent to one side in his chair and those claw-like hands that grip his wheels.

"Are you my new driver?" he asks. There is no warmth in his face or voice.

"Yes, I'm Liz," she answers. She holds out her hand for him to shake.

"You're paid to drive," he answers. Liz steps back. He's right. She's been a taxi driver for a while, and it suits her if she just has to ignore him. He wheels himself to the car and round the back where Liz opens up, and the ramps slide out. She pushes him inside and clicks the wheels of his chair into place. The man grunts with the effort of it all. Liz gets into the front and picks up the paperwork.

"I need to check that you're Dennis," she says. She should have done this already, but his demeanor has flustered her.

"That's me," he answers.

"I'm to take you to your brother's out at Withernsea."

"Let's get on with it then," he answers. Liz turns to look at the man she has in her cab. He stares past her through the windscreen and she starts the engine. If he's trying to make her feel uneasy, she doesn't care. This is easy money.

They taxi out down the back streets, across Beverley Road over the iron bridge on the river Hull and towards the east. They pass the best and worst of the city as they go, lads in caps pulled by pit bulls on chains, an old man struggling at his walking stick, the Kurdish woman with a patterned headscarf chatting into her mobile, the smell of the cocoa factory, a kid on an electric scooter with a cig hanging out his mouth. As they go, the landscape around them changes, on the stop start traffic of Holderness Road, Liz watches as the Saturday shoppers walking on the pavement get fewer and fewer, the shops become terraced houses, then bigger terraced houses, then red bricked semis, and, as they break out past the village of Bilton, they are free of the city. Here, there are dog walkers with fluffy Labradors and posh trainers, detached houses and finally, the open fields of East Yorkshire corn and yellow rape swaying in the wind under the big and blue sky. Liz glances back at the passenger as he looks through the window and out at the landscape around them, he smells of old sweat masked by deodorant.

"I used to live out here," he says.

"How come you moved to the city?" asks Liz. He said he didn't want to talk, but everyone likes to be asked questions and Liz is good at making them, even though she doesn't really want to know the answer.

"I'm not talking to you," says the man, "I'm just talking to myself." She glances up at him through the rear-view mirror and sees his eyes staring out over the fields. He is difficult.

"I grew up in a village near here, I did, me and two brothers and my mum and old boy. I used to ride my bike all over these roads, right along the coast, fishing and visiting. If I knew then what I know now..." His voice has the quality of a whine.

Liz does not respond. She could answer with something lighthearted but it's clear that Dennis is not a chatty man. She follows the satnav on the car dashboard and goes left towards Tunstall and their destination. There's a static caravan park here with rows of white, corrugated iron rectangles next to each other. Some have been tarted up with little gardens and signs indicating that they are permanent residences, others look like prisoner of war dwellings from the 1940s. She pulls up outside one of these. The sky is blue and the deserted caravan park looks out of place in the wild rural landscape. Liz gets out and the door to the caravan opposite opens. A tall man walks to greet her, he has the same miserable expression as his brother with a flabby body and the same style glasses. He looks as unfriendly as her passenger.

"I'll need an hour with him," he says.

"Sure," she answers.

In an hour she has Dennis back in her light blue Berlingo and despite having time with his brother, he wears much the same expression. It's been a sweet hour for Liz – she parked the taxi a mile away and walked along the sandy, deserted beach with the tiny cliffs that are crumbling away into the sea. She breathed in fresh air and smoked a secret roll-up, thought about freedom and how, if he could walk like a normal boy, she would bring Joel here and watch him run into the water and splash around, how she would get a sheepdog, and they would walk all the way to Hornsea with it. Back in Hull, she will have to pick up Joel and her life will no longer be her own, for she will be a slave to his. They drive down the country lanes towards Bilton and the busy city road that will take Dennis home.

"You always carry wheelchairs, do you?" he asks.

"Are you talking now?"

"There's nothing else to do."

"My son's in a wheelchair." Dennis scoffs at this.

"Poor bastard," he whispers. Liz eyes him through the rear-view mirror.

"He's not a poor bastard," she says.

"What kind of life does he have?"

"He's not as miserable as you," says Liz.

"How old is he?"

"Eight."

"What's wrong with him?"

"Cerebral palsy." Dennis openly laughs. As someone with problems, he believes he has the right to mock others, as if his despair gives him currency and even wisdom.

"Can he talk?"

"He has cognitive difficulties." Dennis shakes his head. "What can he do?"

"He can feel," she answers. Dennis scoffs again.

"You mean he can't do anything?" It's an ugly thought. Dennis comes from a world of sensationalized newspapers and angry sound bites, he has not been trained to look at an issue from all sides. Liz doesn't answer.

"He's a vegetable, is he?" asks Dennis. Liz just drives. From his superior viewpoint, he launches into a mini speech and his voice has a dull and dreary quality. "What's the point in a kid like that being in the world? I mean what can he do? He'll just sit there sucking up money and time. Don't you think it might be better if we let nature take its course?" Liz has heard this before from more eloquent people, seen it online as well, thought it herself and there are many arguments against it. She wonders whether she should engage the man in discussion, but he will have his own issues. She's a driver, as Our Dave has often told her and she doesn't need to change people's minds, just drive the car.

"He might as well do himself in," says Dennis. They are approaching Holderness Road and Liz feels some of the city rise within her.

"You might as well do yourself in." Liz is never rude to anyone, but this grim, miserable man has touched upon a vein of truth that makes her angry. He does not respond as she would have hoped.

"Well, it's all in hand," he whispers over her shoulder. "Our kid's setting it all up for me. Once a week, I'm to go out to his caravan and he gives me a puff of something from his gas tank – and every time it makes me weaker and weaker and slower and slower until one night, I'll go in my sleep and nobody will know how or why, and they'll put it down to me having that disease or something else. My brother can have my dad's war medals and I'll be gone and the world will be a better place without me." The man's tone is cold, as if bitterness has

28

eaten him completely. Liz looks at him in the rear-view mirror once more, sees his piggy eyes staring at her under the eighties style wide glasses. They are back in Hull proper and the streets are thickening up with traffic as the houses shrink from detached to semis and then to terraces once more.

"Why don't I drive you out to the Humber Bridge and you can throw yourself off there?" asks Liz over her shoulder. There's some of the cruel honesty of this city in her voice. "It'd save me having to drive you every Saturday." She looks again in the rear-view mirror; Dennis smiles back at her. This is the kind of talk he understands.

They drive back along Endike Lane and Liz pulls up outside Dennis's maisonette bungalow. She gets out, opens the boot and pulls him and his wheelchair onto the pavement. Since their little chat ten minutes previous, the man has been quiet.

"How many puffs will you have to take of his gas?" asks Liz as he wheels himself away on those claw-like hands.

"Dunno, six or seven at most," he answers. He turns the chair to look at her. "It's my way out of here."

"What kind of gas is it?"

"I'll find out for you. Do you want some?" Liz takes a deep breath. People round here say things they don't mean all the time, especially for fun.

"Maybe," she answers.

CHAPTER THREE
Dilva

It's Monday morning, before school. Dilva kneels beside Aziz in the front room of their shabby terrace on Westbourne Ave. He is meant to be her husband. His thin body doesn't fill the whole armchair and his eyes are watery above a wide moustache. Aziz is breathless with his skin tight against his cheek bones. She checks his pulse. It's weak. He's ill.

"I'll put you on the nebulizer," she says. He manages a smile. It has been a long night with him. She made up chicken wraps and Kurdish scones for the kids the evening before and they are in the kitchen stuffing them into their school bags. "I have to go to work," she says. "I'll be back at twelve." He reaches out and touches her hand.

"Thank you," he says. Aziz is not her husband, nor her family, not even a cousin. He's from a long way north of where Dilva comes from, a village near Zahko, they don't speak the same dialect even. It was convenient for them to travel together when they left Kurdistan, for him and for her, and, after all this time, he might as well be her husband, albeit one that she has grown to love in a brotherly way.

"You just go out and do what you need to do," he croaks. She has never asked him his story, and he has never asked her about hers. It's as if, the place they both came from is a dream, of course they celebrate Kurdish new year Nawroz, they talk of the people they knew, the music they love, but never of bad times, or the troubles they lived through. Perhaps Aziz here didn't experience the same things that Dilva did, he's not a soldier and as far as she knows, he was a farmer. He looks pale and his skin has a yellow tinge.

"You'll call me if you need me," she explains. He nods. "It's Monday, and I can't be late."

It's just past eight. Dilva walks from her house along Westbourne Ave. She lives in one of the terraces right at the end that don't have car parking spaces so Aziz parks his car wherever he can. He doesn't drive or deliver pizzas anymore because there's something very wrong with his lungs. Until she and the children arrived in Turkey, Dilva had never seen him before. They had an arrangement and now that he's sick, it's Dilva that has to go out and make enough money for him and the two kids. They aren't really hers either, Mohammed is ten and he's her brother, the little one, Layla is her cousin, she's seven. There are a lot less questions if they say they are married and the children are theirs. Aziz used to smoke and the doctors say it is emphysema. She is worried for him. Dilva has to put all this out of her mind, it's her first day at the taxi office for Our Dave. She's nervous.

She gets to the end of the street and turns left at Chanterlands Ave. This has been a good road for Dilva, there are other foreigners here, some Poles and Lithuanians, and a big Syrian security guard outside the Nisa supermarket. Dilva has an education, she can read and write very well in Kurdish and Arabic and spent a year at the University of Duhok where she studied maths because she was going to be a teacher. Other things got in the way, and now there's a new path to follow, one that she did not expect to be on.

There's the suddenly loud wailing noise of an ambulance behind her approaching through the light pre rush-hour traffic. Her stomach drops and she spins her head, her nostrils flare and she steps quickly around the corner of Bengal Pride takeaway and puts her back against the wall.

Things have happened to Dilva in the past that caused her significant stress and these events linger on in her brain. Her heart begins to pump, she clenches her fists as panic washes over her, sweat begins on her skin. She knows this is just an ambulance, but the noise and the shock of hearing it triggers emotions and events from nearly three and a half thousand miles away. She cannot afford to have an episode now, she needs the job and the money and to make a life here. Our

31

Dave has given her an opportunity, but she is cruel to herself, her mind will push these panic attacks onto her when she can least deal with them. She fumbles at the handbag on her arm and unzips it, there's a bottle of water that she removes. She unscrews the cap as she shakes, takes a gulp and rests with her back against the wall breathing heavily. She closes her eyes and, for a split second, she is back there:

It is July 2017. Dilva is eighteen years old and rides in the back of a Humvee armoured truck. She is Peshmerga, the Kurdish army whose name means 'those who face death first'. She joined with her older brother in the mountain village where she is from, and they travelled to fight ISIS. She is a long way from home and at the city of Mosul where the Americans are attacking. Her brother is far north of here. Dilva has a helmet over her eyes and a dusty AK47 in her gloves. The chin strap is too tight and there are the booms of shells in front of her that are so loud they shake her chest and all the organs inside.

She has to get out of this.

She didn't fight that day to end up panicking to death.

She takes a deep breath and screws the top back on the bottle then puts it back into the bag. She has to control this. Dilva has been in real danger before, many times and there is no threat here, maybe that's why her brain allows her to shiver with fear. She walks on along the street now the ambulance is gone and tries to regain her composure, and in a few minutes, she is standing on the opposite corner to Avenue Cars. Dilva mops her head under the jet-black hair with a tissue. Our Dave told her to go in round the back.

Dilva knocks on the back door and, after a wait, Bev opens up. She scowls when she sees it's her.

"Made it on time for your first day?" is her comment. Dilva wears no expression. Bev does not intimidate her. She knows when people are a threat and when they like to talk hot air.

Our Dave appears behind Bev and opens the door further.

"Come on in then, lass," he says. Dilva follows. Bev goes back into the main office and in the little galley kitchen, Our Dave stands in front of Dilva. "Do you want a brew?" he asks. "A tea? The kettle's just boiled." Dilva shakes her head. She just wants to do the job. Our Dave has already taken copies of her driving licence and she's done the taxi driver course up at college. She'll be driving his taxi, the grey Ford Galaxy that handles like a bus.

"I can come with you if you like today," he says. "Just to be there, as support." Dilva blinks up at Our Dave with her brown eyes. He has already explained that she is needed in this office, and if she can do a good job there will be a lot more work for her. Dilva does not want to screw this up. It's not just about money.

"I can do it," she whispers. Our Dave nods.

He beckons her through into the main office and she follows. Our Dave has owned a taxi company for a long time, even before smartphone apps, and he knows that drivers need to talk to each other. Liz sits in one of the comfy chairs with her legs crossed and a mug of peppermint tea in her fingers covered in hippy rings. Bev is talking into her mobile at the desk. Her voice is clipped and sharp. She puts the phone down and looks up as Our Dave and Dilva enter. Our Dave explains:

"We come in 15 minutes early Dilva, before we go out for pick-ups. You'll be paid for this time. It gives us chance to make sure everything is as it should be." Dilva nods and Our Dave shows her an old armchair against the wall. She sits down on the edge of the battered seat with her knees together, leaning forward. Her long black hair falls over her shoulders and the dark pupils of her mahogany eyes examine the office at Avenue Cars. She sees the open laptop next to Bev, the room is not modern, but it's not dilapidated at all. She looks through the grate opposite the laptop to the waiting area for punters and sees that it's clean.

"Bev, it's a normal Monday for you," explains Our Dave. She'll collect the rich kids with behavioral problems and taxi them down to the special school, then, she'll swing round and down to Cottingham to pick up two more lads who normal schools can't or don't want to deal with.

"How was that fella on Saturday?" Our Dave asks Liz.

"A bit difficult," she answers.

"We knew that. Was he any trouble?"

"Not really." The grim man in the wheelchair gave Liz something to think about. It has kept her awake at night and she feels tired, but in another way, electrified.

"It's pick ups for you to the special school at Ganton." Liz nods. She'll deliver a lad in a wheel chair like her Joel to another special school. Our Dave turns to Dilva.

"I've explained it all to you, lass," he says. "Up to Beverley to get those Sudanese girls and bring them to school here in Hull." Dilva nods. The three ladies who are sitting down look at each other for a moment. They have nothing in common at all apart from their jobs, and the fact that they work for Our Dave. Liz stands up first with her peppermint tea in her hand, she makes her way to the galley kitchen and rinses her mug under the tap before putting it back in the cupboard, and she is off out the door. Dilva stands up next and Our Dave, unhooks a car key from the wall to pass it to her. She attempts a weak smile as she takes it.

"Good luck on your first day," he says with warmth.

"Don't crash," calls Bev as Dilva makes her way to the back door and out through it.

This leaves Bev and Our Dave inside the office. She stands up and the mask of confidence and bravado slips away, her brow frowns and her nostrils flare.

"What's happened to that bloke from Friday night?" she asks.

"It's all been taken care of."

"It's all been taken care of?" she repeats. "It's not a puddle

34

of cat piss, Our Dave."

"It's been sorted. Nobody will know what happened and it's got nothing to do with you."

"What did you do with his body?"

"I got rid of it?" She swallows as she hears this.

"Where?"

"Never you mind."

"I was there, Our Dave, I did it. If the coppers come scratching round in a few months' time, then I'll be to blame. Better that I just say what's happened and come clean."

"Too late," says Our Dave. "If you'd wanted to come clean you should have done it from the start and left me out of it. Now I've got involved we have to see it through. You don't tell anyone. It's like it never happened."

"Who was he anyway? What did he want with me?"

"It wasn't you he wanted, Bev. It was me that was meant to be driving the taxi that afternoon."

"How do you know?"

"I found something in his briefcase. Instructions. He was there for whoever was driving down Pacman Lane at that time. It's usually me."

"So you put me in danger when you asked me to do that run for you." Our Dave looks pale at this. His hand goes to his forehead in worry.

"I would never do that, not to anyone. I don't know why he'd target me. It's been years since anything has gone down."

"What do you mean?"

"It's been years since I've been mixed up in anything like this." Bev's eyes widen.

"This is a taxi office, Our Dave, on Chants Ave, in Hull, opposite Dundee Street fish shop and next door to Steve's Cycles. What would they want with you? What are you mixed up in?" His big face winces in worry. It's difficult and awkward too. He cannot explain everything to Bev because he has hidden it so well for so many years. He will have to step outside his role of benevolent gentleman for a moment.

"Leave it at that," says Our Dave. His voice is calm and without the music it usually has. He steps a little closer to her. "Please, Bev. I would never let anything happen to you. Leave it at that. You asked me to help you and I did and I will again, but I need you to keep your mouth shut. Don't go saying anything."

"What is going on?" Bev has never seen this side of him.

"I just need you to forget everything. Can you do that?"

"I'm a curious sod, Our Dave." The big man takes a breath. She is trying to make light of a serious situation. He shakes his head. Bev is suddenly aware of him standing in front of her; the smell of his aftershave, his smart pale shirt tucked into his jeans with the collar open. He is a good few feet taller than her and his blue eyes are calm but serious. She senses menace under all this, somewhere. She steps back.

"I best be on my way," she says.

"Aye," says Our Dave.

"I don't have to worry about anything do I?" she asks.

"Just as long as what happened is all forgotten," he whispers.

Once these streets felt foreign to Dilva, the smells and the sounds, the bite of the wind, the narrow eyes of the locals, the houses and roads that all look the same as each other with so many rules to follow that it made your head spin. The language was all rapid fire 'th' sounds and she was confused, but not afraid, at least. Dilva has learned a lot in the two years, so much so, that when she watches Kurdish magazine shows, the places they report on look distant and the people strange.

She follows the satnav in Our Dave's sensible grey Ford Galaxy, goes along the bypass towards the little town of Beverley. There are houses along the side of the road, small holdings, some with horses in the fields and big landrovers parked in gravel drives. Dilva turns right and goes up a small street, stops at her destination in front of a red brick detached house and gets out. There are three black teenage girls all in a row dressed in green school uniforms. They stand outside a big door. They are ready to go, and behind, there's a blonde middle-aged woman in running clothes with a wide and perfect smile under wrinkled eyes.

"Are you here to pick the girls up?" she asks.

"Yes," says Dilva as she approaches.

"I was told there'd be an Arabic speaker," says the woman.

"I speak Arabic," says Dilva. "Where are you from?" she asks the girls.

"Sudan," answers a big one. The accent is different but clear to Dilva.

"I'm here to take you to school and make sure you get there with safely, I am Dilva. Do you understand me?" she asks. The eyes on the big Sudanese girl soften as she hears this. She nods and so do the other two. The blonde lady behind them smiles wider.

"They've only been here a few weeks, they don't speak any English at all, nothing, only hello and thank you. Me and Frank have fostered for a few years but we've never had anyone from Sudan. They're as good as gold they are." The woman uses rapid-fire jargon that Dilva struggles with, so she just smiles.

"I don't know how you do it," continues the woman, "speaking all them languages, it's so clever, I mean I did French at school and I got an O level in it as well but I can't understand a thing if I go on holiday!" Dilva nods and smiles as she retreats to the grey Ford Galaxy. There's the sound of a drill from somewhere behind them, and her heart jumps at the foreign noise. She feels the fear starting in her stomach and rising up to her throat. She has to keep busy and distract herself from the fear somehow.

The three girls get into the back of the car. Dilva waves at the middle-aged woman as she turns round and drives back towards the city the way she came. The morning traffic is busy. The Sudanese teens sit in a row in the back with their seat belts over their chests and blank expressions on their smooth, calm faces. Dilva watches the traffic in front of her and, at the crossroads with the Pilot Pub on the corner, they stop, they are first at the lights with a line of cars behind. There are pedestrians waiting to cross, a woman pushing a pram, an old man with a paper under his arm and a cig in his white beard. The dull summer sun is hidden in the grey sky above, and there's the distant drone of a dance track in another car behind.

Dilva begins to drift.

With nothing to concentrate on, her mind starts to wander off to places that it should not go, places that she knows will damage her if she lets them. Is it punishment that she is looking for? Does she feel guilty for living through those times when others who were better than her, did not? Her hands are suddenly tight on the wheel, her heart begins to beat and she struggles to take a breath. The fear begins in her legs. It's happening. Just when she didn't want it to, just when she needs to be normal, just when she has a chance to have a life.

She's back there.

They are in an American Humvee again. It is 2017. This is Mosul in Northern Iraq. There are two of them inside, the man from Kirkuk and Dilva. She wears the uniform of the Kurdish army, the Peshmerga, those who face death before others. The helmet is heavy on her head and the strap bites at her chin. There's an AK 47 on her lap. Driving, the man from Kirkuk has kind eyes and a wry smile, he says he can play the saz and that he's a musician. He is not smiling now as they drive the back streets of Mosul. There have been heavy airstrikes on a city that has been under ISIS control for two years. These two travel through civilian roads on the way to the centre and, parallel to them, on other streets, there are more soldiers in similar vehicles making their way through the smashed-up houses where people still live. ISIS are being flushed out street by street and house by house. The vehicle has been shot at already and the windscreen has a huge crack up the front behind the wire mesh. Dilva does not know if this is new. There may be soldiers in the houses with RPGs or grenades, petrol bombs or assault rifles. This is a dirty war, as if there has ever been one that is clean. Dilva is so afraid that she struggles to breathe, her hands grip tight on her gun as they bump along and then, there's a click somewhere far off and a dull boom from the ground underneath them. She is blown upwards and the helmet on her head crunches against the roof of the vehicle, as it flips, there's the roar of fire and confusion.

It is happening, again. She is back there, again, on the streets of Mosul in 2017. She is being blown up again. The man from Kirkuk who says he plays the saz and is a musician is having his head smashed against the front windscreen, again. She cannot breathe, again. She is going to die, again.

There's a tap on her shoulder and she turns, it's the big Sudanese girl with a concerned frown:

"The light is green now, sister," she whispers. Dilva wipes the sweat from her face. A car beeps behind at how long she is taking and then, as if nothing has happened, she pulls away along Beverley Road.

It's midday. Dilva has dropped the Ford Galaxy back at the car park behind Avenue Cars, exchanged pleasantries with Our Dave, and, she is once again walking down Chaterlands Ave on her way home to her terraced house. She feels a mixture of sickness and excitement. She has done what she did not think possible and, if she can drive that car today, she can drive it tomorrow and the next day, she can make a life for herself and the kids and Aziz too.

Dilva unlocks her front door with a yale key and pushes it open. There's the noise of the TV blaring out and the smell of tobacco. She goes past the front room, the curtains are drawn and a face illuminated by the TV screen looks back at her and smiles. She grins back. He looks better.

"You shouldn't be smoking, Aziz" says Dilva.

"I just had one," he answers. She pauses at the door.

"It'll kill you, you know."

"It already has." She shakes her head. Dilva cares for him because that is what she does.

"I'll make us some lunch," she says as she walks to the little kitchen. There's banging on the wall in the front room, they are dull thuds that drum in repeat bursts of three. It's their neighbour who says Aziz has the TV on too loud. "You better turn that down," she calls.

"He's been banging all morning," comes the wheezy reply from the dark front room. She sighs. She and Aziz travelled together across Turkey in the back of a truck, and when they got to the Greek border, it suited Dilva for him to be her family as it suited him. He looked thin and gaunt even back then. The banging is harder on the wall again from next door.

"You better turn it down," she calls once more. Dilva opens the fridge to see what they have. There's more thudding and shouting from the house beside them. She hears their neighbour's front door slam and Dilva shuts the fridge. She senses something not quite right and steps into the hall where she sees the large figure of the man from next door appear behind the frosted glass. He bangs and shouts.

"Turn the bloody noise down," he yells through the door. He's a big man who wears combat trousers and has army boots and khaki vests that show off his not quite defined arms. Dilva has seen him in the little garden behind his house sharpening a knife with a stone. He plays loud music at night and there are strange men who deliver things in the early hours, on bin days, Dilva has seen his black recycle box full of beer cans and bottles. There's no wife and no children either.

She goes down the hall, the last thing she wants is trouble, and opens the door to reveal the man outside. He is easily over six foot in a white vest under an army green shirt and yellow desert trousers. His face is flushed red. She can see he is trying to be nice.

"I can't take it, love," he says. He is polite. "Do you think you could turn it down?" Dilva nods.

"I'm sorry. We will," she answers.

"It's every day, all night, until late."

"I'm sorry," says Dilva.

"I can't take it," he says. He is still calm. She can smell cigarette smoke from him and what might be alcohol too. His square jaw is unshaven, his short black hair is ruffled.

"I'm sorry," says Dilva again.

"Do you understand that?" There are those that become more aggressive when they perceive weakness. His eyes swim a little. Dilva has said hello to him a few times, she didn't have him pinned as anyone particularly horrible.

"He could do something useful with himself," says the big man. "Rather than just sitting there watching TV all day." There is just a trace of anger on his voice. Dilva moves to close the door but he steps suddenly near, putting his hand on the wood to keep it open. He pushes the frame back and she steps into the little hall as the door opens fully. There's menace in his silence, and also, under his shirt and tucked in the side of his sandy coloured trousers, is a black handgun, the like Dilva has seen before - but never in this country. The big next door neighbour clocks that she has seen it.

He wants her to.

He wants her to feel the unspoken threat that it carries but he is not prepared for the reaction. Like the hammer hitting the back of a bullet and powering it down the chamber of a gun, Dilva launches at him. It's an action she is powerless to stop, and as involuntary as breathing or a heartbeat. Her hands go out, not to his face or the parts of his solar plexus that could hurt him, she is only concerned with one thing – that black gun tucked in his belt that he made sure she noticed. He did not expect this. There are many things that run through his head as he sees Dilva with her long black hair charging at him. What has he done? Should he hit a woman? He instinctively puts his arms out to stop her, but she dips under them and crashes into his stomach. It sends him backwards, tumbling out through the door with her on top of him. As they fall, her hand folds around the handle of the gun and she tugs it free of his belt. His big body thuds onto the concrete path with her on top of him. Dilva is in control of this situation. The big man is winded, but this is not over. She brings the handle of the gun up and then down into the man's face, into his nose, this should break the bone easily, but there's something not right about the pistol. It's not heavy enough and so the blow to the nose isn't nearly as destructive as it should be. She grips the gun in two hands as she sits on his chest, her index finger feels for the trigger and, without the slightest pause, without even a heartbeat to consider that she might be about to kill a person, she pulls the trigger, but not once - over and over. It is hardwired into her. The durable plastic mechanism does nothing but click as she pulls it again and again. There is no bullet, no gun and no dead body below her. She tosses the toy weapon to the side and stands up, looking down on the man who a minute before stood at her door with a gun tucked in is belt. There's hatred in her eyes.

It's been an eventful day.

The neighbour says his name is Ryan and he sits at the round table in Dilva's kitchen with a tea towel to his nose to stop the bleeding. He doesn't seem angry, more curious, as if he has learned some sort of lesson from an unexpected teacher. Dilva can see that where his powerful arms might once have been ripped with muscles, they are now just turning to fat.

"I'm sorry," he says. It's his turn now. Dilva sits in one of the brown chairs and Aziz in another next to her. "You can pack one hell of a bloody punch," he adds. On the table in front of all of them is the plastic gun that Dilva smashed into the man's nose. Aziz has coughed a good bit into his hanky but Dilva is quiet as she looks at the big man sitting in her kitchen.

"Why do you have a plastic gun?" she asks.

"Protection," he answers.

"It can't fire. How will it protect you?"

"People get scared when they see it – you did." Dilva nods and raises her eyebrows. Aziz hasn't turned the TV off in the front room and it blares out into the kitchen.

"I'm sorry I hit you," she says.

"I deserved it. I deserve everything I get. Where did you learn to fight like that?" Dilva shrugs her shoulders as if she doesn't know.

"She's Kurdish army," says Aziz. "Peshmerga." The man who said his name was Ryan removes the bloodied tea towel from his nose and looks at his attacker with a mixture of surprise and awe. He knows the Peshmerga.

"I was forces too. Afghanistan, 2003." Dilva stares blank at him. She does not want to swap war stories. She feels exhausted. Ryan stands up and reaches for the gun on the table. It's actually a desert eagle replica and cost £79.99 plus £5.99 postage and the details are all correct except for the weight of it - it's too light. Ryan picks it up and tucks it in his belt under his shirt. Now that Dilva knows it's not real, and it can't kill anyone, it might as well be a teacup.

"I'm sorry to have bothered you," he says. He has the makings of a polite lad does this Ryan, albeit a little rough around the edges. He likes to think that his name is a reflection of the Chris Ryan SAS books, but he cannot be sure why his father called him so. The old man left when he was very young. "I've not been myself for a long while," he adds. Aziz coughs into a handkerchief and Dilva rubs his back as he does. Ryan watches the thin man with balding hair and sees that he is too sick to do much of anything at all.

"I'll see myself out, and I'll wash this tea towel." Dilva stands up too and nods. She watches the big man clump down the hall to the front door, open it up and leave, closing it gently behind him.

"Have you got any of those cigarettes left?" she asks Aziz. He nods. "I think I need one."

CHAPTER FOUR
Our Dave

Our Dave goes to the allotment most evenings, today is no different. It's just a few streets away and like lots of things, with just a little bit of constant effort, great achievements can be made. Dave drives down the backstreets past terraced houses and a huge Victorian school on the left. In front are two iron gates that open out to the hundred or so plots. This is Ragland Street allotment, home to the fair and good of this part of the city. It's busy on a Monday night, and Joyce from one of the plots nearer the entrance pulls the gates open so Our Dave can drive through. He gives her a smile and a wave as he passes at three miles an hour. She beams back from under her grey bob. It's a hundred yards to Our Dave's plot at the end, he passes rectangular gardens on either side, there's a chicken coup, rows of cabbages, fruit trees in lines, little sheds with garden benches and a pagoda. The waiting time is three years long to get a plot, unless you know Carl, and then it's about two months. There are many kinds of garden here, some given over to flowers with winding paths around fishponds, others just for the veg with onions stalks growing in straight lines and the white flowers of potato plants, some are overgrown with neglect, others packed with green houses and some with large sheds with tables and chairs outside. Here is a home for many, and it can be beautiful or useful or left to rot.

At the very end of the track, Our Dave parks up outside his own plot. There's a waist height poly tunnel on one side of the path and veg growing on the other. He gets out and inspects the plants as he walks to the shed at the end, Our Dave is already aware that there is a man sitting in one of the wrought iron chairs by the round table. He is not meant to be there and will have climbed over the fence at the end to get in. He is dressed in a filthy grey hoody and black cargo pants, there's a beany on his head and his face is drawn and thin. He's a character Our Dave is familiar with.

This is Daz.

It is 1991 and Darren is 15. He's a Beverley lad, but not from the rich end, and he's been dragged up by a single mum and a big brother Leon, who is harder and nastier than he could ever hope to be. Just like his older brother has a swagger, a smirk and danger to his stare, Darren has only wide-eyed confusion at the world. He's not very hard, not good at school, not handsome, not intelligent or funny, he is, in every way super normal and yet, there is a hidden passion in him. Ten years ago, when Darren was five years old, his mum bought him a remote-controlled car and the first thing he did was take it to pieces and put it back together again to see how it worked. He's good at this sort of thing. When his mum took her eyes off him, he would take anything apart and put it back together again, a toaster, the Mega drive, a Walkman and then, a few years later microwaves, and when his elder brother was 16 he brought home a moped scooter. Darren took this apart as well, and then put it back together again after he'd cleaned it. He knows about motors, not because he's had them explained to him, but because he's looked inside them. He likes the sound they make, and he likes to watch wheels spin.

It's early spring and he is walking home in the new darkness of seven o'clock, the traffic is thin on the suburban street. A single decker bus passes and slows, there isn't a bus stop here, so Darren does not know what the bus is doing as it pulls up with the engine running. The double doors hiss open and the driver steps out into the night street. He's moon-faced and wide-eyed with a letter to post in one of his fat hands. No doubt he has stopped the bus so he can drop that in the letter box just behind where Darren walks. He brushes past the young lad.

This is the moment.

There is in front of him, a new reality, a crossroad, and a decision. The doors of the bus are open and the engine ticks over as the driver moves to the post box a few yards up the street behind him.

Darren can steal the bus.

It is as if the universe is offering him a doorway to another world. In many ways this is the moment that all his problems begin and, perversely, it is also the moment he finally becomes real and not a bit part in another story. Darren becomes who he really is and always will be. He steals the bus.

The chain of events the bus theft led to were life changing, first off, after he was arrested, charged and released, Darren's older brother stopped hitting him. He was no longer known as just his kid brother – but his kid brother who nicked a bus, just because he could. His mother said that she could not deal with him anymore, even though this was not true at all, and she sent him to live with his alcoholic dad in Hull. Here, he became Daz, and got slapped up and down by the old man. It made him realise that his elder brother was infinitely less tough than his father.

At 16 Daz joined the army just to get away, and they made a mechanic proper out of him, as well as a pisshead. He was there for ten years and when he was discharged, he didn't know what to do, so he drifted back to Hull and ended up on Chants Ave where his dad used to live. For a time, Daz slept rough in the cemetery at the end of the street, that was until he met Our Dave, the bald man bought him cups of tea in Chants Café Bar and they chatted about this and that. When Our Dave found out he was a mechanic, he took him down to the garage on Richmond Street a few minutes' walk away and they had a chat to the owner. Daz does not really know how it happened. It just did. That afternoon he ended up changing the cam belt on an old VW van which is not an easy job, for some. They gave him a job and he was there a while until the drinking started to get the better of him and then he tried brown and then skag. That was that. He went back to sleeping in the cemetery and robbing where he could, he drifts in and out of the hostel on Princes Ave. There's a place for drunks that he goes to as well. He comes back to get money off Our Dave because he knows he's a soft touch.

Our Dave makes his way to the front of the shed and sits down in a wrought iron chair opposite Daz.

"How are you, Dave?" he asks.

"Good, you?"

"You know," this means he isn't doing very well. His eyes are shifty. When Daz speaks you can see that his teeth are already rotting in his mouth, a biproduct of using heroin.

"What can I do for you, Daz?" he asks.

"I'm here to talk about business." Daz's leg jigs as he sits there. He's maybe a drug addict, but Daz is intelligent and notices things that others are too busy to see. He knows a little bit more about the city than those regular folk who go to work and their allotment, and to the pub on Friday night.

"What business?"

"Your business." Our Dave wrinkles his nose. He is not sure what Daz is getting at or why he has managed to get into the allotment. Our Dave has a range of different businesses that he keeps going, the taxi office, houses and shops he rents out, and something else that he keeps quiet, a business he has been running since the mid-nineties - the smuggling of illegal booze. It doesn't have any of the glamour of the drug trade, there's no need to source the stock from dangerous foreign enterprises, no strippers or cocaine or suitcases full of money or any of the razzle dazzle of gangster films. However, it is illegal and Our Dave does make a hefty profit, he sometimes needs to get his hands dirty and he needs to pay people off, organise shipments, as well as have a distribution network. Over the years he's had to fine tune this, and ordinarily, everything is smooth, but he's also learned how to deal with problems as they arise. From time to time, Our Dave must also deal with his competitors.

"I was talking to a bloke," says Daz. Our Dave puts his hand over his mouth in thought. This doesn't sound like the kid he tried to help a few years ago. "Times are changing, Dave." It's actually Our Dave. "The bloke told me, the way you do things needs improving."

"What are you on about, Daz?"

"A bloke paid me to come and have a word with you."

"Who?"

"I can't say."

"Has he paid you yet?"

"Not until I call him and tell him what you said."

47

"Why can't he talk to me?"

"He doesn't want you to know it's him."

"I'll give you 20 quid to tell me who he is."

"I don't know him. I've never seen him before." This is a bit of a worry.

Our Dave's distribution network has taken a long time to build. Some booze comes in straight from Europe on trucks right here to Hull, it comes with trusted loads and drivers who ship it as grain imports or wood. Our Dave learned a long time ago that it's not good shipping beer – it's too big and bulky, so it's all spirits, and it doesn't stop in Hull. It goes out across the country to nightclub companies who put the rum, the whiskey and the gin in all their pubs and clubs from Newcastle to Glasgow. It's not even knock off stuff either, it comes from the big factories just outside Dusseldorf that produce spirits for the whole world. That's not just it either. There's all the stuff coming in from America, the bourbon that comes in via Liverpool and goes off to the specialist whiskey shops in the richer parts of the country. Then there's the malt whiskey that comes direct from Scotland in small batches that the producers know about, sometimes in yachts direct to Hull marina or pleasure boats into Bridlington, and Our Dave's lads, whoever they are, circumvent international trade duties and get it out to America or Japan at a fraction of the cost to the producers. That's just the start. There's the gin company in Cottingham, and the Wolds Whiskey company, a quarter of everything they make goes through Our Dave. Everyone does well and he makes sure they all get paid.

Daz will not know any of this. Nobody knows any of this. Nobody but Our Dave.

"Cut to the chase," he asks Daz.

"He wants to buy your business and if not, there's going to be a bit of a struggle." He rubs his face and over his eyes.

"You ok to take a message back to him?" asks Our Dave.

"Yeah, that's what I'm meant to do."

"Good. Tell him no more messages. If he knows who I am and where I am. Tell him I want to talk face to face. None of this." Daz nods.

"Can I have my twenty quid?"

"What for?" asks Our Dave.

"I told you who the bloke was."

"No, you didn't."

"I did, I told you I didn't know who he was."

"That isn't the same." Daz does a big sigh:

"I did my thing, Our Dave, it was you that said you'd give me twenty quid."

"Where you living these days?"

"Just off Hessle Road." This is near the docks and the place where, in the seventies, they used to haul in fish that was worth more than gold. It's not what it was back then.

"You stay away from the Dairycoates Inn, Daz,"

"I go in there all the time." Daz grins and shows his rotten teeth. Our Dave examines his face because he knows that users are good at lying to get what they want. There's someone he knows who runs that pub, a woman who, like Our Dave, has been mixed up in all sorts for a number of years. Her name is Ann Leatherhead and she is left over from times long gone, she's a strong woman, into her sixties now and the last of the Hessle Road lasses who looked after the bains and the money. Leatherhead has been running hard drugs into Hull from the docks for many years. Perhaps she's sent Daz here. Our Dave stands up and feels for his wallet in his back pocket. He opens it up and takes out two twenty-pound notes. Before he hands them over, he wants to say something.

"You know if you went back to work at the garage, you'd make more than you'd make on the streets." The words are lost on Daz already, he sees the money and his mind sees the bag of gear he can buy from the back door of the Dairycoates Inn. He snatches the notes and makes off past the rows of veg in neat lines. Joyce will let him out.

Our Dave sits back down on the wrought iron chair. Things run through his mind. Who sent the man who Bev killed? Who paid Daz to talk to him? He will have to assume they are not from the same source, and that they know something about his business dealings outside the taxi office. He is in a position of weakness. There's more. How could

49

anyone know who, where or what he is? Nothing in Dave's life is connected, and anyone he deals with thinks he's working for someone else, from the Whiskey makers in Orkney to the men who make cotton candy moonshine from murky bayou water in Louisiana.

Dave takes his watering can with him to the tap at the end of the plot, he sets it on the floor and begins to fill the green tank. Maybe it is time to sell all this, but what else would he do? People rely on Our Dave too, there are those at the taxi office who need their job to put food on the table, customers who have used him for years as well. Also, it would be impossible to sell his operation to someone else, how could he? There are forces moving against him.

He's had it too easy for too long.

CHAPTER FIVE
DI Lyndsey

It's nearly five o'clock in the afternoon and Bev sits in her classy white Mercedes in the car park. She's outside the thrift supermarket waiting for her daughter, Chloe, to finish her shift behind the tills so she can drive her home. Since Our Dave returned it to her, it's got that new car smell. The place where the man hit his head against the dashboard is clean and smooth. It all looks brand new.

Like always, Bev is early. She digs into her leather handbag for her phone and swipes her pass shape to bring the screen to life. When she got in after the incident the other night, Bev downloaded the dating apps again, all of them, and she reposted photos of her there, one of her on holiday in a bikini, one with a drink in a pub, one in a flower garden and another with her friends where their faces have been scribbled out. Like always, the messages came thick and fast, hundreds and hundreds of them from men near and far, and like always, it's Bev's job to weed out the ones who aren't tall enough, aren't funny enough or handsome enough either. It's not easy. A few years ago, she went on a series of dates with all sorts of men, ignored the majority after the first meeting and slept with a few. She swore she'd rather be alone than with the wrong man, but here she is again, scrolling through the faces of the fellas therein, the handsome, the filtered, the funny, the smart, swiping left every time. She stops at a picture of a blond man, he has blue eyes and is standing by a lake. The sun is going down behind him. He is called Lars, 47 years old, Groningen, Holland, 502 miles away. She reads his profile, factory owner, likes rock music, two older teenage lads. He looks good, and he is so far away that he will never contact her, and so, without a thought, Bev swipes right. They match. She smiles with her face lit up by the phone. It's a game to take her mind off what happened.

She puts her phone down and looks across at the big supermarket where her daughter works three days a week. Shoppers waddle to their cars pushing full trolleys of groceries.

Her phone buzzes. It's Lars, the Dutchman with blond hair.

"Hello, great pictures! I'm in Holland, a little bit far from you!" She smiles and her thumb works quickly on the screen as she types.

"It means you can't ask me out."

"HA!... What are you doing tonight? Maybe we could get a coffee?" She smiles and shows her straight white teeth.

"Okay, where are you taking me?"

"I know a place, they serve a great cocktail called an Old Fashioned." Bev likes whiskey. Because this man is far away, she can flirt with him without fear he will be a friend of anyone she knows. It's just harmless chat, and that's all she needs.

"Would I have to dress up or down?"

"Definitely up."

"How come your English is so good?"

"It's not. Do you like a man in a suit?"

It continues like this for a few more exchanges. He is quick and light-hearted. She goes back to his profile again to look at the pictures, zooms in to see that his teeth are straight and white, the photo does not seem like it's been altered, his arms have the smooth definition of muscle under his t-shirt. There's a picture of him strumming a guitar. Bev likes this, she wonders what it might be like to be with a man who could play.

There's a tap on the opposite window. It's Chloe. Bev presses the button and unlocks the car door so she can get in. Her phone buzzes again and she answers Lars. Chloe sits down and watches her mum pump a message into the screen.

"You ok, love?" she says as she types. Chloe can see the familiar red screen of the dating app under her mum's fingers.

"Are you dating again?" she asks.

"Just chatting," answers Bev as she puts her phone back in her bag. "Nothing wrong with that is there?"

"I guess not," says Chloe. "It's just where it leads to." Chloe has a wise head on her shoulders. She has all of her mother's street sense as well as a good education. She should be in Uni but Bev has convinced her she doesn't need to go.

They drive back through the stop start traffic of the city to their house off Chants Ave. Bev and Chloe live on Lynton Ave in a whitewashed end terrace with a gravel drive where she can park the Merc. It's next to a ten foot that runs behind all the houses. She reverses the car into the spot and as she turns off the engine, she notices a black Ford Fiesta parked opposite her house. She gets out and so does the man inside. He's wearing a work suit and a black tie without his collar done up and has frizzy curly hair cut short around the back of his head and ears, but left to grow a little longer on the top. Bev watches his approach. Chloe goes to the front door and lets herself in. There's something not quite right about this man walking towards her on Lynton Ave in the afternoon sun, he isn't aggressive but is here for some serious reason. He smiles when he reaches her car but it is more perfunctory than friendly.

"Is it Bev Thorne?"

"Who wants to know?"

"DI Lyndsey, Clough Road Police Station. Can I ask you a few questions, Mrs Thorne?" Her legs are jelly and her stomach turns in a grumble of fear, yet there is no change of expression on Bev's face at all.

"Can I see some ID?" she asks. The man nods and goes to his inside pocket to produce a leather wallet which he holds open at her. Bev doesn't know what she's looking at.

"There you go," he says.

"It's Miss Thorne, actually," she answers. "What do you want to ask me questions about?" Bev has had problems with the coppers before after she hit that man in a pub all those years ago. They're nothing but trouble, like Our Dave says, they're the biggest gang in the city. Does he know about the man who was killed in Bev's car a few days ago? If he did, then Bev would be taken in, there'd be no friendly visits from a plain clothed officer.

"Just a friendly chat."

"You can go to a pub for that. I'm busy." The copper with the curly hair looks down the street and then back to Bev standing next to her white Merc.

"Honestly, it would be better for you if we had a chat, and it's nothing to worry about. We just need some help with our enquiries." He looks too young to be a copper, but then again, everyone looks too young to be anything these days. She knows the less she says to this man the better, but if she looks like she has got something to hide, he might think that she has.

The curly-haired copper who says his name is Lyndsey follows Bev through the house to the little kitchen at the back. There's a round table and three chairs.

"Can I sit down?" asks the copper.

"Yeah, make yourself at home." There's a sarcastic edge to Bev's voice. The man pulls back one of the chairs and sits. Bev leans back on the sink with her arms folded. Her heart is beating quickly and there's a lump in her throat. It must be about the man in her taxi from the afternoon before, the one that Our Dave said he would get rid of.

"Nice house," he says. "It's a good area round here, not too expensive and a good community feel." Ordinarily, Bev would ask this young copper to get to the point or be on his way.

"I'm busy," she says in lieu of this.

"Yeah well, I'll get to it. There's a young lad from Kirkella, James Boyce, only 16, he goes to The Zone school on Anlaby Park." It's not about the body. Bev's insides flutter in relief.

"I know him," she says. "I drive him to school sometimes."

"He's gone missing."

"Right. It's not always me that drives him. Our Dave, Dave Wilkinson, the man who owns Avenue Cars, he drives him more than I do."

"I'll be on my way there next. Have you seen James in the last few days?"

"No."

"He's stolen a substantial amount of money from his father and also a car, a grey Audi, quite recognizable. Have you seen it?"

"No."

"When you last saw James, did he give you any information about where he might go or what he might do?"

"I know he hated living there. That's it."

54

"What kind of a lad is he?"

"Misunderstood. Bright. A bit of a twat. He'll be back, I should think. How come you care so much? Kids go missing all the time and the police don't give a toss." She feels a little more herself now she knows it's not about the body.

"His dad's someone important."

"So he's pulled out all the stops to get him found then."

"That's the thrust of it," says the curly haired copper. "If you see or hear from James at all, you'll let me know, won't you." He fishes inside his jacket and pulls out a card, then puts this down on the table face up. There's his name, DI Lyndsey, with the police crest in the corner and his number along the bottom.

"I will for sure. I hope you find him."

"So do I, his dad's having kittens. How long have you worked at Avenue Cars?"

"A long time. Longer than you've been in the police force."

"When did you start there?" Bev looks down on this man with curly hair and sees that this is not just a bit of banter, he genuinely wants to know.

"Started in 2005 when Chloe was little."

"How long have you known Dave Wilkinson?"

"The same amount of time, I guess."

"How do you find him? Is he a good boss?"

"He's a very good boss." Bev doesn't really understand the line of questioning.

"That taxi office has been around a long time."

"It has, Our Dave bought it from some Turkish fella in the late 90s." Bev should be careful what she says, she shouldn't offer any information that isn't specifically requested, after all, she did kill someone a few days ago, and her chat with Our Dave in the office this morning has unnerved her.

"He does a lot of work through the council. That's the business now, isn't it?"

"Yeah. That's about right. We don't have to pick up drunks on Friday nights anymore. Other cab firms can do that."

"I've heard a few things about Our Dave," says the copper.

"What?" This young man looks up at her with his pale blue

55

eyes in earnest.

"I've heard he's got his fingers in all sorts of different pies."

"What does that mean?"

"It means that he does different types of business other than taxiing."

"Not to my knowledge, he doesn't. He's got a good reputation around here has Our Dave, and not just with me." Bev feels a little of her anger rise.

"I've heard that too. Dave Wilkinson, pillar of the community, always willing to help. I know for a start that he employs criminals." The copper lets that last line hang there as he stares at Bev.

"Does he?"

"Well, there's you for a start." Bev's lip curls in anger. "Smashed a pint glass in a man's face - you could have killed him." His voice has menace in it.

"I paid for what I did."

"Yes, but you've still got a record, love, we still know what kind of a person you are."

"What's this got to do with that lad who went missing?"

"Nothing. I'm just ascertaining what kind of taxi company you work for and what your boss is like. You know I could make things difficult for a woman like you?" Bev's smooth blue eyes focus in hatred at him. "I mean, have you got an enhanced DBS check considering that you're working with vulnerable people?"

"Of course I have."

"And it didn't pick up what you did?"

"It was 20 years ago. I was just a bloody kid." The man tuts in disgust.

"One of the lads at the station says he met you off a dating site a few years back. He told me he came back here. Told us everything you did. I won't go into it."

"That's not illegal and it's none of your business." He is not a pleasant man.

"Wouldn't it be terrible if a policeman logged a complaint against you, for say, verbal abuse and if you got arrested, that would shaft your DBS check and you'd lose your job. That'd be a problem for you, wouldn't it?" Bev flares her nostrils. He is threatening her. It feels just like it did the other day with that passenger on the way to Brough, the one who had his head smashed on the dashboard, suddenly someone goes from being okay to unreasonable, all in the same movement. Ordinarily, Bev would tell him to piss off out of her house but there is something definitely wrong with Our Dave of late and of the way he got rid of the man's body for her. She has to protect herself and so, she will not tell this copper to get stuffed because she is too afraid of what he could find out.

"What is it you want?"

"Tell me everything you know about Dave Wilkinson."

"There's nothing to tell. He runs a taxi business and he does it well and he gives people round here chances too."

"Like you?"

"Yes, like me. You've got a lot to learn, lad," she says. He grins. There's definitely something disagreeable about him.

"I've been watching Avenue Cars for a long time, Miss Thorne. I know there's something a bit off about it and I need to find out what it is." She swallows. The copper continues: "I think you know a lot more about what goes on there than you're telling me. You want to be a bit careful."

"You ask anyone up and down Chanterlands Ave about Dave Wilkinson and they'll tell you what kind of man he is. Ask anyone in this town. It's you who wants to be careful officer, he's someone who people like and respect." DI Lyndsey stands up. He's only a little taller than she is. His pale blue eyes are expressionless as he looks at her.

"I won't do it, whatever it is," she answers.

"It's nothing hard. I want you to find out everything you can about Our Dave. Listen to who he talks to, watch where he goes and who he meets and if you see anything that you think isn't right, let me know. You've got my number on the card."

"He's looked after me, has Our Dave, I won't spy on him."

"I've asked nicely," says DI Lyndsey.

"I won't help," she answers.

"You might have to. You might have to save yourself, or

57

your daughter." Bev swallows.

"Out of my house," she commands in a whisper. "You should be out looking for that James kid."

"He'll be back," says officer Lyndsey. "I'm happy that I got to talk to you. Whatever you can find out for me, Miss Thorne, I'm counting on you. I'll be in touch."

He closes the door behind him as he leaves.

Bev doesn't move for a moment. She looks down at the white and green lino tiles on the kitchen floor with her arms still folded. The policeman has made her feel like a dumb slag. It gives her a nasty taste in her mouth and reminds her what it's like to be married. In her bag on the table, her phone buzzes. It's Lars, the Dutchman from the dating app.

"How's your afternoon?" it reads.

"Marvelous," she replies with her quick thumb, "I'm lying down in the garden in the sun." This is a distraction for her. It gives her a chance to sweep the rest of the world under the carpet while she responds to this blond Dutchman.

So it goes on.

She messages him as she cooks fish burgers and homemade coleslaw for her and Chloe, she messages him between washing up and cleaning, and while she's having a glass of wine. She messages him while she's not watching a film, and as she sits in the bath. She messages him as she lays in bed on her side, with the screen illuminating her face in the darkness. She tries not to think about the policeman with his curly hair who has threatened her, and tries not to hear the veiled menace on his East Hull accent.

Lars is a sweet man. He runs a factory with his brother. It's a small operation. He's also divorced with two sons who are at university. Lars likes football and melodic punk like Green Day, he doesn't know why he is on the dating app. He doesn't want a one-night stand either. His messages are peppered with humour and Bev flirts with him, safe in the knowledge that he cannot come round to her house or suggest they meet up because he is across the sea in Europe. In between the messages she thinks of the policeman again, she will not spy on Our Dave for this officer, even though she knows too that there is something not quite right.

She will have to tell Our Dave.

It's Tuesday. Bev gets to the office of Avenue Cars a little late. She couldn't sleep and not just because she was sending messages to Lars the Dutchman. They have swapped numbers for real and she has been sending him pictures, not smutty stuff though. He sent her some snaps of his holiday in Malta last year and she sent pics of the camping trip to Northumberland that her and Chloe had at Easter. She goes through the back door, through the little galley kitchen and into the taxi office. There's Liz sitting on the edge of her chair with a mug of green tea cupped in her hands opposite Dilva who sits at the table. The Kurdish woman looks a lot less scared than yesterday.

"Survived your first day, did you?" asks Bev. Dilva looks up at her without expression. Our Dave has his face in the laptop screen and is sitting where Bev usually sits, in front of the grate. He takes off his glasses.

"Did you hear about that James Boyce?" she asks. "The rich kid from Kirkella?"

"What about him?" says Our Dave.

"He went missing yesterday, pinched his dad's Audi and stole money too."

"I didn't hear that, I picked him up from school and dropped him home. He seemed in a better mood than usual." Bev frowns.

"Did you get a visit from a copper yesterday, Our Dave?" The man shakes his bald head. Bev swallows. She glances around the little office, first to Liz and then to Dilva.

"Time for us to go," says Liz, she nods at Dilva. In a few moments, they have both left through the back door. Bev stands looking down on Our Dave. He takes off his reading glasses.

"So, James Boyce didn't go missing?"

"Not as far as I know."

"A copper visited me yesterday and told me he had. A curly

59

haired kid," Bev pulls out DI Lyndsey's contact card from her back pocket and sets it on the table in front of Our Dave. "He wasn't a nice lad, he said you were up to something illegal and that I was to watch you. He threatened me." Our Dave picks up the card and looks at the name on it. She can see him thinking as he does, as if, she's not quite there. This is a man who managed to dispose of a dead body a few nights ago as if it were an old mattress. Bev is afraid again, more so than when she spoke to the curly-haired copper.

"Just what is going on, Our Dave?"

"What did you tell him?"

"Nothing. I don't know anything. You're a sixty-year-old man who runs a taxi office, staffed by lasses, there was nothing to tell him."

"About the other night?" She shakes her head.

"I didn't say anything about that." Dave sits forward and rests his elbows on his knees.

"I'll not say much, Bev, because the less you know, the better it is for you. Someone wants this business. They want me to sell up."

"Are you taking the piss? This is Avenue Cars, Our Dave, we're not exactly printing money here, are we?"

"It's not just that part of the business they want."

"Who are they?"

"That's just it, I don't know."

"Why don't you just sell and have done with it?"

"It's not as easy as that." Our Dave looks down at the contact card for DI Lyndsay with a frown. He did not expect war to come so quickly and from so many angles, there are lads in the police station on Clough Road that he has known for years, he tells them things as they happen down Chants Ave, minor incidents or anything nasty that he spots. They trust him. Our Dave is beyond reproach as far as they are concerned and so, this copper must be someone new and someone paid to take an interest in Our Dave's affairs.

"He told you that James Boyce had gone missing, did he?"

"Yes. Just so I'd let him in the house, I think."

"How old was he?"

"Young, in his twenties."

"Plain clothes?"

"Yes. Nasty grin too. Made out that I was a slag. Told me a lad at the police station met me one night off one of them dating apps."

"Is that true?"

"Yes." Dave looks up at her. He knows Bev well, and sees that her nostrils are flared when she says this.

"I'm sorry you got mixed up in it. It's going to get worse before it gets better. Ignore anything he's told you."

"He wanted me to find out what you're up to, where you go, who you speak to on the phone. What should I do?"

"Nothing for the time being."

"I hate to say this again, Our Dave, but what is going on? What is all this about? This is a taxi office."

"It's not just a taxi office, Bev. It never has been. The less I tell you the better it is for you, I promise."

"You helped me in the past, you helped me when nobody else would. You can trust me."

"I didn't really do it for you, Bev. I needed someone I could depend on, and that was you, you just couldn't see what you were worth all those years ago. I'm not sure you can see what your worth now." Our Dave has a way of getting to the truth of a problem. "If I need your help, I'll ask for it. Not a word to anyone about this neither." Bev swallows.

"What happened to that man's body from the other night?"

"Nobody will find him if that's what you're worried about."

Our Dave drove Bev's white Mercedes down to the Energy Works Power Station incinerator on Cleveland Street that night, made a late call to someone who was in bed and told him that he had a load of gear that needed burning. Our Dave has done this before with booze, and the man on the other end of the phone made a call to someone else. Then, like he was dropping a rolled-up carpet at the tip, Our Dave drove through the automatic gates and to the open door of the big, hot furnace where they ordinarily burn clinical waste. Security turned a blind eye just like the cameras. He carried the dead man through and, at the open hatch, he shoved his body inside and he was gone. No need to tell Bev this.

"It was murder," she says.

"It was manslaughter, and self-defense at that. He would have done something to you if you hadn't done it to him first. There are some bad people in the world."

"Maybe you're one of them," says Bev.

"I am, if I have to be. Sometimes you need to pull up the weeds, you need to cut back the roses to make them grow stronger."

"It was a person's life."

"It was you that killed him." She takes a deep breath in through the nose when she hears this. It's true.

"Why did you help me?"

"Because if I hadn't there'd be coppers all over this place, and then we'd all have to face the music. All of us. I've got people who depend on me, Hazel at home, all you who work here. I can't let it all just fall apart." Bev had never considered that Our Dave is anything more than a kind eyed older man who runs a taxi office that doesn't make a great deal of money. Now she sees he's more than that.

"You'll be late for your pickup," says Our Dave.

"Should I be worried?"

"A bit," he answers. "I'll make a few calls today and get it sorted. I'll find out about our mate DI Lyndsey too."

"What do you want me to do?"

"Carry on as normal."

CHAPTER SIX
Dilva

Aziz is on the nebulizer in the front room. The clear face mask turns liquid into a mist that he can breathe in. It soothes him. Dilva brings him coffee and some of the biscuits she made last night. It's Saturday and so the kids are not at school, and Dilva is not at work. The two of them are upstairs playing on the games machine that Dilva bought with her first week's wages from Our Dave. When she brought it in last night, she was a hero and she felt it too, full to her chest with pride and with a big beaming smile. She can hear them upstairs shouting and cooing at the TV screen they set up in Mohammed's little bedroom.

She goes back into the kitchen and sits down at the table opposite the cooker. She is making their favourite - upside down rice that you do in one pan with roasted veg at the bottom and rice on top, her grandma used to make it. It has been a good week, the Sudanese girls she picks up each day are sweet and funny, she feels safe when she drives them because they are more frightened of the world even than she is. The attacks have been there, in the background, threatening to strike her down and suck her back into the horror, but she uses distraction tactics, plays the radio, makes herself recount vocab lists in English, sings a song that she knows and, in some ways, she can keep the flashbacks at bay, but they are always there, ready to strike at her when she is least expecting.

There have been other passengers too, there's a community group of African ladies and hospital trips for another Kurdish family that live on the other side of the city. It's easy. Our Dave is straightforward, not kind, that would be too stupid a word, Dilva has the sense that he needs her and that's why she's employed, it's not charity – at least that's what she hopes. She's getting used to the other drivers too, the tall woman with short hair and the big smile who calls herself Liz, is a sycophant but well meaning. The blonde one who looks like a prostitute still hates her, but Dilva doesn't care. Aziz has turned the TV up and there's loud Kurdish music, it's traditional beats mixed with hip-hop, she rises to her feet. She doesn't want a repeat of Monday with their big next-door neighbour.

"You'll have to turn that down," she calls and then thinks about the noise that her two younger cousins, who are meant to be her kids, are making upstairs. She doesn't want to see that man from Monday again, or make him angry, but more than that, she wants to avoid getting angry herself. Dilva doesn't want to be the woman that she was made to be, once upon a time. Aziz is not turning the TV down and so she gets up and goes out of the kitchen to the front room, as she does, she sees a big figure outside the frosted glass of the front door. It's that neighbour, the man who called himself Ryan. She pauses and sees him knock. This time, it's not a thump, but a respectable tap with the knuckle on his index finger. If Aziz could get to the door without wheezing himself half to death, she'd make him do it. Like most things, it's better for Dilva to just do it herself. She walks a few paces and opens up.

There he is. All six foot two of him. His hair looks like it's been washed and he's had a shave so his big face is smooth and clean. He has a checked shirt tucked into army style green trousers and still wears the boots, but they have been cleaned and shine up at her from under her front step. She tries not to smile. This usually leads men on. In his hand, he has a packet of something.

"I couldn't get the blood out of that tea-towel," he explains. "So I bought you a new set." He hands over a plastic packet of striped cloths. She nods in thanks. There's the smell of aftershave, not the expensive stuff that Dilva smelt on men of wealth back in Kurdistan, but the cheap aroma of UK pound shops. It's better than sweat. She looks up at his face and sees that his eyes are a bit swollen from where she hit him on Monday. That's what happens when you get smacked in the nose.

"How's your face?" she asks. "I'm sorry." Dilva wanted to go around and apologise again in the week, she wanted to take some sort of offering, maybe alcohol or upside-down rice, but Aziz said it would show weakness – as if he knows. She is sorry

64

for what she did to him, not because she hurt his face so much, it would have hurt his pride to be struck by a woman. She gets the feeling that this Ryan, who has bought her a replacement set of tea towels, is not as mean as he looks, nor as mean as he thinks he is.

"My face is fine. I'm sorry if I frightened you, with the gun." He stands there on the step longer than expected. Dilva should say thank you and close the door. He is nervous, he's not looking at her but down at the floor. "I get those rages too," he says. Dilva frowns, she's learned not to say she doesn't understand, it frustrates people and given time, they will usually paraphrase what they mean, or it will become obvious. "I mean, I get angry too, like you did the other day, and I don't know why. It might be a little thing, like the way someone looks at me or a loud noise, or a smell even." She stares at him from under her smooth black hair and with her high cheekbones. "I was a soldier too," he says.

There is something impenetrable about Dilva standing with her hand on the open door of her house in Westbourne Ave, there's the sound of kids playing in the gardens behind them on a trampoline, and the noise from Aziz's TV blaring out Kurdish hits. Ryan has begun a light sweat. He knows why he is here, telling this Kurdish woman more than he has ever told anyone before about how it feels to be Ryan. It's because she bested him at his own game, she disarmed him and she beat him and she was not scared of it either – she is not afraid of him.

"I know someone who can help you," he says.

"I don't need help," says Dilva. She is calm. Ryan takes a leaflet out from his back pocket and passes it to her, she looks it over but doesn't take it. There's a big square QR code on the bottom right to scan with your phone, and at the top it reads Hull and East Yorkshire Trauma Centre, there's blurb that Dilva doesn't understand. This is for those who have been touched by war or accident, who have found a dead body or survived a grisly car crash. Dilva has been offered this help before, but that would mean living through the whole thing again. She won't do that. She takes the leaflet and smiles. It's her best one but she senses that this man can see through it.

"Thank you," she says.

"Where did you serve? Who trained you?" he asks. She shakes her head.

"I'm not good at English," she answers. This is a good line to use, when you don't want to explain yourself.

"They can get you an interpreter. I'm only saying, because I couldn't deal with it for a long time. They helped me, and they can help you."

"I don't need any help."

"I thought your English wasn't good."

"I don't need any help, but thank you." She moves to close the door and Ryan steps forward and puts his big hand on the frame to stop it from closing.

"You can have your TV on as loud as you like, now I know you, I don't care. If you need anything. I'll be next door. I'm always there." He keeps his grip on the doorframe but his tone is not threatening. "Do you understand? You don't have to go through this alone."

"I understand," she says. She closes the door and watches the big figure move away from behind the frosted glass. She swallows. He saw her as she really was on Monday, a maelstrom of fierce anger and panic, screaming violence and aggression that she controls so it is as sharp as a razor. She puts her hand to her head and rests her back on the wall. There's the sound of the Kurdish music and the kids playing on the Xbox upstairs. She is afraid that he has seen through her so easily and that she let him do so, Dilva has to keep her problems to herself. That's what she's been taught to do, that's what her mother did, that's what her grandmother did. Why should Dilva be any different to those strong women? Like her grandmother used to say, a tree stands alone.

CHAPTER SEVEN
Liz

Liz drives her roomy blue Berlingo taxi out into the flatlands past East Hull. Dennis is in the back, with his wheelchair fastened to the floor. Joel is at the childminder's and even though Liz is at work, she is free.

Dennis is not a nice man at all. Liz can usually find something to warm to about most people, but not this one. He hates everything, the weather, the city and the world, but more than anything else - he hates himself.

"Have you had a good week then, Dennis?" she asks, knowing that he'll give a shitty answer.

"Middling to crap," he answers. He smells of old sweat but he's tried to cover this up with some sort of deodorant, again. Liz opens the window slightly to let some air in.

"Do you mind, Driver?" he says. "The cold gets to me." Liz closes the window again and looks at her passenger through the rear-view mirror.

"I thought you'd like that," says Liz.

"What?"

"Something that gets to you? I mean your brother's giving you something that will sort you out. That's what you told me last week."

"Aye, he is. I'll get some more of it today. I hope you haven't told anyone, if you have, I'll just say you're lying. They'll believe me, you know."

"I haven't told anyone." They have left the city already and the land is flat and colourless around them, the big sky is voluminous with grey clouds rolling in slow motion above as the car travels out along thin roads flanked by tall hedges.

"How's your lad?" Dennis smirks as he says this.

"He's good, thank you," answers Liz. This is not true. Joel has had trouble this week. As he grows, he becomes more frustrated and angry at himself and the world, he throws things on the floor and makes hooting noises like a monkey, smiles and dribbles his food down his bib on purpose. He bangs on the wall in bed at night, shits himself as soon as she has changed his nappy. Liz says these things to herself, but there will be no menace in Joel's actions, he does not know what he is doing in many ways. She feels cruel when she thinks like this, just like Dennis back there.

"How's his CP?" This is the abbreviation for cerebral palsy, the condition that affects a child's brain. CP can range from mild to extreme. Many live a normal life though their brain doesn't tell some of their muscles to move as they should, so a kid may shuffle when she walks, they might slur their speech but otherwise they are all there. Other cases are more extreme, like Joel.

"He's perfect as he is," says Liz in response to Dennis.

"He really is a vegetable then, is he? If he wasn't you'd have said so. It's not him I worry about, he'll be fine, having his arse wiped for his whole life. It's you I worry about and your husband." Dennis looks out of the window at the flat scenery of the countryside. "Are you married, Driver?" he asks. Liz speeds up slightly, because the best part of the day is when she drops Dennis off and has an hour to herself. The quicker she gets there the better.

"I'm single," she answers. Dennis gives a huff as if this is somehow pathetic.

"I bet that kid split you up," he says. Liz looks again in the rear-view mirror and sees Dennis's piggy eyes and his curled lip. He enjoys hurting her.

"You don't have a right to talk about my son, or my life. I'm a taxi driver, not your friend or someone you know. I'd prefer it if whatever you think about children or people with disabilities you keep to yourself. Alright?" Dennis beams back at her. "Just because your life is shite, doesn't mean everybody else's is."

"Now we're getting somewhere," says Dennis. "That's it, tell it like it is. I'm not your friend at all. I don't have any friends, and I'm not talking to you, I'm just talking out loud."

"You're asking me questions."

"You don't have to answer them."

"The quicker you get enough of that stuff your brother gives you, the better."

68

"That's the way," says Dennis. "Admit it, I'm not needed here or wanted either, and I'm doing something about it. Your lad doesn't have a choice."

"What would you have him do, Dennis? Kill himself?"

"How can he? You should do it? You brought him into this world, should be you that helps him out." Liz feels her teeth bar in anger. She wants to spit venom back at this man, but she will not. Liz knows what pity is and she knows how it feels to have it for yourself and for others, she reasons that Dennis will not really care about what he says, he just wants to inflict as much damage as he can. Liz should see this man as a challenge.

She pulls down the lane to the caravan park that looks deserted under the grey East Yorkshire sky, drives along to the caravan at the end where his brother lives and comes to a halt. The door opens and his brother steps out into the air. He looks as miserable as Dennis but at least he can walk. Liz gets out and opens the boot so the man can get Dennis from the back.

"About an hour, same as last week?" says the man.

"Sure. Look after him," says Liz. It's clear she doesn't mean this.

"I will," it's clear he doesn't mean this either.

Liz spends an hour on the beach a few miles away but the sense of freedom she wants is marred somehow by the conversation she has had with Dennis. What would Liz do without her boy? What would be the point of her? She would not have to work driving a taxi and she would not have to drive at all. She could go back to riding that old bike with a basket on the front ringed with plastic flowers. She could meet someone. Rather than staying in when Joel goes to bed, she could go out for a drink along Princes Avenue where there are trendy bars and colourful people. She could be free, like she used to be. After all, who does Joel matter to? His father doesn't care. Liz's mother is in an elderly home back in Newcastle, and her father is long dead. She has no brothers and sisters and no uncles. There are no cards for her and Joel on birthdays, just Facebook messages from friends who Liz used to know well but doesn't know well at all now. Who would miss him?

She looks out to sea and fancies she can see a huge tanker out in the mist somewhere. It makes her feel small to be on the beach there, with the sky wide and huge overhead, and the horizon stretching to forever in front. She should be feeling thankful for the life she has, the home and friends and family, but her mind is cruel. What is Dennis's brother giving him? How is it going to kill him slowly?

They drive back to Hull under the same grey sky. Dennis is quiet. His flabby hands rest on his thighs as he looks out of the front window. The landscape is changing back into the streets of East Hull and they hit traffic on Holderness Road.

"Did your brother give you more of his gas?" she asks.

"He did. It was delicious."

"What's he giving you?"

"That's for me to know. Why are you interested anyway? Do you want some for your lad?"

"I was thinking I could get you some more, we could get the job done a bit quicker on you." Liz has lived in this part of the world long enough for their rough humour to have rubbed off on her. Dennis grins.

"If you think you can get the job done faster, Driver, without any blame falling on anyone, then be my guest."

"You're full of shite," says Liz. She does not usually swear but this seems to come from somewhere deep within her.

"You could come and finish me off, if you want, lass," whispers Dennis through his barred teeth. "They key safe number is 1234, you could let yourself in and smother me with a pillow or something. You'd be doing me a favour." He sits back into his wheelchair after he delivers this.

"You've got a lot to learn," says Liz into the rear-view mirror at the man.

"What would you know about me?"

"Nothing. I've known people in worse situations than you. You've had some bad luck, you're in a wheelchair and you're

70

ill. It doesn't mean your life is over." Liz at once wishes she hadn't said this, she can see the snarl of anger across the man's face as he hears her words.

"Put yourself in this chair, in this body for just half an hour and you wouldn't say that. How dare you?" She should not be arguing with him, not in this taxi while she is at work, he is a customer and her feelings should not come into play. She has to work to find the good in this situation, like she always does.

"I know someone who can help," she says. "There are counsellors at Joel's crèche, people who've lived through the same as you, they can help. All this stuff you're telling me, it's not going to get you any better."

"If I wanted any help, I'd ask for it," he barks. "You're not paid to be a psychologist, love, you're paid to drive." The conversation is ugly. He is right. She has no place to do this. Liz stops at the junction opposite the Humber Pilot pub where the lights take a while to change. She looks in her rear-view mirror and sees Dennis, with his face red and looking out the window.

Who is she to know his pain, or to know what's best for him? She feels guilty, like she always does.

CHAPTER EIGHT
Our Dave on Chants Ave

Our Dave walks along Chanterlands Avenue. There's a tall lad with a beard outside the expensive supermarket selling the Big Issue, Our Dave gives him a smile.

"Now then, Tyler," he says as he moves past. It's late afternoon on Saturday and the shops are shutting. The bakery opposite has an empty front window and a woman in a yellow pinny cleans it with a cloth. Our Dave passes along the street. There's Broomstick, a crystal shop, then Lavender Moon that sells books for holistic healing, there's the Indian restaurant Gold Spice, he looks in the window to see if he can see the owner Mahmoud but doesn't spot him. A man driving a sleek black Lexus waves and Our Dave nods back.

This is his street.

He passes a hair salon, a wedding dress shop, an Italian takeaway and a Kurdish barber. One of the Kurdish lads is having a cig outside and leaning on the glass of the shop. Our Dave gives him a thumbs up and the lads smiles. He knows this street does Our Dave, he knows who's who and what goes on, he knows that Shelly from the wedding dress shop has just lost her dad, he knows that Naz who he just passed is an Iraqi Kurd and that Asef inside cutting hair is Iranian. Our Dave knows that Stephan from the letting agency he is passing across the road is in financial trouble. He knows the figure in a long black fur coat and dark Elvis glasses walking towards him is JT from the band Black Kes, and that he is hungover because of the way he walks.

"Where's your e-scooter?" asks Our Dave.

"The handlebars fell off," says JT. He sees that the man in dark glasses has a bruise under his quiff on his forehead.

"Not while you were riding it, I hope."

"It's all rock and roll, Our Dave," says JT with a sweep of his hand as he moves on down the avenue.

Our Dave walks on past the key cutting shop and the Chanterlands Ave café. Outside is the large figure of Ryan, sitting at one of the tables, he has a big book open in front of him and he's engrossed in it. Milly who owns the shop collects his cup and gives Our Dave a wave as she goes back in. There's a line of three people waiting outside Steve's Cycles, and he can see through the window of the Italian restaurant next door, Michaela is setting the square tables with napkins. Our Dave is not a mafia boss. Nothing like that. He's seen the Godfather films, Goodfellas, The Krays and those modern blockbusters where the action moves fast and the gangsters are colourful and full of humour. It's not like that at all. Our Dave knows this street, not because he intimidates the people here but because he helps them. Mahmoud from the Indian Restaurant has a long-term loan from Our Dave which bought his tandoor oven. He boarded out the fitting room in Shelly's wedding dress shop. Our Dave did Steve's shopping for a month while his wife was in hospital.

The money he makes from his booze business, it's not for him, it was never for him. It's for others, and this is where his power comes from. At first it was so his mam could pay the electricity bill or get the shopping, then it was to help his brother buy a car, it was for his son to go to university, it was for Hazel his wife so they could go on holiday, it was for a camper van he could drive down to Dorset in the summer. Then it was about the business, because the money the drivers make on the council jobs is not nearly enough to pay them what he does. The money is for the rent on Lisa's tattoo shop which Our Dave convinced her was paid for by the council. He is tired of seeing poor people lose just because they are poor, and so, Our Dave does his best to see that those who work hard are kept safe from the cruel world of banks and laws. That's why he has a property on Westbourne Ave and two terraces on Perth Street that he lets out for a pittance to families who wouldn't have anywhere else to go.

He stops outside the front door of Avenue Cars and there's a curly haired man in a mid-price suit eating an ice-cream. He's nearly finished and there's just a lump left in the cornet.

"Are you Dave?" he asks. "Dave Wilkinson?"

"That's me kiddo. Who's you?"

"DI Lyndsey, Clough Road Station. I wondered if I could

73

come in and ask you a few questions."

"You can ask them out here if you want," says Dave. The man takes a final lick of his ice-cream and then bites off a bit of the cornet. "Maybe I'll let you finish your ice-cream, kid, and then you can come in and have a word." DI Lyndsey wipes his face with the other hand and drops what's left of the ice-cream into the bin on the street.

"I'm ready," he says.

"Bit young to be a DI, aren't you?" asks Dave.

"Connections," says the young man. "I've had people help me out so I can get my foot on the ladder and move on up. Shall we go inside?" There's something not to like about this lad, straight away, he's got a manner of speaking that makes him seem more familiar than he should be. Our Dave goes along with it. The curly haired copper takes out a tissue to wipe off his face. Our Dave unlocks the back of the taxi office and they walk inside. It's dark after the bright sunlight. DI Lyndsey looks around then stands in the centre of the back office with his hands folded over his not cheap but not expensive suit.

"I don't just work for the police," he says.

"Oh aye?" says Our Dave. It's condescending. He sits down against the wall in one of the chairs and crosses one long leg over the other, looking at the DI with his curly hair.

"I'll keep this really simple, shall I, Dave?"

"If you like, son," he answers.

"There are certain players who know about your business. I don't mean this taxi office, I mean the business that brings controlled substances into the country and distributes them far and wide. I think we both know what I mean. This isn't a police matter because there's no evidence of wrongdoing. You probably have some of Clough Road station on your payroll anyway."

"What do you want from me?"

"This is a cease-and-desist order. Stop your trading and supplying as soon as possible."

"Who do you work for?"

"The Doyle Family."

"The Manchester Doyle family?" asks Our Dave.

"Yes."

"I know Patty, we go way back to the seventies. I'll give him a call and get all this nonsense sorted out straight away." Our Dave does know Patty Doyle. Many years since, he had a job as a trawlerman on a boat named the Cuckoo that sailed out of King George Dock in the early seventies, he wasn't quite tough enough to stand the rigors of the sea and so he only did one trip. It was enough for the lads at the dock to recognise young Dave as a good worker and he was apprenticed to a ship fitter where he learned to be a carpenter. He learned too, how things could be brought into the country, and, in part, this was his apprenticeship. There was a young Manc Irish lad, a driver on the docks who Our Dave knew took bits and bobs up to Manchester. They became friends and, many years later, he climbed the ranks of his family, right to the top. Our Dave and he had an understanding. Dave brings in booze and he gets left alone.

"Things have changed there," says DI Lyndsey.

"How so?"

"Patty's dead."

"Who's taken over?"

"His grandson, Robbo." Our Dave takes a deep breath.

"So this is his decision, is it?"

"Yeah, out with the old and in with the new."

"What if I don't stop?"

"There'll be consequences."

"I've been threatened before," explains Our Dave. "I know how to look after myself and I have friends too." DI Lyndsey raises one of his eyebrows under his curly hair.

"This is a taxi office on Chants Ave, you only have three drivers, four including you." Our Dave stands up. He's six foot one these days and towers over the officer as he approaches him.

"I'm going to give you a chance, son, because you're young and you're too arrogant to look at things as they really are. One day, something is going to happen to you, something terrible, unimaginable, it might be the death of someone, an accident, an episode in your mental health, I don't know what. Until that happens to you, you'll be blind, just like you are now. I don't know how a Hull copper has got mixed up with the Doyle Family out of Salford, but you have to get yourself un-mixed up with them, especially now Patty doesn't run it anymore. Go back to whoever handles you, tell them Our Dave said he won't stop, tell them he's ready for whatever they can throw at him; and then, you run, get out of Hull and get as far away from Manchester as you possibly can, because, once you are in their pocket, there's no getting out, except in a box."

There's the impassive look of concern on DI Lyndsey's face as he hears this. Then he smirks.

"You don't have to worry about me, Dave. I know what I'm doing and this is a new world with new minds. The Doyle Family don't break people's hands, this is the 21st century, not an episode of the Sopranos. They want your business. It's as simple as that. First, there'll be a police investigation of your dealings, led by me, it'll be all forms and phone calls and looking at your bank details. I can do it all from my laptop in the office, mate. Then there'll be interviews of the people who work for you. I know some of what you do already, I know you have Dave Adam Haulage running teak furniture into Hull and across the UK, and know it's not just furniture they're bringing in. I know there are spirits on those trucks, Our Dave, a lot of people do. So that's what will happen, and you'll just get banged up, nobody will get shot or killed, it'll just be paperwork, and you'll get nicked."

"I've been at this game a long time, DI Lyndsey. You'll investigate me and then you'll have to investigate my links too. Some people won't like that. People who've helped me in this city won't like it at all, because nobody is squeaky clean in the eyes of the law. Your paper chase will end up with you, son." DI Lyndsey looks up at the tall man, sees his earnest eyes and his bald head. There's solid reason to Our Dave. "Have you got a wife, a girlfriend, a boyfriend, anyone?" DI Lyndsey is confused.

"What's that got to do with this?"

"Everything. I'm guessing you've got paid some already by the Doyles and this new fella at the top, or someone under him."

"Maybe."

"What do you need the money for? If it's something reasonable, I can help. Money for someone who needs it, someone who's in trouble."

"Are you trying to bribe me?"

"No. If we can avoid this and you can get what you need then everything can go back to how it is. You might not have worked it out yet, but having friends is better than making enemies, even if it does cost to start with."

"If you must know, there isn't anyone, Dave. There's just me. I want the money for holidays, designer suits and whores, expensive dinners in posh restaurants and cologne. I want the money so people can look at me and feel jealous. That's what I'm doing this for, because I'm someone, not a no one like you." Our Dave shakes his head.

"You've suffered, I'm sure you have, kid. This isn't going to make whatever happened to you any better."

"Don't try to stall me with all this, Dave. You'll either stop now, or the Doyle Family, and me, will come down on you."

"How long have I got?"

"A day."

"It would take months to close down everything. Even if I was going to."

"You've got a day. As long as you show willing, I'm sure Mr Doyle will see you're a man trying to do the right thing."

"Once this goes wrong, he'll take it out on you, DI Lyndsey, you do know that?"

"Are you going to play or do you want war?" Our Dave sighs. Maybe it is time to stop all this. Perhaps now's as good at time for him to cash in his chips and tell the wagons to stop rolling, but there are too many people who depend on him, not just his wife, Hazel and his son down in London. There are the girls in the taxi office, the drivers at the haulage firm, the Scottish distilleries, the Cottingham Gin makers, the couple who live in his house down Westbourne Ave. He can't close up shop and he won't be intimidated.

"It'll have to be war, DI Lyndsey. The Doyles won't be

happy about it."

"You're making the wrong decision."

"Maybe. You've messed it up already. You probably told him all about me, this taxi office, this street, the bit of business you think I do. You told him it would be easy, straightforward even. It's not going to be."

"It's a different world now, old man. You best move aside or you'll get shoved over."

"Let yourself out, mate, won't you?" says Our Dave.

DI Lyndsey does his grin, turns on his heels and walks through the galley kitchen and out into the car park.

Our Dave boils the kettle as he unpicks the visits from seemingly two different forces. First, there's Daz who says his benefactor wants to buy the business, then, there's this copper who works for the Doyles in Manchester who says they want him to close up shop and stop running booze. He puts a teabag in a cup and pours on the hot water as he thinks.

Do they know about each other?

CHAPTER NINE
Bev

It's morning. There's a message on Bev's phone. It's from an unknown number and it just reads 'slag'. She deletes it and looks out of the window at her garden out back. She's suffered abuse before, lots of times and worse than this too, but it's not nice however hard you think you are or pretend to be. The phone buzzes again and she swallows as she picks it up. It's from Lars.

"How are you today, beautiful?" She smiles as she begins to pump in a reply. Lars is never rude to her, never pushy or overly dirty, unless she is. He always replies in good time and has messaged her every morning when he wakes up since they first got in contact. Chloe comes down the stairs and into the kitchen, she flicks the switch on the kettle to boil it.

"Who are you texting?" she asks her mum. "Another bloke?" Bev puts the phone down on the table and looks up at her daughter, not in anger but in resignation. Chloe doesn't dwell on it but turns back to the rumbling kettle.

"You don't mind if it is, do you?" asks Bev. Chloe frowns.

"No. You've never asked me that before."

"You've never been old enough. It's not the sort of thing I wanted to talk to you about. Not when you were younger."

"It's your life, mum," says the girl. She's tall and slim with straight black hair from a centre parting. Bev says she should dye it, but Chloe says it would make her look cheap.

"I'm not trying to meet any man, Chloe. I want someone long term, someone I can make a life with. That's all I've ever wanted." This is honest.

"You had enough chances," says Chloe as she fills her mug with hot water.

"What's that supposed to mean?"

"It means that you've had a lot of men." Chloe is not as naturally predisposed to tell the hard truth like her mother is, but she has her moments.

"No, I haven't," says Bev. "I've had a few boyfriends since we left your dad, but not that many." Bev blinks as she thinks

79

about what her daughter just said. There's the insinuation that she is less than wholesome because she has kissed a few lads. It's the kind of thing Bev's mother would say, she didn't expect it from her daughter.

"Come on, Mum," says Chloe in mild despair. She turns to look down on the blonde-haired woman sitting at the table in the kitchen on Lynton Ave, the make-up around her eyes makes them look bigger than they are. "You had a lot more than a few. Those are just the ones that I know about."

"Do you think I'm too easy?" Chloe and Bev have been through too much together for word games. The thin, young lass casts around the room with her eyes to look for an answer that will be both truthful and won't offend. "Don't answer that," cuts in Bev. "There's no need. I know what I am, and I know what I have been. I don't regret what I did, and you shouldn't judge me for it either, that's what your bloody granddad used to do. I'll tell you this though, the next man I'm with will be for good." Chloe gives her a half smile as if she doesn't think this is quite true. It is hard for Bev to see this on her daughter. She stands up and goes to the window to look out on the garden.

There have been a lot of men. Before she was married, Bev slept with a few fellas, fell in love with one or two but chose her husband because he was well-dressed and always seemed to have money, this is not to say that she didn't love him, she did, but in the end she wanted more to life than a half a bottle of vodka every night watching the telly and getting slapped when he was drunk. When they got divorced in the early 2000s, Bev felt a sense of liberation, and with the aid of dating sites and her wry smile she was pursued by men from all corners; not just working-class lads, but lecturers, policemen and men of position. She became complacent at how easy it was. Because she had a job driving a taxi, she didn't need them either. It was a sense of power and freedom, but there was always the desire for intimacy as well. Bev dreamed of someone she could trust and depend on rather than screw, and while there were a string of men who would happily marry her, they were never quite right.

"I would never get anyone to replace your dad," says Bev. "and I would never have had anyone move in here with us."

"You don't have to explain yourself to me, mum," says the lass from behind.

"I'm explaining it to myself as much as you, Chloe," she turns and looks at her daughter. There's something special there, it's an intelligence that gets things done and looks at things in a new way. Bev will never keep her, she has to let her go into the world where she will thrive.

There's a crash from behind them. The top glass panel of the little conservatory shatters and collapses into the room below, Bev jumps forward and her arms go out to protect her daughter as Chloe drops her coffee mug in shock. There's another crash, and a second brick comes in through the side panel and hits the clock on the opposite wall, glass shatters across the room. There's the buzz of a scooter in the alleyway next to the house as whoever threw it speeds away.

Bev does not know where to look for a moment as her brain processes what has happened. She dashes down the hall to the front door, and as she opens up, she sees two figures on a twist and go moped flying off at speed down the avenue. Instead of helmets they both wear black balaclavas. Bev slams the door and returns to Chloe who stands in shock. She looks down and there's half a brick on the kitchen floor.

"Some little bastard has just chucked that through the conservatory window," she whispers. Bev looks up at the damage to the room. Two panes are broken and shards are scattered over the little settee in there.

"Who would do that?" asks Chloe. She sounds worried.

"I don't know," says Bev, but she does know.

It's something to do with Our Dave alright.

It's the start of war.

CHANTERLANDS AVE
Afternoons

It's twelve o'clock. From down the ten foot at the top of Newstead Street, and picking up speed as she goes, comes a goth girl riding a black e-scooter. She wears a short skirt and fishnets, dark fingerless gloves and her nails are painted jet black also. The eye makeup is smooth and tapered. There's no helmet. She doesn't check for traffic as the scooter moves onto Chanterlands Ave proper - she does not have to. Like the teenagers who weave their mountain bikes in and out of cars in this city, she has a godlike sense of knowing when to slow or turn without seeming to notice anything at all. In her ears studded with piercings there are two shiny black buds pumping music directly into her brain.

She passes rows of terraced houses and the expensive supermarket on the right-hand side. There's no need for her to slow for the old woman stepping onto the zebra crossing, instead, she uses it to get onto the other side of the road where she mounts the pavement. There is no expression on her face as she wizzes down the path. The little speedo on the handlebars reads 15 mph. She weaves in an out of the pedestrians.

The goth girl passes the Avenues library with the chiropody practice on the opposite side and crosses in front of Dove House charity shop - there's a new display in the window of used toys. She avoids an old man with a walking stick coming out of the Avenues Pub and speeds on past the medical centre and the singing school in the upstairs flat. The goth girl applies the brakes at Westbourne Ave, and makes a sharp turn, still on the pavement, she banks in a smooth well-rehearsed manoeuvre and crosses the road to the other side.

Shop assistants have done most of their work already, but the takeaways will just be firing up their ovens, Adrian at the pub checks barrels and his stock in the beer cellar. The chip shops turn on the huge friers, and once it gets to three, mums and dads will flock down to the primary school behind the cemetery to pick up their kids. Chants Ave will flood with traffic and people making their way up or down.

The girl on her e-scooter moves back onto the road. She cuts in front of a car so the driver has to break sharply. She is not going to stop. She finds a space so she can squeeze between a parked double decker and the oncoming traffic. She is expressionless yet as the speedo climbs to 20mph and the handlebars rattle. By the time she has got the scooter to Park Ave she is doing 25 and glides along like some sort of dark Valkyrie as she passes the petrol garage. She's going to visit a lover perhaps, or to band practice, or to get a new tattoo.

That's the afternoon. It's full of promise.

CHAPTER TEN
Dilva

It's five o'clock in the afternoon. Dilva knows this because the Kurdish news channel has just started with the seven o'clock bulletin. The kids are sitting down to eat their tea of upside-down rice which they like, and Dilva has just taken a big bowl of it through to Aziz who is watching the TV. The sound is not too loud today. Now that they know the big man, Ryan, who is their neighbour, and after Dilva's fight with him, they are both more respectful of the amount of noise they make. Dilva allows Aziz to eat in the living room because he is ill, but the children eat in the kitchen with her, like her mother and grandmother made her do when she was young. She goes back in and sits down opposite as they go at their rice. Mohammed talks about football at school and Layla explains something about her Xbox game in Kurdish that is poor and broken, their language is interspaced with English words pronounced like they were from Hull. Dilva looks over at the dish with the rice on it and thinks there is a lot left, her mother would have plated that up and taken it to a neighbour, so would her grandmother. Dilva stands up and reaches down a bowl, she begins to spoon some of the rice into it. She might be in a different country, but that doesn't change where she has come from and what she thinks is right.

In two minutes, she stands outside her neighbour's front door with the bowl in her hand. She taps on the glass and waits. Ryan opens the door. He is wearing a khaki vest that shows his arms and his face is mistrustful. When he sees it's Dilva, he smiles. She hands him the rice.

"What's this?" he asks.

"For you," she says. He looks confused. "We're neighbours," she explains. He takes the bowl in one of his big hands and she looks past him to the house behind. There are pizza boxes on the floor and empty beer cans, books and crisp packets strewn on the sofa. She notices that he is unshaven. Ryan sees the look of pity on her face, but he does not feel threatened by it, more ashamed.

"I need to have a clean up," he says in defence. "I've not been feeling great this last couple of weeks." A month ago, Ryan lost another job. He has worked at many places - the animal rescue centre, the DIY store, a night shelf stacker at the supermarket, the plastic factory, and that's in the last year. Before that, many years before, Ryan was in the army. Dilva knows this because he told her and, in some ways, he trades on his past as a serviceman, but it has taken its toll on him, perhaps more than he can know.

"You can come in, if you want," he says. Dilva steps through after him. It's a mirror version of her own house, with the stairs and hall on the wrong side. There's the smell of male sweat and onions from whatever he's been cooking, the radio is on and there are dirty socks on the floor. What strikes Dilva, however, is how little there is in the room, there are no pictures, one long couch, a rug, a TV on the wall but no signs of warmth like cushions or a lamp. Ryan looks confused as he stands there with the bowl of upside-down rice in his hand, he's afraid of her somehow, because, in all these years there's been nobody who has physically attacked him so successfully and at such speed, and with such good reason. He is ashamed that he had the gun, even though it was plastic. Dilva looks at the light mess of the terraced house.

"Are you here alone?" she asks even though she knows it is just him. He nods.

"Now my mum's gone."

"Where did she go?"

"She died." Dilva wishes she hadn't asked.

"I'm sorry for you."

"She was old, it was for the best," answers Ryan. They are awkward in the front room these two, each curious of the other. There is a connection between them, Ryan knows this woman was a soldier but not the full extent of her story, and she knows too that he has served his country but that he is sloppy and lazy and frightened. Those who are afraid make the most noise. She nods down at the rice in the bowl.

"There's chicken in it too," she says. Their conversation is drawing to a close. Ryan does not know the situation, it's in his mind that Dilva is married, and her husband next door will be jealous of her being in his house. In the same way, Dilva thinks that her standing there will be a green light for this British man to think about her in a less than polite way. She steps back. Ryan must act quickly because, he cannot put his finger on it, but there is something about this woman. Her eyes are dark and so calm, and yet, there is rage hidden in her. He is drawn to it and frightened by it too, for in the fight she had with him the other day, there was truth. She saw a gun and she reacted, not against Ryan, but against the weapon and she pulled the trigger at his head so swiftly, like she was cutting potatoes or pouring hot water into a coffee cup. There was no bravado, and for so many years, bravado and bluster are all Ryan has ever been. The plastic gun was part of his hard man act. She steps back towards the door – he needs to know how she became this, and, how he can be it also.

"I see you've got a load of rubbish in the back garden there?" She cocks her head because she doesn't quite understand what he is saying. "All the rubbish in your garden. I could get rid of it for you. I could take it to the tip. Your kids could play there. I've got a car." Her eyes examine him and rather than wonder what he really wants from her, Dilva can see that he's lost. He doesn't look after himself or his house and has nobody to care for either, he wears army clothes and carries a plastic gun, but has forgotten how to fight, he walks like a cockerel down the street with his chest puffed out. He is broken and he wants to hide it from the world. Her yard really is full of junk from the previous occupants, there's a fridge freezer on its side with the door open like a wide mouth, a rotten armchair, plastic bags stuffed with rubbish, an old swing and part of a greenhouse. She won't let the kids out there.

"I could clean it up for you," he adds. She smiles. Her teeth are white and straight and her eyes twinkle. She is not really sure what she is accepting.

"Thank you for this," says Ryan about the bowl he holds.

"It was Iraq," she says.

"What was?"

"Where I saw war." This is the answer to Ryan's question from the last time they met.

"Were you a soldier?"

"Kurdish. Peshmerga."

"Where?"

"Mosul. 2017." Ryan's face is impassive. He knows what happened there and he knows men who fought in the battle. He can see fury behind Dilva's eyes, swimming below the surface like a pike under the still waters of a lake. He has an idea of what will have happened to her. She steps back towards the door, she's been here long enough already and she turns to leave.

"Did you think about what I said, about the people you can call who can help you." Her black eyes concentrate on him.

"I don't need help," she says. Ryan knows this mind frame. He has it. He's been to meetings at the trauma centre where they sit around in groups and tell stories of their experiences but only because he was ordered there by the courts. Ryan is known to thump people he thinks deserve it, and, once the red mist comes over him, he swings his heavy fists and because he is so big, he hurts people, mix this with drink and some of the amphetamines he's been taking on and off and there's a recipe for assault. Ryan was let off with community service and spared the prison time because the man had hit him first. Another condition was he attend the trauma unit.

"I can start tomorrow, if that's okay with you."

Ryan closes the door and looks down at his green combat socks that he got from an army surplus website. He puts his hand to his forehead and closes his eyes. There are flashes sometimes of his own past and what he did all that time ago and all those many miles away, things that he cannot tell anyone because they will not understand.

CHAPTER ELEVEN
Liz

It's Monday morning again. Liz stands at the backdoor of her ground floor flat and has a roll-up. Joel is inside. The smoke curls up into the blue sky above. She doesn't smoke, of course. This is a treat she allows herself once in a while - most mornings and every evening. Joel woke early, about six and so she did too. She'll drop him off in half an hour at the minder and then go to work herself. He's been a good lad today and at odd times, Liz found herself laughing with him, as she washed him in the shower, as they wrestled on the bed. She takes another puff on the roll-up. Her phone buzzes in her pocket, it's on silent as it usually is. She looks at the caller's name. Mathew. She swallows. This is the blond man who moved to London to pursue an academic career that could not be missed. What could he want? She presses the green button and holds the mobile to her ear as she frowns in concern.

"Yes," she answers.

"Liz."

"Yes." There's silence on the other end and she can almost hear him swallowing.

"It's Mathew."

"I know that," she replies. She has found, instantly, her tone of contempt.

"I just wanted to catch up."

"It's been a while."

"How's Joel?"

"He's fine, growing up. It was his birthday last month." She can hear the pause on the other end.

"I just wanted to let you know a few things."

"Go on."

"I've been offered a position at the University of Osaka. That's in Japan."

"I know where it is."

"I just wanted to let you know that I'm leaving next month, and I probably won't be back for a while."

"Why are you telling me this?"

"Just so you and Joel know where I am." Liz drops her roll-up on the ground and crushes it out with one of her sandals like she is grinding him into the stone floor of her garden path.

"We didn't know where you were before, so what difference does that make?"

"You knew I was in London."

"I've got your phone number, Mathew, that's all. Is that really why you're ringing?"

"Yes, I just wanted to do the right thing." If Liz was Bev then she would launch into a tirade of hatred now, she would explain how Mathew has never done the right thing for her and Joel. Liz is more level-headed, but she can still wound him.

"Is it to ease your conscience?" she asks. She hears the silence of him squirming on the other side.

"No," he answers. "What do you mean?"

"I mean that you never have any contact with your son." He coughs on the other end.

"We both agreed that you'd bring him up, Liz. I've helped financially, but you do realise that the work I'm doing here in London, and soon enough out in Osaka is crucial to the world. We're making breakthroughs that have never been dreamed of." This is Mathew's way. He will turn the world to his advantage. Like she has realised before, the tone of his voice, the excitement on his breath as he speaks tells that Mathew is not remorseful of what he has or hasn't done, because he was doing it for the best all along. "I would have loved to stay there to help you with Joel, but there are bigger things at stake here, Liz. You knew that, you knew who I was and what I did. Don't hate me for it. I thought you were better than that." Liz looks down at the phone screen and presses the red button to cut him off. He calls back and she presses the red button once again.

In the kitchen, Liz makes herself another roll-up with more tobacco than usual. She lights it with fingers that fumble with a mixture of shame and anger.

Bev is already in the office when Liz walks in. It's still Monday. She has a look of mild thunder across her face as she glances at her mobile screen.

"Where's Our Dave?" she asks.

"Off somewhere on business. How was your weekend?" asks Liz.

"Shite," says Bev. Something has rubbed her up the wrong way for sure, so Liz smiles and puts her handbag down on a chair, she'll choose not to tell who called her this morning. She knows what Bev would say anyway, she's already told her to get onto the child support agency and squeeze Mathew for the correct money he should pay for his son. Liz knows she ought to.

The door from the kitchen opens and Dilva walks into the office that is bright with morning sunshine. She smiles.

"You're late," says Bev. The Kurdish woman fixes Bev with a cold stare. It's one minute past eight. So, she is one minute late. Dilva knows how precious people in the UK are with time, and that for some of them, it's more important than anything. She's not going to let this blonde woman get the better of her and looks down on Bev with her cool, dark eyes and there's that rage just below the surface, like something terrible hiding in the mist. Bev can sense this but is too tough to care.

"Keep looking at me like that, lass and I'll split your lip." Bev stands and the chair scrapes on the wooden floor. Dilva takes a slow breath. If this woman attacks, she does not know what she might do.

"Just what is your problem with her?" asks Liz. Something has got under Bev's skin, like it does.

"I don't know who she thinks she is, coming in here like she owns the place." Liz's face is flush with disdain. This Kurdish woman has done nothing wrong but Bev carries on anyway. "She's just ignorant. The least she could do was learn English, she's been here long enough." Bev knows that it's not as easy as that, but she has been rattled by the brick through her conservatory window, the man she killed a few weeks back and the slimy young copper DI Lyndsey.

There's heavy knocking on the back door of the office, the one that leads to the little galley kitchen. Bev walks past Dilva and gives her a black look as she does. It might be the postman with a parcel. Bev goes through the kitchen with the kettle clicking as it boils and opens the door. There's an ugly face she does not recognise under a black beanie hat, he's got a thug grin and is a few inches taller than her but young. There's another man behind him dressed in a dark bomber jacket and with a beard. The two of them have hard man scowls.

There's something wrong.

The brick through her conservatory, the man she killed, Our Dave's strange behaviour and now this - it's all linked. Bev does not have time to say anything as the man erupts into violence, shoves open the door and steps inside. He's wearing builder's gloves. He grabs her by the shoulders and pushes her down the galley kitchen, against the wall. Her back slams against the calendar that's pinned there. One of Bev's knees goes up to catch him in the balls, but this lad is not the kind of opponent she has fought before and sidesteps it – he's not angry or drunk, he's on a job. He catches her by the throat and holds her against the wall as the rough material of his gloves scratches her smooth skin. The man behind him makes his way into the taxi office and Bev can hear Liz scream. She tries to twist her way out of the grip but he uses his body weight to pin her by her neck. He produces a silver snub-nosed pistol in his right hand and he shows this to Bev's wide eyes.

"This is a message for Dave," the man's accent is Manc and nasal. He leans into Bev's throat with his hand and her legs struggle as he does so. In the main office there's a loud bang and shouting, Liz is screaming and there's the scrape of a chair. The Manc in front pushes his hand further into Bev's neck. She can smell his aftershave, it's expensive, she sees his haircut is freshly done. "You tell Dave that this has just begun, alright? You got that? This is just a warm up for what's coming later on? Do you understand? Nod if you get me?" Bev nods. He pushes harder. He has opened her legs with his, so he can get in closer still and push his groin against her. She can feel him rise.

There's movement in the galley kitchen behind them. Bev can make out the dark hair of Dilva as she walks through the door, she has a vacant look to her as she picks up the kettle from the far end that has just boiled. The Manc is too busy thinking about his groin and Bev's blonde hair to notice anything, besides, he's been told there are only women here. Bev watches as Dilva paces up behind him, noiseless and calm, her eyes are wide, as if she's in a trance almost. Her nostrils flare and she is breathless. She has already done something to the other man. Now she will deal with this one. Ghostlike, she moves behind him and yanks the collar of his coat, pulling him back just enough and then, tips the kettle of boiling water over his head. He makes a shrieking sound as he goes down on his side and Bev watches Dilva's impassive face as she follows with the rest of the boiling water, making sure she has got it all on him like she was pouring a cup of tea. The snub-nosed pistol clatters to the floor and he screams in shock and pain. His face is bright red and the skin is already bubbling up in welks and white blisters.

There's the sound of footsteps behind them. Whatever Dilva has done to the man with the beard in the main taxi office, it has made him afraid enough to run. A figure dashes through the door of the kitchen out to the car park. Dilva sees the man, drops the kettle and springs after him. Bev watches her disappear around the door on his heels, blinks a second as she realises the woman just saved her, and then follows after them through the door. Bev now understands the level and calm stare that Dilva gave her, it wasn't arrogance - it was fear. Liz appears in the kitchen with her eyes wide in terror.

"Phone Our Dave," says Bev. "I'll get her," and she is out the door after Dilva.

It's early Monday morning and the traffic is just picking up. Secondary school kids walk in groups with big backpacks. There are students standing at the bus stop outside the cemetery and power mums out for a jog. The man Dilva chases is quick but she injured him in the office. In the melee she hammered a biro into his thigh and smashed his head into the laptop screen. He won't be as fast as he ought to be. She sees him with his black bomber jacket open as he sprints down Chants Ave past the supermarket. The red mist is over Dilva's eyes and she can hear the roar of rockets from all those years ago, and the rattle of gunfire from her memories. She is sweating and afraid. She has to get that man. It's all she can think of. She sprints after him on her cheap trainers with her knees powering her forward and her face cold.

Thirty seconds behind her is Bev. She's not unfit but hasn't been running since she went out with a lad who was into marathons. He convinced her to join him at East Hull Fitmums jogging sessions where she was put in the two-mile group. Bev cannot mess about, she has to keep up with Dilva. She spots the jet-black hair some way off as the Kurdish woman runs across the road. A sandy coloured Range Rover slams on its brakes and horn as it skids to a halt to stop itself crashing into her. Bev sees the man she is chasing too, with his bomber jacket open as he runs back over the road, through the morning traffic that is slow and thick, and turns down into Lynton Ave, Dilva disappears after him and out of sight. If she is to catch them, Bev must speed up, she sticks her chest out, and just like she was taught at East Hull Fitmums, she gives it legs down Chanterlands Ave at five past eight on a Monday morning.

On the quieter side street, Dilva nears the man she chases. He stumbles as he goes down a little alley behind a double garage. There are blue wheelie bins standing guard outside back garden gates; the man dodges the first and crashes into the second knocking it over, he falls onto his back as the recycling spills from the bin next to him. In three steps, Dilva arrives, her knees crash into his chest as her weight falls down on him, her fist crunches into his cheek and there's a weak pop as something cracks. He's stunned. She steadies herself with her knees over each of the man's shoulders, pressing into the arms. She is about to hit him again when she notices a half broken red wine bottle that must have rolled out of the wheelie bin. She sees opportunity and picks it up. Just like when she pulled the trigger in Ryan's face a few days before – there is to be no pause, no consideration for the act she is about to perform. In this state, Dilva is free, there's no future or past, no worry or doubt, just the cold calm rage of what she has to do. She maneuvers the bottle so the jagged edge along the underside is pointing down towards the man. She's going to ram it into his face.

A figure dives at her before she can deliver the blow and she crashes off under the mid weight of a thin woman with blonde hair. It's Bev. Dilva drops the bottle and they roll, the two of them, for a moment, across the uneven stone floor of an alley on Lynton Ave. Bev scuffs her cheek on the concrete and comes to rest on her back, above her is Dilva with her long hair falling over her face as her hands go around Bev's throat. The grip is expert, the thumbs are on her windpipe, not designed to threaten or frighten, but intended to kill. Bev roars out into the morning as she feels the pressure build.

"It's me, it's me," she calls, as if this will help. Dilva is not her friend, ten minutes previous Bev was ready to split her lip. Dilva maneuvers her weight on Bev's body to get a better grip, between her long black hair she gets a glimpse of the woman below her. She sees the frightened eyes with the dark smooth eyeliner. Dilva has never killed a woman before – she's never had to. She releases her hands and just as quick as the rage took her, fear takes its place. The Kurdish woman scrambles backward off Bev and her hands go to her face in concern as she stands. The man who crashed into the bin further up the alley gets to his feet and limps away at speed, Bev watches him disappear as she sits up. In front, Dilva has her red face in her hands in shame and worry.

Bev got this girl wrong.

The four of them sit around the little table in Avenue Cars. On the stone floor there are smashed pieces of plastic from the laptop Dilva battered one of the men with and broken porcelain from the mugs that were knocked off the tables. The men who attacked them are long gone, even the one who Dilva poured a kettle of boiling water over. Once Bev had got Dilva back to the office, Our Dave appeared looking grey – he pleaded with them to make the morning run as usual, so that there'd be no police involved, and that, at 12 o'clock back in the office, he would explain.

It's 12 o'clock.

This is the first day that Bev has thought about having a cigarette since her divorce in 2001. Liz has had several roll-ups out the back door and Dilva sits on a chair in the office, emotionless with her lips a thin pencil line across her pale face. Now Bev knows the Kurdish girl is as screwed up as she is, maybe more so, she likes her a lot, she's a sister even. Bev has made her a cup of tea without milk, as she says she likes it. They watch Our Dave rub his big hand over his bald head, like he does.

"Are you going to spit it out then?" ask Bev. It's clear he is going to spit it out, that's why they're here, but Bev just has to prod, it's what she does when she's nervous. Our Dave looks grey still.

"I never thought it would come to this," he says.

"Come to what?" asks Bev.

"You'll just have to let him speak," says Liz. She has managed to sit with one of her legs tucked under the other.

"I'm being taken over, girls. It's a simple as that." Bev huffs. Dilva has not moved at all and Liz does breathing techniques she learned at Tuesday night yoga, as she tries to understand. "What I mean is, my business is being taken over. This taxi office along with it."

"This is your business," says Bev.

"Not really," he answers. "This is kind of the front for my

real activity and it has been for a long time."

"What's your business?" asks Liz. He might as well be honest, he's got this far. These girls are the people that he trusts most in the whole of the network he's built up over the years.

"I smuggle booze. Mostly through the port here at Hull in grain trucks or inside plastic toilet components from Holland or Poland, sometimes inside furniture. I bring in whiskey too through the fishing boats at Hornsea and on the yachts on the marina here as well. The money comes through the taxi office and the mechanic down the road, some of it through a letting business on the properties I have. I just give it away as well, sometimes. I've got a load of old fifty-pound notes buried at the allotment." There's silence from the three girls after he finishes.

"What about the police?"

"Money goes to the Clough Road Christmas Party every year, and I pass a few quid to policemen here and there. Lads up at the port get a good whack for looking the other way. This is alcohol after all, nobody really worries, and there's always a few extra bottles for someone. What's to care about? There are far more powerful men and bigger fish than me bringing in a lot more under the radar."

"You don't pay tax on it, then?" asks Liz. Our Dave shakes his head. Liz asks obvious questions sometimes.

"So who were the men who came here this morning?"

"Lads from the game."

"The game?" asks Bev.

"It's the old school name for what we do."

"Are you taking the piss?" asks Bev.

"I'm not taking the piss," says Our Dave and there is a degree of mettle in his voice. "The game is organized crime, Bev. What do you think pays your wages? Picking up kids from school or running blokes in wheelchairs to hospital visits doesn't exactly make a lot of money. It doesn't make enough to run this place, that's for sure."

"What's there to run?" asks Bev. "Look around, Our Dave, it's hardly Las Vegas." Bev is naturally cruel and unless you know her, you'd think her heartless. Our Dave could hit back with a nasty remark of his own, but he is not like that.

"Turns out my quiet operation has come to the attention of two different parties. That copper who you spoke to Bev, DI Lyndsey, he works for a Manchester firm, they want me to stop business so they can move in. There's more. Someone right here in Hull wants to buy me out as well. I have an idea of who it is, but I'm not sure." Bev paraphrases.

"You run an illegal booze smuggling operation? There are gangsters from Manchester who want you to stop doing business and some other gang who want to buy you out." She has a way of saying things straight. "You're definitely taking the piss." The last sentence is rhetorical.

"You've been here for twenty years or more, ever since I came here to uni in the nineties." It's Liz. Our Dave ignores this obvious outburst. It will take her a bit more time to get her head around the situation.

"The point is that you're involved now," continues Our Dave, "as much as I don't like it." He looks greyer than normal, there are bags under his eyes. "I didn't think it would happen like this and quite this fast. I'll get onto that copper and tell him it's all over. I can't have normal people like you in the line of fire. Once I call him, they should back off. I'm just sorry this happened, girls." He looks to each of their faces, Dilva with her impassive stare, Liz with a look of terror and Bev with her hard, defensive frown.

"What about the police?" asks Dilva. "What about the men who attacked this office?"

"They'll be gone, there'll be no police," explains Our Dave. "It shouldn't have happened," he says. "And it won't happen again, because I'll give him what he wants."

"What about the pistol that lad dropped? What have you done with that?" Bev leaves no stone unturned.

"I put it in the drawer under the microwave," he says. She tuts as she looks away.

"It's not a pair of scissors. What if the police come sniffing round? You need to get rid of it." Our Dave is not flustered by Bev's words.

"I will, just as soon as all this blows over. This is what's going to happen," explains Our Dave. "You'll still keep on as normal for the time being, but I can't have people trying to hurt you. I don't know what'll happen in the long run. Maybe it's time for things to change. The most important thing you can all do, is not to say anything about any of this, to anyone, not even people you trust. You understand that?" He looks to each face and gets a sullen nod from Dilva, a more expressive sigh from Liz and a scowl of agreement from Bev. "I'll sort it out, one way or another, you just don't go worrying about it, and keep driving like you always do. There'll be no more bricks through windows or threats or strange men attacking the office. Things will go back to normal soon enough."

When the girls have left the taxi office, Our Dave walks through into the front waiting room with wooden seats around the outside. It's deserted. He looks at the grate over the little window for the receptionist. This room is a museum now, a leftover from a past long gone. Avenue Cars is dead and it needs to be buried as well, it's all disappeared to mobile phone apps. Time was, this waiting room would be full of people and you never knew who they were going to be. Our Dave had fourteen drivers at one point, all coming and going, here and there on their radios and the phone would be ringing every two minutes. Everything comes to an end after all. The fish factories across this city closed up many years ago when the arse fell out of the docks, the estates that housed the workers are getting pulled down, the little shops on Chants Ave that have been here forever are closing. It will soon be autumn. Our Dave feels melancholic but philosophical, when the leaves on his potato plants at the allotment start going yellow, he pulls them up and digs out the spuds. Things die and change and that's the way it is. He puts his phone to his ear. It rings a few times until someone picks up at the other end.

"DI Lyndsey," says a youthful voice.

"Tell him I'll stop," says Our Dave. There's a pause on the other end.

"That was quick," says the officer. "Just like that. What made you change your mind?" His tone is playful. Perhaps he doesn't know that two men attacked the office earlier that day or that someone threw a brick through Bev's window or that a week ago, a man tried to kidnap Our Dave but got the wrong person and is now, ashes on the incinerator floor.

"We had some visitors, and I don't want any more. You get on the phone to Robbo Doyle and tell him that I'm giving up. I'll start to wind the organization down as soon as I can but some of the things will take time to drop off, there are shipments and containers and if they just stop people will get suspicious."

"I'll put it to him," says DI Lyndsey on the other end. "He's a reasonable man, I think. I'll do what I can."

"No more heavies. I'm someone who has a history, officer. I wasn't always as calm as I am now. I'll do whatever to protect any of these people, do you understand?"

"I do know about what you've done, Dave," his tone is condescending. "I'll explain."

"See that you do."

"Hopefully, I won't have to speak to you again about this, Dave. I'll drop by for a social visit sometime, though, just to make sure you're doing okay." Our Dave pulls the phone from his ear and hangs up. He's surrounded once more by the ghosts of the taxi business past, the cackle of laughter and the stink of fags. He's going to do something he doesn't want to do. Since his father died in 1981, Our Dave has managed everything himself more or less, he's asked for advice many times, but he's never asked for help. In such a situation as he is in, there is only one person in this city who can help him. If he is in their debt then he might as well close the business down anyway, but, these are dangerous times. He'd rather be in debt to her than some young prick from Manchester. He's felt her hand in all this already, perhaps with Daz, the skag head.

He's going to see The Leatherhead.

There's a pub at the end of Hessle Road called the

Dairycoates Inn. It doesn't fit with the industrial units on the same street and the busy main road, it's a building that has been pulled straight out of the 19th century. There are green tiles around the huge windows and, inset as a display piece into one of the outside walls, is a picture of a ship's anchor with the words 'Anchor Brewery'. The world has changed around the Dairycoates Inn, the terraced streets have been torn down and replaced with warehouses, there's a flyover right opposite where the trucks, lorries and cars drive out of the city all day long. Everything has changed around her, but she has stayed the same.

Our Dave has parked down the street and walks to the little pub with a frown of concern. It's just past two in the afternoon. It's been a while since he has been here. The lady who runs this pub is not someone to be messed with and he thinks suddenly as he gets to the door, that he is too old to do this sort of thing. What would Hazel have said if she knew he was walking into the lion's den?

Inside, and even at this time of day, there are a dozen or so drinkers. This is where shift workers come for a few before they go home to sleep. It's an honest boozer with regulars and steady, well-kept ale, at least at the front. Round the back, at the kitchen door, the chef will sell you a range of different narcotics, but he won't sell to just anyone. Here in the bar there's a big older man with tattoos under his rolled-up sleeves sipping on a pint. He looks at Our Dave through mean eyes. Once this man would have worked the trawlers. Not so today. The boats this old timer knew are long gone and lots of the culture too, but not all of it. Like the Dairycoates Pub itself, parts of the fishing industry are still there and still strong. The bar girl walks to Our Dave.

"What can I get you?"

"Is Ann upstairs?" he asks. She looks back at him with a blank expression.

"Aye, who should I say it is?"

"Tell her it's Our Dave."

He goes up the stairs and there's the smell of fags, bleach

and flowery perfume. The last time Our Dave was here it was 2005, the winter, and he didn't ask a favour, he just struck a deal. If she left him alone, he'd leave her alone too and that accord has stuck until the present day. He rounds the corner and there she is, sitting at the head of a long table in the kitchen. This is Leatherhead. She's a dinosaur like Our Dave. People say that she got her nickname in the sixties when she fell from the back of a motorbike without a helmet and got off with just a scratch - because her head was made of leather. Our Dave knows a different story - it's because of her face, even back then it was wrinkled and worn, now it looks much the same. She's a big one, six foot when she stands up and overweight with black dyed hair and piggy eyes, a real patty slapper as you might say, but very far from being stupid and very far from being someone you should trust. She's having a coffee and she sets the mug down to look up at Our Dave as he enters. There's a red-headed girl next to her with a laptop open, she's in her twenties with smooth skin, a proud nose and bright eyes.

"Now then, Wilkinson." She's one of the few people in the city who calls him by his real name.

"Now then, Ann," he replies, he knows what the Leatherhead was called before she became all this.

"Sit yourself down," she says. Our Dave pulls one of the chairs out at the other end of the table and sits down, all polite. The kitchen is pretty much just as Our Dave remembered it, orange lino tablecloth, eighties style light oak cupboards with metal handles, Leatherhead herself is in a long flowery top that shows her flabby arms. The girl with the laptop is new.

"Have you got an assistant now, Ann?" he asks.

"This is Kasia, she's Polish. She handles lots of things on the laptop here. We're just in the middle of a business meeting." In other UK cities there are gangs - families who run areas of Liverpool and Manchester like the Doyles, disaffected poor and old school gangsters in London, the warrior Welsh in Cardiff and up in Scotland tight knit Glaswegians who'll cut holes in your cheeks. Not so here. There's only one force on Hessle Road, it stretches up to

North Hull and over to the East, this is the Leatherhead. Drugs that run in through the port go through her, so does the delivery of them, not through her of course, because Ann Leatherhead doesn't believe in drugs but through her group of runners and small dealers, she sells everything from MDMA to weed. She remembers their last meeting in 2005 and what they said, Our Dave smuggles booze, and she does everything else and in return, he supplies the spirits to all her venues, including right here at the Dairycoates Inn.

"Business good?" asks Our Dave. Leatherhead takes a glug on her mug of coffee.

"Never better."

"You?"

"I'm having a few problems."

"I heard."

"Did you now?" It's not a question. Our Dave must play Miss Ann Leatherhead carefully. There are few in the city who know as much about him as she does.

"I did. Someone's making a play for your end of the business."

"That they are lass. What do you know?"

"Plenty. I'm sorry, Dave, would you like a brew?" Our Dave does not want to be here any longer than he has to, but if he's to get anything from the Leatherhead, then he'll have to show willing.

"Aye, that would be grand."

"Make Our Dave here a tea, will you Kasia," says Leatherhead without taking her eyes off the tall man who sits at the end of the table.

"Are we okay to talk?" asks Our Dave as he looks at the Polish girl who has gone to the plastic eighties kettle to boil it.

"Kasia knows everything about what I do, Dave, she's Polish, been here a few years now. She's like lots of Poles, you give her a job to do and she'll do it, she'll do it proper as well make no mistake, she's got no imagination at all though and she's as miserable as fuck, but she does okay for me." As she prepares the cup, Kasia looks over her shoulder at Our Dave with a scowl in response to the Leatherhead's insults.

In the seventies, Leatherhead's father was a trawlerman, one of the rough ones, he did time for glassing someone in the Halfway House pub. They sent him to jail where he got friendly with the wrong sorts, things just spiraled from there. When he got out, he sold whatever he could get his hands on to whoever would pay him, opium, cannabis resin, porn, handguns, stolen petrol. He wasn't a nice man, particularly, and as a low-level gangster, he got knifed to death at a petrol station in the early eighties. It was only natural that Ann Leatherhead should take over from him, she'd watched everything he did, and knew how he did it too. There were a few altercations, of course, as Ann took her father's young business to a new level. Our Dave heard about lads who were found frozen to death in fish factory cold rooms. Strong women are the norm around Hessle Road, with the men off fishing for so many months at a time, lasses held this community together, and Ann Leatherhead is the perfect example of the fishwife, big, warm to her friends, organised with an eye on her money and the future, terrible to those she does not know or worse to those she does not like. Our Dave knows how it used to work, and like her, he knows how it works these days as well.

"Who wants me out? I've heard it's the Doyle family of Manchester." She smiles at him like he's a child.

"That's what I've heard as well, but it's not so the new son Doyle can step into your shoes. There's someone else who he's doing a favour for." Our Dave wants to ask her who it is, but this is too crass. He has to tread a little more carefully around her. She's been in this game longer than he has, and that's a long time. Kasia sets a mug of tea down in front of him on a cork coaster, she looks like she'd be more suited to teaching in a primary school, Our Dave notices her sensible flat sandals and unpainted toenails.

"I heard old Cyril passed on." This is an acquaintance of both of them from the old days, the landlord of the Halfway House pub in the middle of Hessle Road. It's a way for Our Dave to keep the conversation light so he can get to the answers he needs.

"Aye," she answers. "I didn't go to the funeral."

"There weren't many there."

"There's not many of us left." The Leatherhead has the fatalistic view of the world that those connected with the fishing industry do, it's a simple turn of fate that will send your brother or your father to the bottom of the frozen North Sea. Death is not a strange thing for the Leatherhead.

"I need your help, Ann. Who wants me out the way?" She examines him with her cold fish eyes, they look like they are dead but there is life and humour hidden in there.

"You know I like you, Our Dave. I always have and we've had our agreement about business in the past. You do your thing and I do mine, I liked it that way. It was like I had a friend. Things are changing and we have to change with them, there's a new way of doing business."

"Is there?" Our Dave is not being sarcastic when he says this. The Leatherhead looks at Kasia who is typing away into her laptop, her voice is suddenly soft.

"You can leave us now, Kasia. I'll call you when I need you." The Polish girl does not smile at all as she leaves. Leatherhead has another sip on her mug and sets it down with a thump.

"What's changed Our Dave, in case you hadn't noticed, is that we're all being robbed, and not by gangsters or organised crime syndicates or drug barons. Now we're being fleeced by banks and electric companies, supermarkets and gas stations. There's a fella out at Kirk Ella by the name of Boyce, he lives opposite the golf club on Pacman Lane, he's on the city council, calls himself a businessman but he got all his money from his posh father who owned lots of the fishing ships down here in the eighties. Boyce is a ponce and he's never worked a day in his life. His type are moving the world straight." Our Dave does not quite understand what she means. Leatherhead leans into her explanation. It may take him some time to see what she's getting at, especially as he has been in the game for so long and the rules will be engraved on his heart.

"Profit will come from regular stuff that folk need, Dave, water, fuel, food and the businesses that we have both done well from will not be the same. Weed'll be legal in the next few years, you can buy it on any street corner now – other drugs will follow, and they'll remove the criminal element from the lot of it and big business will make all the profit. Folk like me and you Dave, we're all that's left of the old ways. Boyce wants to be part of that new breed. There'll be no need to pay off coppers to bring in what you want, you can get the laws changed so anything will be legal. That's why Boyce wants you gone, Our Dave, only he hasn't got the balls to bump you off like he should do. That's why he's got his friend Robbo Doyle from Manchester to put the frighteners on you and your girls." Ann Leatherhead mops her creased brow with a napkin from her mini handbag hanging over the chair. It has excited and tired her to give such an explanation. Our Dave considers this, he does not really know what she is getting at. He knows Boyce, he knows him because it's his lad, James Boyce, that he picks up from school. This fella would have known he would drop James off the other afternoon. It might have been Boyce senior who employed the man in a suit to do something to Our Dave, and then got it wrong with Bev. It's making a bit more sense.

"They rob people fair and square now, all legal and above board. Not like in our day," says Ann Leatherhead.

"Are you thinking of giving up?"

"I'll have to soon enough, Our Dave. I can't keep going forever. It's getting harder and harder to import stuff, there's cameras everywhere and the squeeze is on. It's all getting more difficult and at my age, I can't really be arsed. I need to find other ways to bring the money in."

"You could always open a taxi company." They both know the only people who make money from this now are the big tech giants.

"I might just take over yours," she says.

"You'd be welcome to it."

"Did you send Daz to talk to me, Ann?"

"I did. He's a regular here." By this Leatherhead means that he buys heroin from the back door of the pub. "I wondered how long it would take for you to guess it was me." Ann wipes the sides of her big mouth. There's an element of Jabba the Hut to her. "I'm taking over your operation, Dave. You'll keep the taxi business and I'll take the rest. You'll explain all the workings to Kasia and she'll pick up where you leave off. I need to diversify. You've had a good run, and now it's time for you to give up. You and Hazel can go on holiday somewhere if you like, you can retire."

So here it is. There are two sides.

On one, the Doyle Family and their boy Boyce who want him to shut up shop – they have the copper DI Lyndsey on their payroll and thugs who will break windows and attack the girls in the office. On the other side, there is Ann Leatherhead who wants to take his business, she controls Hull with a much heavier hand than the Doyles do, but so far, has not raised a finger against him. Our Dave is trapped in the middle. He stares across the orange lino of the table at Ann Leatherhead.

"What if I refuse to sell?"

"You know what happens, Our Dave. That's a stupid question to ask me. You'll end up shut in a freezer room in one of the fish factories. I've got a favour to ask of you, and then, I'll consider everything square between us."

"Everything is square between us," says Our Dave. "I don't owe you anything." She grimaces. Ann Leatherhead gets what she wants.

"We need it to go smoothly, don't we, Dave? I mean, you don't want anything to happen to you or your Hazel, do you? How long have you been married now?" The man takes a deep breath.

"46 years."

"It'd be awful if something happened to her, especially now you're about to retire. I need you to do me a favour." Our Dave knows what's coming. Leatherhead is ruthless, and she'll have a simple and terrible solution. He plays along.

"What do you want me to do?"

"You'll have to bump Boyce senior off, Our Dave. You'll have to get rid of him." He looks Leatherhead dead in the eyes and she does not blink. "Don't pretend you're all shocked, it's not as if you haven't done that kind of thing before. I need him gone. He's stepping on my shoes by moving in on you. You just get rid of him, like you used to get rid of people."

"That was a long time ago. I'm older now."

"It's either that, or something worse for you and yours. Have Mr Boyce come to some sort of accident, like you used to, go back to thinking like you did in the late seventies."

"I'm not proud of what I did, Ann."

"You don't have to be. There's a job to do and someone's got to do it. If you get rid of Boyce, you, your taxi office girls and your Hazel will get left alone."

"So you'll take my business, and you expect me to do someone in? What do I get out of it?" Leatherhead's face is full of creases, it's impassive and deep-sea cold in the gloom of her eighties style kitchen.

"You'll get to live, Our Dave. Do you need a bit of time to think it through, lad?" He swallows. Even after all these years, Leatherhead can still make him feel like a little boy.

"What's to think about? I'll do it. I'll kill him." The Leatherhead smiles and shows her white, fake smile:

"I'll give you a week to get it sorted then, Our Dave."

"A week?" he asks.

"Aye. A week." Our Dave looks down to his wrinkled hands clasped on his lap. He thinks of the girls in the taxi office, if he does not get this right, it will be them that Leatherhead will come down on.

"Consider it done, Leatherhead," he says. She nods.

"Now fuck off out my pub."

CHAPTER THIRTEEN
Bev and Dilva

You shouldn't really drink on Monday night. Bev tries to have Monday and Tuesday night off wine, she'll have a couple on Wednesday, a few on Thursday, then Friday and Saturday are fair game because it's the weekend, and there'll be a few glasses to come down with on Sunday night.

It's been a right day, so, she's okay to knock back a couple. Bev walks down the ten foot by the side of her house, along the back of the street towards Westbourne Ave. In her right hand she carries a bottle of flavored gin, and in her handbag are two little bottles of posh tonic that clink as she walks, brisk. She's going to do what she ought to have done a few weeks ago when Dilva first started. She's going to be her friend. Bev imagines what the Kurdish girl must think of her and she is sick with embarrassment. Without a thought, Dilva defended her this day and by God, there have not been many who have ever done that.

At Dilva's house, she walks up the long path to the front door and raps on the glass. There's the telly blaring in the front room and the sound of video games from upstairs. Dilva opens the door. She gives Bev a weak, almost ashamed smile.

"Can I come in?" asks Bev. She gets straight to the point. "I need to say sorry," she hands over the bottle and Dilva takes the smooth glass in her hand. "I thought we might have a drink and a chat," says Bev.

In the kitchen, Dilva has set the bottle of flavoured gin on the table and she is boiling the kettle to make a drink. Bev sits in one of the sensible chairs and examines the house. It's clean and in order with a big clock hanging on the wall, a well-scrubbed sink and the smell of spices she is not familiar with from something in the oven. Dilva pours two little cups of black tea and then sets these on the table, one in front of Bev and one in front of her. The blonde English woman looks embarrassed to be there.

"I don't drink alcohol," says Dilva, "but, thank you."

"I should have thought on," says Bev. "I want to say thank you for what you did this morning, from Liz and me." Dilva nods and smiles at this. She slides a box of expensive looking chocolates across the table, they have already been opened.

"Take one – they are from Liz. She came before." Bev tries not to scowl at the fact that Liz beat her to it. Where middle class educated Liz has gifted expensive chocolates with a posh grainy feel box, Bev has managed a cheap bottle of flavoured gin and only lemon because that's her favourite. It's not selfish. Bev means well and she had pictured the two of them having a drink and becoming closer, Bev wants to help her. She suddenly realises that this Kurdish woman might not want or need her friendship, she can look after herself and her family. What would she need a middle aged, bleach blonde woman for?

"You also helped me," she says. "I was going to kill that man. Why did you stop me?"

"Because you'd go to jail for it, you'd lose all this, your husband, the children, all of it. It wouldn't have been fair." The conversation withers. Bev is worried that she will not be understood and will therefore offend. She goes onto small talk:

"How long have you been married?"

"He's not my husband. He's my cousin." This second part is not true, but Dilva lies to make the story sound less farfetched. "He's ill. His lungs." The sound from the front room blares out into the house, Dilva turns round and shouts something in Kurdish to Aziz and the volume goes down, but not by very much. "He cannot work and they won't pay him benefit." Bev's mind adds up the facts.

"Are they your children?"

"The small one is my brother, the girl is my cousin also." Bev likes her more now she knows this. "Are you married?" asks Dilva.

Bev shakes her head. "I was, but that was a while ago now, and we kind of drifted apart and so we decided to split up, it was for the best for both of us." This is the kind of shite that she spins when she does not want to sound like an idiot for

109

marrying a man who turned out to be as wet as tissue paper when he was sober, a thug when he was drunk, and who she had to get rid of. She doesn't want to specify either that there have been other men and most of these terrible, unfulfilling and rude. Dilva nods as if what Bev is saying is true. "I'm seeing someone else now, he's Dutch. He's a businessman, in industry. It's early days but he seems nice." Bev fiddles in her bag and pulls out her mobile phone, she clicks a few buttons and brings up the best picture of Lars, the one she looks at when she feels lonely, the one where he's dressed in a suit and smiling his big white smile. Dilva looks him up and down and nods in an approving way.

"Does he live with you?" Bev shakes her head.

"He's in Holland at the moment," she offers. She does not want to say that she has never met him before, and that she has never even heard his voice. Dilva nods and smiles but she does not understand who this man is meant to be. She knows that Europeans have boyfriends and that their families are different from where she comes from.

"Do you have children?"

"Chloe," she's eighteen. "She might be going to university," although Bev has discouraged her from doing this.

They are worlds apart these two and both of them sense it. Bev reaches out across the kitchen table and she takes Dilva's hand in hers. This is the only natural thing that has happened between them. Bev is not afraid of revealing how she feels to those who deserve it.

"If you ever need anything, I'm here, you've got my number, anytime of night or day, even if you just want to talk, I'm here." Bev means this from the bottom of her heart, as true as she loves her daughter and as true as the tears she wept at her mother's funeral. She can imagine the poisonous looks on the city streets outside for this young lass, the sneaky comments on buses that she should go back to wherever she's from, not that they know where that is. She looks into the soft brown eyes. The one thing that Dilva could never stand is kindness. She puts the back of her hand to her nose and her eyes well up, Bev holds her hand tighter. It's not the first time the Kurdish woman has cried silent tears, but she doesn't do it in front of people, she doesn't feel safe to. She wipes her eyes. The man in the front room begins coughing loudly and it breaks the moment as his hacks and heavy breathing overpower the sound from the Kurdish news channel. Dilva goes to him, and Bev follows, standing at the door, she watches as the woman fits a nebulizer over his face, sits him up and turns the machine on. Aziz continues to cough and each one rattles his little frame under thinning black hair. Dilva rubs his back and looks up to her guest at the door. Both women are embarrassed that they are not as strong as they pretended to be.

"Do you need any help?" she asks, but this is a polite offer only. Dilva shakes her head and adjusts the dials on the machine that delivers drugs into the frail man's body through the mouthpiece to his lungs.

"I'll see myself out," says Bev.

Bev walks down the ten foot that connects Westbourne to Lynton Ave. She goes past the hedges of blackberries just out of season and pumps a message to Lars into her phone as she moves.

"Do you have time for a call?" she asks and puts the device back in her bag. She checks to see if it has been read before she opens her front door – it hasn't. Chloe is in the kitchen with the radio on. She's cooking curry in a wide frying pan over the hob, it smells sweet. Our Dave has been over already and taped up the broken windows in the conservatory with carboard, the glazier has been called. Bev has already wondered what kind of man will get sent round to fix it and then remembers Lars in Holland, then remembers that he hasn't text her back yet.

"What's wrong with you?" Chloe knows when something is the matter with her mum. Bev will not tell the truth, it's not what she does. There are a number of reasons why she's upset: the attack on the taxi office this morning, a man howling with pain as a kettle of boiling water was poured on him, her past treatment of Dilva, Liz bringing chocolates when she brought

111

gin. Instead, she mentions what is not so important.

"He's stopped texting me," she says.

"That bloke from Holland?"

"His name's Lars."

"He'll be married, mum," she replies.

"He's been divorced ten years."

"Have you spoken to him yet?"

"Not yet, but we text every day, I've sent him some pictures."

"Have you now?" says Chloe with her eyebrow raised as she stirs her curry in the frying pan.

"Not those kind of bloody pictures," Chloe knows her mum. Bev did send him some nudes, but tasteful ones. "And anyway, I can send whatever sort of pictures I like to anyone."

"I'm not saying that it's wrong," says Chloe. Bev puts her bag down on the table and the bottles of tonic that she never got to use clink inside.

"How long have you been texting him?"

"Two weeks… no, three weeks." It's actually a week and a half.

"Everyday?"

"Lots of times. He's special."

"For fuck's sake, mam, he lives in Holland, and there's no chance of you meeting up."

"We might meet in Manchester. He doesn't have much money at the moment, there's a problem with his business. He owns it with his family and it's not doing too well."

"He'll be married, mum. He'll be married and you'll be a bit of fun for him, someone he can chat with and send mucky pictures to. I'm not saying it's wrong, but you have to go into this with your eyes open." Chloe has the strength of reason on her side, she's levelheaded, smart and realistic. It's not that Bev is a bad catch, she's a fine-looking woman with a sharp wit, but when it comes to men, she's as daft as a brush. "Have you thought about that, mum?" asks Chloe.

Bev sits down in one of the chairs next to the dining table, rests her elbows on the wood and puts her face into her palms. Her eyes crease up behind them and she tries not to cry. It's not about the man in Holland who hasn't yet text her, it's everything that has happened the last three weeks; it's the thud of the man's head as it hit her dashboard when it killed him, it's the man who held her up against the wall in the taxi office with his aftershave in her nostrils. It's looking up at Dilva's face above as the Kurdish woman is about to murder her. Bev cannot contain all her worries and fears in herself forever, as she has done all these years, sometimes they come spilling to the surface in tears and she cannot stop them. Chloe comes to her and they embrace there in the kitchen. She is thankful to have her daughter and thankful too that she is not going away to university.

It takes Chloe ten minutes to get her mother back to normal. Bev eats the curry stopping to check her phone every so often. Then, she checks every ten minutes until she goes to bed and lays down in the darkness staring up at the ceiling. She looks at her phone every two minutes until she goes to sleep.

That Lars from Holland is just like every other man she's ever known. Just like Chloe said, he's probably married and this is all just a bit of fun for him. Right now, he's probably showing the pictures Bev sent him to all his mates.

She feels cheap.

It's a familiar feeling.

CHAPTER FOURTEEN
Poor Dennis

Liz has had a difficult week.

She has smoked a lot more roll-ups and taken to spraying herself with perfume after each one, so there's a haze of cheap pound shop scent around her black hair and smiling face. Joel had to go to the doctor's because he had a chest infection and he hasn't been sleeping well. He coughs a lot and Liz has to go to him in the night and rub his back till he calms down. Sometimes, when he is facing away from her on the bed, she can see his hair and fancies that he looks like his father. It's like always. She is guilty of hating the boy who needs her. It makes her hate herself. At three o'clock this morning, she stood outside the big back door of her house and blew the thin smoke from her roll-up into the night air, with the moon above looking down on her like some nasty school teacher who knew Liz's thoughts.

It's Saturday again. She thought the job with Dennis would give her time off from her life but the man is actually a drain on her spirits. He makes the world dark and bleak around him and unlike anyone Liz has met in recent years, she is afraid of him because of this. It's as if he can see the darkest parts of her without trying.

Liz pulls up in her Berlingo in front of his bungalow and switches off the engine. She rummages in her bag for her perfume and gives herself a quick spray. It's more habit than a wish to smell nice for Dennis. Normally he is waiting for her and all ready to go. She looks at his front door. It's closed. Liz does a big sigh as she gets out. In a few steps she is looking through the frosted, patterned glass to see if there is any movement inside. She presses the doorbell, stands back, and folds her arms as she waits with her eyes narrowed in mild passive aggressive anger. She can see her reflection in the glass of the front door.

She waits a minute, and then presses the doorbell again, hears the shrill electronic clang around the ground floor flat and steps back with her arms folded once more.

She's not going to wait.

If he isn't at the door in another minute, she's off. Dennis would be the first one to complain if she was late. Liz blinks in the weak Saturday sunshine. She's put the idea into the back of her mind but it wriggles its way to the surface. All Dennis's talk about doing himself in. What if it wasn't just talk after all? What if he's done it?

She tries the door. It's locked. The key safe is a silver box next to the doorbell, it's a chunky square of metal with a pad of numbers. Dennis told her the code previous and said she could let herself in and smother him with a pillow. What if he's in trouble? She pumps in the number 1234 and the front of the box falls open. There's a key within. She fits it in the Yale lock next to the frosted glass, turns it and pushes the door open.

There's the smell of rich and warm sweat that is old and rotten. The heating is on, even though it's warm outside. She closes the door behind her and calls into the silence of the flat.

"Dennis," Liz's voice is not loud even when she tries. The sound travels down the hall and around the corner into the front room. There's no response. She swallows as she moves down the hall and turns into the kitchen. It's deserted and there are no pots in the sink, and a clean hob, like a fake kitchen in a showroom with nobody living there. She frowns. On the marble counter next to the sink is an envelope. She approaches. There is a handwritten name on it and her blood runs thin as she reads her own name in scrawl - Liz. She puts her hand to her mouth. He's done something. Blood rushes to her head and her stomach turns, she staggers as she backs out of the kitchen until she is next to the toilet door. She pulls it open.

There he is. Dennis. His head is slumped down on his chest and his fat arms hang, limp and uncomfortable over the side of his wheelchair. He is dressed but there's a wet patch over his groin. Liz reaches out to touch his hand and it's cold. She squats in front of the man, his eyes are open as he looks down at his fat gut stretched tight against his blue shirt.

He's dead.

Liz stands up and feels sick. Her mind whirrs and her stomach grumbles as she gasps for air. As nice as Liz may be, she is still a pragmatist, she has a son she must take care of, and, should anything befall her, what would become of him? She discussed this death with Dennis. He told her he was going to do it and he told her how he would do it too. Liz scrabbles to the kitchen to the letter lined up next to the sink. She pauses. He did tell her that he was taking poison, that his brother gave him it in a kind of gas, and that it would kill him slowly because he didn't take too much at once. He said he would give Liz some for her lad, and she agreed he should – this was messing about, stupid talk, like people do around here. It wasn't meant to be serious but as she stands there in the deserted kitchen with the smell of bleach in her nostrils, there is a dead body in the bathroom next door and, maybe he did kill himself with special gas from his brother and maybe he did mean it, and maybe also, Liz meant it too – that she wanted some for her son.

She takes the letter and pulls open the envelope. There's scrawl across the little square of paper she takes out, ugly and poorly formed like the way Dennis spoke:

'Liz, there's something for your lad under the sink.'

She stands in the kitchen for a minute with the paper in her hand and her mouth dry. She feels the world around her, hears the passing of a car outside on the street, the tick of the clock on the kitchen wall, her stomach lightly complains under her heart beating shallow in her chest. She squats down and opens the cupboard under the sink, there it is, the item he left her. It's a blank white aerosol spray can with a plastic cover to go over your nose and mouth fitted to the top. She is afraid. What if someone finds this letter and the spray can? What if the police decide to examine the contents, and that the gas inside really is what has killed him? What about Joel? Darkness draws over Liz's brain as she thinks, a black mist, terrible and evil. She could help her lad and herself, and just as suddenly the darkness is buried and she sees drinks with friends in bohemian pubs, nights out in Leeds, days away in London, and holidays to India, all possible when he is not there.

Liz opens her handbag and slips the envelope inside, she picks up the spray can and puts that inside also. She does not quite know what she is doing, or, what she is going to do, but she is red faced as she picks up her mobile phone. She's not Bev, she's not going to call Our Dave, this is beyond him. The voice on the other end gives her a list and she chooses police. When a woman's voice comes on, she speaks clear and bright.

"I'd like to report a death," she says.

A policewoman arrived within 20 minutes. Liz sat in her car while she waited so as not to touch anything inside after she had answered questions for the phone handler. The policewoman was very nice, very thorough. Liz explained it all, in detail, everything she knew about Dennis, the trips she had with him in the car, his brother out on the coast and his struggles with his illness. She told too, how Dennis had explained the key code so she could let herself in. She had even looked a little upset and the policewoman calmed her down by touching her shoulder.

It's half past two now. Liz is driving back along Princes Avenue and turning into Park Lane towards the child minder's to collect Joel. At least she will never have to see Dennis again. She stops outside and puts on the handbrake, then turns off the engine. Her hand goes over her eyes and her forehead wrinkles underneath the fingers in worry. She can see the image of Dennis, dead in his wheelchair with his legs at a funny angle and Velcro shoes, his groin wet with his piss and his fat face looking down at his stomach. These tears are not for Dennis – they are for the poison in her bag, and for her son, Joel.

Ryan turned up at just after nine in the morning. It's Sunday. He banged on the front door in his heavy-handed way and Dilva answered. She wanted to offer him a drink but he was too quick to explain his plans as he pointed to the yellow estate car parked down the road. She caught some of it – that he was going to take the junk away in his car.

She watches him work from the kitchen window. He is a

bit taller than six foot and wears army boots that he has tucked his grey tracksuit bottoms into, he's got a khaki hoody and gloves as he tugs at a rotten metal swing on its side. He's calm as he works there on the Sunday morning, there's no anger, just methodical workmanship as he struggles to unscrew the rusted iron hinges to take it apart. Upstairs, she can hear the shouts of the two kids on their games, and their voices are smooth and comforting. There's the smell of coffee in her nostrils and, in the front room, she can just hear the faint snore of Aziz. She hooked him up to his nebulizer and he has fallen asleep. Dilva feels calm too. Safe and warm somehow. She sets her coffee down and there's a bang from the back garden as Ryan lets one of the sides of the old iron swing crash onto the other. Dilva catches her breath suddenly, her hands clench into fists. Just when she feels calm she attacks herself, as if she needs to be punished.

It's happening again.

She is back there.

The ringing is in her ears. It's Mosul 2017. The Humvee she rides in has been hit from underneath by a mine and the world is the wrong way round as she comes to her senses. It has been blown upwards and onto its side. The back doors have come open and the smoke from outside billows in. It's acrid yellow with the smell of rubble, petrol and explosives. Dilva is crushed in the side of the truck with the helmet over her eyes. She looks over to the driver, the lad from Kirkuk who said he was a musician, he leans over the wheel and is not moving.

There's a hollow clanging coming from outside the truck. Thuds hit the top and side. A bullet spiders the front windscreen. She's being shot at. There's a voice from the smoke and from outside the open back door of the big truck. This is the worst part of the memory. A voice in Arabic yells out into the buildings and rubble around and outside, the accent is foreign, Syrian maybe.

"There are rats inside," it calls. "Stop your firing, you shits, get the rats out!" Dilva feels panic. Her hand goes to undo the seatbelt at her side and she sits up. Her truck was headed into the centre of Mosul, and around the city there are more than a hundred thousand troops, Iraqi army, American, French and various forms of the Peshmerga, the Kurdish army, some from over the Iranian border, some from as far as Turkey. They are all there to rid the city of ISIS who have been pushed back into the old town. Even as Dilva and the man from Kirkuk drove down the tiny, half bombed out streets, there were snipers in the taller places, hiding in amongst the everyday people, some of them have shaved their beards so they no longer look like extremists. This is still an occupied city, and there are still pockets of them, and these are the men who scream at each other from outside the Humvee on its side. Dilva's heart pumps, and she releases the seatbelt, her hand goes for the pistol at her side, but she does not have time to draw it before a figure, lithe and nimble, appears out of the smoke behind her from the doors that have come open. The man grabs her by the shoulder and yanks her backwards, he begins shrieking as he does so, a kind of hollow, evil whooping. As he pulls her back, Dilva manages to tug the pistol free from the holster, and shoots it over her shoulder so he disappears back into the smoke through the open door. The voice comes again, closer perhaps.

"There's a rat in here!" Banging begins on the outside of the truck, rocks or rifle handles clang on the metal and the huge vehicle rattles from the blows. Dilva looks forward in terror as something smashes against the front windscreen. The toughened glass does not break but it shocks her momentarily. She turns back and there's the figure again, right on her, he grabs hold of her shoulders and yanks her backwards. He is howling again.

Dilva has to control herself.

She is not there.

She is not being dragged from the Humvee truck on its side, it is not Mosul in 2017. The faceless howling men are not going to hurt her. This is not happening now. It happened, but it is not happening now. She is not there anymore. The banging is loud around her, and suddenly, it is real, she is not in Mosul and her lungs are not full of smoke, her nose is not bleeding from where someone hit her, and she is not being dragged along the ground by her hair after they ripped the helmet from her head.

Her face looks up to the back door of her kitchen here in her terraced house off Chanterlands Ave in Hull, and there is Ryan, his big hand banging on the glass as he looks in with a frown of concern. Dilva is not back in Mosul, but the emotions are still with her. Ryan opens the door and looks inside.

"What's up?" he asks. Dilva's face is red with fear and her eyes wide. Her hands grip the side of the chair she sits on with white knuckles. Ryan has seen the look on her face before as her pupils examine him. It's the same expression she had just prior to when she attacked him, like a feral cat trapped in a corner. Ryan holds his hand up.

"Don't go nuts," he says. "I just smashed some glass from the old greenhouse. You didn't want it anyway." Ryan might as well be speaking Chinese for the speed of his delivery and the words that he uses. His tone is more friendly than angry and curiously, it brings Dilva back to herself somehow. It's the kind of tone her grandmother used. She stands and she is shaking, her heart pumps shallow in her chest and her legs are hollow. This is fear. This is what it does to you, and if you let it, the frenzy will swallow you up, even though you know there is nothing here but safety. She takes deep breaths. Steadies herself. She has children to look after, a pretend husband to care for, she must keep this together.

"I'll help you move the rubbish," she says. You have to keep at the war, to keep the war from getting at you. That's how you stay alive. Ryan can see she is upset but does not want to say anything, not for fear she will attack him, more that there is nothing to say. There's only the job, no time to talk – what good can that possibly do.

"I've got some spare gloves," he says.

Dilva is strong in a methodical way. It's clear that she has done some manual labour but not nearly as much as someone like Ryan. She helps him carry bigger panes of glass down the ten foot and into the back of the yellow estate car, others she carries herself. The work makes her feel better and the fresh air too. At the back door of the terraced house, in front of a garden that is starting to look unruly rather than an actual tip, Aziz steps out and sits on the step with an unlit cigarette in his mouth. He fiddles with his lighter. Dilva walks over to him:

"You shouldn't be smoking that," she says in Kurdish.

"I'll die anyway," he answers. "There'll be less for you and the children to worry about."

"I'll have to pay to have you buried, and they won't be able to dig a hole in the ground big enough for your fat head." Since she has been driving a taxi, Dilva has learned this mean double talk from Bev. It's the art of being slightly horrible to each other and it works well in Kurdish. Aziz likes this kind of chatter too and he takes the cigarette out his mouth as she approaches.

"Why is that gorilla from next door helping us?" he asks. He catches Ryan's eye and gives him a wave. Ryan waves back. He will not be able to understand them.

"He's lost and lonely," she answers. "A bit like we are. He was a soldier as well."

"Do you like him?"

"What do you mean?"

"When I'm gone, you'll need someone to look after you."

"A man?"

"Yes."

"This is Europe, Aziz kaka. A woman does not need a man to get on here."

"Maybe, I didn't mean that." Aziz is one of the wise ones, perhaps we all are when we are so close to the end. "I mean, you'll need someone to love you."

"I have children."

"They'll grow old and leave. You need someone to care for you and for you to care for as well. It's as important as the sun in the sky." Dilva turns and looks at Ryan dragging a piece of iron from the broken greenhouse out into the ten foot. It scrapes the floor as he pulls it out onto the street.

"He's too big, too ugly, too rough. What would he want

121

with me?" Aziz smiles at this.

"You're always so quick to put yourself down. You're a fine woman, my Dilva." She does the smile that she has seen Bev do, the one that means someone's taking the piss.

"You're a liar because I look after you," she says.

"Will you let me smoke this cigarette?"

"You know I can't." Aziz does a half-arsed sigh and slips the lighter back in his pocket. Ryan approaches. He is much bigger than either of these two, and while Aziz feels the slight shudder of intimidation, Dilva does not. Ryan has played the role of a thug so many times that it has become part of him, and in this dark-haired Kurdish lass, there is no nonsense, and a levelheaded controlled rage. He is mesmerized by her.

"The car's full. I'm gonna drive to the tip." Dilva nods. The idea that there is a place to dump rubbish and junk is alien to both her and Aziz. She nods.

"You are going to eat here tonight," she says. She has a sense of her power over this man. He cocks his head.

"When?"

"You drive. I cook. When you come back, I'll give you food." Ryan nods and smiles.

Dinner is awkward. The two kids are almost completely silent as they eat their chicken and rice. Ryan sits at one end of the table and Dilva has given him a fork to eat with. Her, Aziz and the two kids use their fingers and bits of the flatbread that Dilva cooked. Ryan is out of place here. He knows that he should try to make polite conversation but he cannot find the words so he goes at the rice, which is good.

"He eats so quickly," says Mohammed in Kurdish without looking at the man.

"Don't make eye-contact with the gorilla," answers Aziz, "or he'll eat you up as well." Dilva shakes her head at this.

"He is our guest," she says.

"Are you kids at school?" asks Ryan. Mohammed responds in flawless Hull that neither his mother or Aziz understand.

"I'm at Northwood," he answers. This is a big orange school that has had money thrown at it to improve the place.

"I went there," says Ryan.

"It's a proper shithole," says Mohammed. Neither Aziz nor Dilva register this as foul talk. Ryan wrinkles his nose. He is a rough lad but he would never use language like this near his mother.

When they have finished, Dilva pours black tea into small cups for Aziz and Ryan. The kids disappear upstairs and, after he's taken a few sips, Aziz rises to make his way to the front room. He is slow like an old man, his chest rasps and he splutters on his way out of the little kitchen. Dilva leaves and settles him, when she returns, Ryan is standing by the front door, ready to go.

"I'm going. Tomorrow, I'll cut the grass down and make it look like a garden. You'll be able to sit out there."

"Why do you help us?" asks Dilva. She has smooth and level eyes that are not afraid of him, and everyone is afraid of Ryan, not that they should be.

"I don't know," he answers. "Maybe I like you. Maybe I want to help you. You need fixing." He swallows. He is speaking his mind as he never does. Perhaps it's the sweet sugar of the tea or the spices in the rice, or her calm eyes, or the fact that she cannot be intimidated by him. Ryan has done things too, looking down the barrel of a gun, he pulled the trigger on those that did not deserve it, and he carries it with him, in bravado, strapped to his proud chest.

"You need fixing as well," she says.

"There are people who can help you. I told you."

"I don't need help."

"You do."

"I do it alone. I always have."

"You can't do it alone. I know. Whatever happened, it'll catch up with you. You need to talk it out." For a brief second, Dilva sees herself being dragged from the truck in the dusty streets of Mosul with the sound of the whooping in her face as she is pulled along the concrete, but there is no fear strangely, with this earnest man standing in front of her. She does not really remember what happened to her that day, only that she woke up in an American field hospital sometime later with a broken shoulder and a bullet wound through the side of her torso. Her knuckles were raw from fighting, and there was dried blood under her fingernails. She feels embarrassed that Ryan can see through her, and that he can understand that she suffers.

"Thank you for your help," she says in the hope it will make him back off. He looks down at his feet and then up to her face, then to the door handle, then back to her mahogany eyes.

"I'm just next door if you need me," he says.

"Thank you," she answers. Her expression has become impassive – serious even. He leaves.

Ryan hears her turn the lock as he walks out the front door and he pauses for a minute to look back at the little terrace, with the lights on in the upstairs windows and front room. He thinks about the woman who disarmed him a week or so previous and her sleek black hair, high cheek bones and smooth olive skin. He swallows again.

It's as close as he has ever come to being in love.

CHAPTER FIFTEEN
Our Dave and Charles Boyce

Our Dave drives west. He goes over the railway tracks on Spring Bank and out, past streets with rows of terraces branching off, cut-price supermarkets and non-descript takeaways. He heads towards the richer end of town. This is a small city, and you can drive from run down, boarded up houses to stately mansions in twenty minutes, and it seems everyone knows their place. Lads from the Hastings on Spring Bank West wouldn't want to drink in the Wheatsheaf up at Kirkella, with its light lunches and décor from the eighties. It's an open prison in some ways, people know where they should be and where they shouldn't, only, there are those that can operate on Orchard Park or in the posh Italian restaurant out at Swanland. Men like Our Dave.

He pulls his grey Ford Galaxy up into the big, gravel car park behind a squat ancient looking church next to a pub. This is the leafy suburb of Kirkella near where he drops off James Boyce. Once upon a time it would have been a village on its own, now it's joined to the city by estates that pretend they are middle class. There are houses here with tennis courts and indoor swimming pools, equestrian properties with stables, huge lawns maintained by gardeners and folk that drive gleaming four by four cars. Our Dave knows people from here as well as he does from the rough streets of East Hull, and they are the same sort of animal with a different way of doing things. Before he gets out, he eyes the cars already parked up, there's a huge gleaming range rover with the number plate VO6 UE.

Charles Boyce is here.

Our Dave enters the pub through the back door and a big glass conservatory. He stands in front of the deserted bar until an older woman comes to serve him. She's in her late fifties with crows' feet at the side of her eyes and weathered hands with long, chipped, pink nails. Dave knows her from years back, like he does most people. She smiles at him. He orders a half of ale.

"How's Hazel?" asks the woman. She must know his wife from somewhere.

"Still drinks too much whiskey," says Our Dave. This is what he always says. He likes single malts and she did as well.

"It's Carol, isn't it?" She beams as she hands over his half pint.

"Yeah. How did you remember me?" Dave remembers everyone. That's honestly how it works with people. You remember their names and you listen, and you're friendly because everyone matters. You never know when you're going to need someone to help you. That's the way Our Dave plays it.

"I bought you a drink once, and you gave me your number." This may or may not be true. Carol smiles wide again. She does not remember either but he is tall, and handsome in a steady, assured older gentleman's way.

"Why didn't you call me?"

"Hazel got there before you," he answers with a smile. Our Dave takes his drink past the dining tables in the large conservatory, he goes into the front bar where there are expensive leather armchairs and brass decorations on the walls, with paintings and pictures that are meant to be from times long gone, but can be bought off eBay for a few quid. A man with a well-pressed light blue suit and an open white shirt sits in one of the armchairs next to a fire that is not on. There's a coffee on the little table in front of him, and the posh biscuit that came with it is untouched. He has short dark hair and crystal-clear blue eyes. This is Charles Boyce, James's dad. He has his legs crossed, one over the other, but the line in his sky-blue suit trousers is sharp and neat. He has no socks on and dark loafers. Our Dave sets his drink down on the table and takes a seat in the armchair opposite. Charles Boyce has watched him enter from the corner of his eye and looks up to him now.

"My lad, James, is quite taken with you. He tells me all the stories you tell him." Our Dave gets himself comfy in the brown leather.

"He says you're a twat." Charles Boyce does not alter his

126

passive expression.

"Is that meant to shock me?"

"If you deal with rough people, you get rough answers. That's what James told me about you, Charles, and you should know that I don't tell lies. There's no point. I'd have to remember them all." Our Dave looks at him with cold eyes.

"Is that why you wanted to meet, to tell me that?"

"Partly." Our Dave only lies to make people feel better. "I wanted to catch up to talk about business."

"So, talk."

"You missed me, the other day."

"Did I?"

"The lad you sent. You won't have heard back from him." Charles Boyce has an entitled face and an attitude. His father and grandfather made a fortune from the trawlers that ran off Hessle Road in the seventies and eighties. It's easy to stay rich when you are rich already. It's natural to think you deserve it too.

"I didn't send a lad, it was a man." he answers.

"Someone flagged down one of my girls who was doing my run with your boy, James. The man threatened her too. There's no damage done, though. There were lads who turned up at my office sounded like Mancs, they didn't come out of it too well either."

"What are you saying, Dave?"

"You can't intimidate us."

"Yes, I already have, that's why you're here. You don't think anything was going to happen to you did you, if that man had got in your taxi? It would have been a bit of roughing up, that's all. I do hope you haven't gone and done anything stupid with him – he was loaned to me by a friend out of Manchester."

"He's probably gone on holiday," says Our Dave. "If it's you that wants my operations to stop, why couldn't you contact me direct?"

"That's not how business is done, Our Dave. My old man and his grandfather, they were like you, if they wanted to buy a fish they went to a fisherman and told him how much they'd

127

pay. It's not like that anymore, you have to generate interest and have strategies. It took you a while to find out it was me that wants you shut down – doesn't that make you think about what I know and who I know?"

"Aye," says Our Dave. He's going to play this one straight.

"Good." Charles Boyce smiles.

"So, you want me to shut down?"

"Exactly."

"So you can take over?"

"In a way. Things are changing. You know it's much better to make laws rather than break them. I met Robbo Doyle down at Hayes Business School in my twenties. We hit it off right away. He's inherited a considerable business now his father has passed on, as did I when my father died. We're not rough and ready street people like you, Dave, although Robbo is a little more rock and roll than I am. We don't get into punch ups and swear. There's a proper way to do things. We've links to those in the government, and with the right pricing and corporate wrangling, we can reduce the tax on any alcohol to almost nothing. It'll all be legal. It's the same for Robbo over in Manchester, once our people get where they need to be, the drug laws in the country are going to change. We're businesspeople, not gangsters. We're not like you are."

"Why have lads visit my taxi office?"

"Just a bit of fun, horseplay, and a language that I know you understand, just so you realise I'm serious." Our Dave picks up his half pint and takes a sip on his beer. He sets it down slowly.

"There are secrets in this city, lad, that you don't know about."

"Do you mean that old witch on Hessle Road, the fat cow who calls herself Leatherhead?"

"Not just her," answers Our Dave.

"How very mystical. I'm terrified."

"I've been in this game a long time, son. Why not just edge me out, I probably wouldn't fight you for it, I'm too old, but to straight out tell me to stop, it feels like it hasn't been thought through. You could at least offer to buy it from me."

"Alright. How about five pounds? You don't need the money. What have you been doing with all the cash you've made?" Our Dave is not going to say he has sunk it into big terraces on Spring Bank West that he rents out for less than the market value, or the land he owns at the bottom of Chants Ave that he won't sell to the big supermarket to open a shop which would kill every business down there. There are the places he never collects rent on, the garage, the unsecured loan to the boxing club on North Hull Estate.

"I'm here to say that I won't be stopping anytime soon." Charles Boyce smiles. He's the kind of man who is right in any situation, even when he's wrong, perhaps it's the way he's been brought up.

"A friend of mine from the police station told me you were ready to give up, and that you didn't want any trouble. Have you changed your mind?" asks Charles Boyce.

"Aye, I've had a change of heart. I just needed a bit of time to set things up."

"I hope you've thought this through. I mean there are people that rely on you. What's your wife's name, Hazel, isn't it?"

"I thought you weren't a gangster."

"I'm not, but when you deal with rough people, you may be required to use a rough course of action."

"If you get involved with the Doyle family, I can promise you, it won't end well. They're not as forgiving as I am."

"Robbo Doyle has the keys to the whole business now his grandfather's gone." Our Dave shakes his head as he takes another drink.

"There'll be a power struggle. If he's anything like you, he won't have the speed or the balls to deal with it." Charles Boyce grins at this. He uncrosses his legs and leans forward so that Our Dave can smell the expensive perfume as he brings his face close.

"You just be careful how you go, Dave, okay?" The tall man nods and stands up. As he steps away from the armchair, Our Dave turns, as if it's an afterthought.

"I saw your James, today," he says. "He told me he wanted

to get away for a bit. I know you two don't get on, so I said he could stop at a place that I know. He'll be fine, he just needs a bit of space, you know what I mean."

Charles Boyce finds his mouth is suddenly dry. He blinks up at the tall and kindly figure of Our Dave.

"What do you mean?"

"He won't be coming home tonight." There's not a trace of menace in Our Dave's voice and no suggestion that anything would happen to James. Colour drains from the thin cheeks of Mr Charles Boyce in his light blue suit. "He'll be fine. I'll look after him," adds Our Dave.

Charles watches the man leave the Wheatsheaf and exchange a kind word with the bar lady, like he did when he came in.

Boyce has been outclassed at their first encounter.

James Boyce sits in the front seat of Bev's big Mercedes, unusually. As this isn't a normal run to his house or school, Bev told him to sit in the passenger seat. The lad is dressed in jeans and wears a scruffy winter coat. Bev picked James up from his house and has driven him across the west of the city. She pulls down Neptune Street and drives straight through the open barriers, goes along the dock side and past a long rusty freighter ship, then continues for a minute until she stops near the end of the dock. In front of her, gleaming yellow and stretching up into the sky, as tall as a church, with two radar antennas spinning on top, is a gleaming boat. This is the Kirkella, a modern trawler.

"Are you sure this is going to be alright?" he asks.

"It's fine. It'll only be a week and then you'll be back."

"And how much will I get again."

"Five hundred quid." James nods as he hears this. "It'll be hard work, but it won't be like it used to be." Bev nods at the sleek, modern trawler, alone almost in the dock. It's the last, golden memory of Hull's fleet of fishing trawlers. "There's a cinema and a gym on board, and internet. The food's good. You work eight hours a day." Bev has been instructed to sell this opportunity to the lad by Our Dave, but, in doing so, she must make it seem more like it's James's idea than hers.

"How come you know so much about it?"

"I went out with a fella who was first mate." He was actually just a regular trawlerman. "Are you sure you're up for it?"

"Course I am. It's what's in my blood. My great granddad sailed these ships and so will I. Not like my old man, he's too piss scared to get his hands dirty. This will show him, won't it Bev? It'll teach him that I can do what I want with my life."

James is sixteen and a half and is not legally allowed to be on board, but that won't matter. Our Dave knows the skipper and it will be okay because there are folks who still turn a blind eye to many things for a few quid.

"It'll say that you are your own man, James, that's for sure." Bev is telling the truth here. "Our Dave sent you a text. He wants me to make sure you got it."

"I did," says James.

"You've to read it to me." The lad fishes out his phone and unlocks the screen. His nimble fingers navigate to the text from a few hours earlier after Our Dave had planted the idea of a week on a trawler in the lad's head, so he could be like his granddad. He opens the message and reads.

"No whistling, never mention the colour green, never talk about pork or pigs, never wash your clothes the day you sail, don't carry any loose change on board." James goes into his pockets and pulls out a couple of ten pence pieces and a pound coin. He drops these into the money well next to the parking brake and looks up at Bev. James doesn't seem scared, in fact, Bev has never seen him the way he is right now, his eyes are bright and straight. He's proud of himself.

"Go on then," says Bev, "fuck off and I'll pick you up when you get back in a week."

He gets out the car, takes his rucksack from the backseat and walks to the steps that lead up to the shiny vessel. He turns to look at Bev still sat behind the wheel. The boat sails in fifteen minutes, and as soon as the steps are pulled up, he'll be committed. Bev knows he'll be at sea for sixty days and not a week, and she doesn't feel bad about lying to him. One day, he'll find it hilariously funny and he'll for sure learn more with the lads on board than he will at the school for wayward kids up at Anlaby. In fact, if he tries his usual, cocky attitude on them, he'll get worse back, from people who have been taking the piss out of each other all their lives.

Bev gives a little smile as she drives away down the dock.

He'll be a posh lad on a trawler for two months, out around Bear Island and up to Svalbard.

It might even be the making of him.

It's just after six in the afternoon. There is still traffic moving outside the front window of Avenue Cars, but not as heavy as before. Bev has finished all her runs for the day and has returned to the office at Our Dave's request. There he is, sitting in front of the open laptop sipping a mug of coffee. He hears the blonde woman come in and closes the screen.

"Did you drop him off okay?"

"He was desperate to get on board," she answers. Our Dave's face looks worried and he sighs with a grimace across his big face.

"He's a good kid. I hope he'll be alright."

"I thought you said you went away on the trawlers when you were his age."

"I did. Over one Christmas. 1971. It was a hell of a trip and it nearly killed me, Bev. I don't say that lightly." Bev huffs at this in an action that communicates her mistrust and distaste for his memory, as if the terror he faced all those years ago aboard a sidewinder is of no consequence at all. Our Dave never talks about himself, and he would never have told this to anyone else; it's why he likes Bev. She pats away the indulgence of sentimental nonsense like emotion or pain, as she's learned. Like the women Our Dave has known and trusted all his life, she won't take it.

"You were fine and he will be as well. He'll grow a bit of hair on his balls. I don't know why you needed me to help."

"I had to go and talk to his dad."

"What for?"

"The trouble we've been having. Seems like he might be

132

the cause of it."

"James Boyce's dad?" she snaps.

"Charles Boyce, aye, but you just leave any worrying to me, Bev." The blonde woman narrows her smooth blue eyes surrounded by eyeliner at Our Dave as she calculates what he's just said. She remembers back to the man she picked up a few weeks ago. The one who bumped his head against the dashboard, and the one who was stone cold dead.

"Was he anything to do with that man I picked up? The one who had an accident? What about the lads who attacked the office, was that him as well?"

"I think so."

"You think so, or you know so?"

"I know so."

"You'll call the police." Our Dave shakes his head. It's his turn to belittle Bev's suggestions.

"DI Lyndsey? He works for Boyce."

"And you got me to put his lad on board a trawler that will be at sea for two bloody months? I've got a family, Dave. I've got Chloe to look after, I can't be wrapped up in your street games or for whatever bollocks you've got going on." He stands up and he towers above her but not in a threatening way at all, it's more to instill calm. Bev will not tolerate unnecessary emotion, but she is concerned about reality and more so than most. She knows what it's like to be arrested, to lose your job or someone you love, she knows how it feels to be hungry and poor and afraid.

"It's all in hand," says Our Dave. "It's been sorted. Charles Boyce and me have come to a very logical and workable agreement that we can both live with. There'll be no more visits from thugs and no more strange men getting into your taxi. It's all done. Young James Boyce getting on board that trawler is part of it. Calm down." Our Dave's measured speech has the desired effect, even if it is not quite the truth. He is fairly certain that the disappearance of the lad will keep Charles Boyce from doing anything horrible, but he can't be sure. Talk of this gives Bev the opportunity to go over old ground.

"What happened to the guy who got in my car a few weeks

back? I need to know." Our Dave does that kind of smile that means he doesn't want to answer.

"You don't really want to know."

"I have to know," she answers. "He was dead, Our Dave."

"I took the body out to the waste incinerator on Cleveland Street. I've got an agreement with the lads who work the nightshift – they don't care what I burn and I give them £50 a pop. It's not as if they think I would burn a dead body. You can rest easy, there's not a trace of him left. It's where they burn medical waste." Bev listens. Reality causes her to examine the information.

"There'll be CCTV of you, Our Dave, there'll be evidence of you driving there. There'll be videos of you doing whatever it is you did." The tall man shakes his head.

"That's the thing about technology, everyone believes it. Don't you think part of that fifty quid is for them to wipe the video evidence of me driving up there? Whatever you can film, you can just as easily wipe. In fact, it proves that I wasn't there." Her big, blue eyes look up at him with a mixture of relief and horror. For the first time in a long while, Bev does not have anything to say.

"It'll all be back to normal soon, lass, you'll see."

Our Dave hopes this is true.

CHAPTER SIXTEEN
Kasia, Leatherhead and Boyce

Kasia first started work at the Dairycoates Inn two years ago. Leatherhead brought her in as the early morning cleaner before the doors opened. Right from the first day she was quick and organised and levelheaded, and the floor of the pub was cleaner than it had ever been, the stools and seats were all brushed down and hoovered, all the bins were emptied and the drip trays as well. Kasia is five foot two with dyed red hair more often than not tied up in a ponytail, she has thin, delicate features and a quick organized style. She keeps her mobile phone in a protective sock so it will last longer. She has a pair of house slippers she brings to use when she works in the pub. She is always on time.

For those first two weeks, Leatherhead watched her at work from the corner of her eye in the pub. The thin girl hardly made a noise as she went about her business in her cleaning shoes, and there was something familiar about her to the old woman. On the second Friday after she had finished her duties and it was time to be paid, Leatherhead called her upstairs to the kitchen. She asked the Polish lass to sit at the opposite head of the orange table while she smoked a menthol cigarette like she does when she talks to folk. Most people will laugh and joke, and Leatherhead can tell a story and listen to one of theirs, it's how you get to know them. Not Kasia. Leatherhead found out she read economics at university back in Poland, has a six-year-old girl, she likes going for walks in the country and reading, but doesn't do smiles. She was impenetrable. Sitting in the upstairs kitchen of the Dairycoates Inn, Leatherhead remembered who Kasia reminds her of - her own grandma.

In three months, Kasia was the bar manager. Leatherhead organised childcare for her little Alicja with friends on Greek Street a few nights a week, so she could be there, and the pub started to change. Like grass growing, you couldn't see it, but there were extra punters at the bar because the beer was better. Kasia had the boiler serviced, she convinced Leatherhead to get the front of the pub whitewashed, the toilets smelled nicer, the windows were clean, there was a big outside heat lamp for the smokers. One morning on the orange table in the kitchen upstairs, in an expensive bag, was a bottle of sweet perfume for Leatherhead herself, a gift. Leatherhead reads insults into everything but she let this one go. Perhaps, she knew she was a fat old woman, and perhaps she knew she could smell better as well, so, she wore the perfume despite what she thought. Part of being clever, and being a leader, is to know when you are wrong.

Within six months, Kasia was running the pub and some of Leatherhead's other affairs. The old woman has been on Hessle Road a long time, which is why she owns a boutique dress shop and hairdresser across the road from Asda, there's a car park and two buildings that she rents out for storage near the docs. Kasia looked into the business and started to move things around and it did not take her long to see the true picture of what Leatherhead's interests were. Her only real question was why, why did a woman like Leatherhead have control of something like this? The answer is very simple. Leatherhead is from a long line of woman who rule these streets, not with their fists or harsh voices, but by the choices they have to make and the people they support. Back when fishing was a thing here, the whole of Hessle Road relied on the dock and the boats that brought in the silver cod from the North Sea. The fisherman were gods who returned to drink and fight and make love to their wives and then, three days later they were gone again and the women were back in control of the kids and the money and the houses and everything else. Leatherhead's grandmother ran a home with five kids, her mother ran a house with six and they did it with traits that she uses today, compassion, humour, honesty and hard work. Of these qualities, Kasia lacks only the humour, but Leatherhead is sure she can learn.

It's been two years and Leatherhead has no idea what she would do without the Polish woman. Business has been good during that time. Leatherhead has a contact in the Netherlands who makes synthetics, ecstasy, mephedrone and other highs newly created by science. This is the way to go in today's market she has concluded, she does not want the hassle of bringing in product from far away countries – she'll let the gangs from Liverpool do that, they can take all the big risks with cocaine and heroin. The packets come in through Albert Dock less than a mile away and she has them distributed across the north of England and up to Edinburgh and Glasgow. It's much better not to sell the stuff around here – people start to ask questions. She still sells heroin out the back door of the Dairycoates Inn, but she wants out of it to be honest.

It's Monday evening at seven and Leatherhead sits in her chair at the head of the orange table while Kasia fixes her a cup of tea. There's a man sitting at the opposite end in the interview spot. He is red faced and his nostrils are flared. Charles Boyce is not the kind of man you usually find in the Dairycoates Inn, on a Monday. Kasia sets a mug of tea down in front of Leatherhead and brings a glass of water over for the man in the sky-blue suit. She's noted that he smells good and that he has no socks. Kasia finds this attractive. She gives him a smile, which looks more like a scowl.

"You told me Dave wasn't a threat." Leatherhead lights up one of her menthol cigarettes and takes a drag. It's odd to see people smoking these days.

"He isn't," she answers.

"He's got my lad."

"No, he hasn't."

"Then who has."

"Why don't you ask him?"

"I thought we were in business together," says Charles Boyce. "I thought we were going to help each other out." Leatherhead frowns.

"I never said that. I said I'd allow you to take care of Our Dave if you wanted to. I said I'd advise you. Do you remember what I advised you?"

"No." Charles Boyce does not take advice. He has too much money.

"Well, I'll tell you again. Don't underestimate Our Dave. Looks like you did just that."

"Where's my fucking son?" he snaps.

"Use language like that in this kitchen, and Keith from downstairs will be up here to throw you down the steps."

"Where's my son?"

"I'm not going to say."

"Why?"

"It's between you and Our Dave. If you want an answer, ask him. I'm not here to clean up a mess that you've made."

"You might think I'm some sort of rich boy who doesn't know how to play dirty, but I've got some powerful friends across the country, people who you would not like." He means the Doyles over in Manchester. Leatherhead sits back in her chair. The smoke drifts up to the strip light and melts into the darkness of the corners. Kasia sits by her side with the laptop open and the light illuminates her face.

"I knew your granddad, when I was younger," says Leatherhead.

"What's that got to do with this situation? My son is in danger, a young life, he's fifteen." James Boyce is actually sixteen.

"I worked in Brekkies on William Wright Dock, started in 1967." Charles Boyce looks at Leatherhead, over the orange table, as if she is talking some sort of nonsense.

"And?"

"Your granddad once came to the factory. He did a tour with some other posh knobs, and they put their little white hats and wellies on. They smelt of ale, the three of them did and the tall one, your granddad, stood behind me and he watched me gut a fish, like I did five days a week, eleven hours a day." She takes another pull on her menthol cigarette, the more he wants the information, the slower she will go.

"Then what?"

"He felt my arse and told me I'd done a good job. It took all my effort not to stab him with the gutting knife I had in my hand."

"Am I supposed to feel guilty about that?"

"If you like. You should feel more guilty about what they did to one of the secretaries from the office."

"That's got nothing to do with this situation."

"I swore if I ever got the chance, I'd fuck him up, for pinching my arse." It's okay for Leatherhead to swear.

"Well now he's dead, and my son will be as well, if you don't help me."

"I don't know where he is," she smiles. "I don't talk to Our Dave. Why would I know? You shouldn't have bothered wasting your time." Charles Boyce's lip curls in anger.

In his pocket, his phone buzzes. He fetches it out and looks at the screen. Someone is ringing him. There's a smiling picture of his son – it's James. He clicks the green button and puts it to his ear as he stands up.

"Who is this?" he commands.

"It's me, Dad," comes the reply on the other end.

"Where are you?"

"I'm on a boat?"

"Where? I'm coming to get you."

"No, you're not, mate." The lad's voice has humour in it. "I'm in the middle of the North Sea. Our Dave got me a job on the Kirkella, the new trawler that sails out of Hull. We'll be there in three days. I'll be back in a week." Charles Boyce swallows as he processes the information.

"You're on a trawler?" he asks.

"Yeah."

"Did he make you get on board?"

"No," James sounds incredulous at the suggestion of this.

"Are you safe?" There's a pause on the other end. James has never been asked a question like this by his father.

"I think so. I start my first shift when we get there."

"It's a factory boat, James, you'll be working in a factory. You won't be able to cope, you can barely wipe your own arse as it is." The instant that Charles Boyce knows his son is not under any threat, he reverts back to type, and is overbearing as well as condescending. James fires back:

"You couldn't do it," he says. "I wish I hadn't called. I thought you'd be happy I'd made a decision and decided to do something for myself." The brave lad, already past Norway and far out into the North Sea hangs the phone up, leaving his

139

father standing in Leatherhead's kitchen. She watches him put the phone back in his pocket with cold cod eyes.

"He's at sea," says Boyce.

"I heard."

"At least he's safe there."

"I wouldn't be too sure," says Leatherhead. "Did Our Dave get him the job?"

"Yes." Leatherhead grins wider.

"Then I wouldn't be too sure. Dave will know people on that boat and they'll have their eye on him, for good and bad. Accidents still happen, Dave still has you buy the bollocks."

"Do you know anyone on board, the skipper perhaps? We could radio and get them to turn round." The old woman shakes her head.

"I told you that I'd advise you, Boyce, and now I'm going to advise you again. Get out of the game while everything is good, while there's been nothing lost and you still have your head on your shoulders." He runs his hands through his black hair and takes a deep breath, the words from Leatherhead melt past him.

"I'll be on my way then, Leatherhead. Thank you for the water and the advice."

"No need to call again, Mr Boyce," says the woman. He nods. Boyce makes his way out of the Dairycoates Inn and into the street. He has to consider his next move, he'll need to consult someone who knows about such things, Robbo Doyle from Manchester. Our Dave will need dealing with, for good.

Perhaps he'll have to deal with old Leatherhead as well.

CHAPTER SEVENTEEN
Unpleasant visitors

Liz stands at the back door and blows smoke up into the Monday night sky. It's her third one. This morning she had a policeman round to take a statement about what had happened to Dennis. She sat him in the front room with its high ceilings and lots of cushions on the two couches, and gave him a cup of peppermint tea. He was sorry that she had found the man dead, and explained that it was not her fault, and too, that Dennis died of natural causes – there was something wrong with his heart and that's what killed him. She nodded in understanding and the old copper left.

Now in the evening, her mind whirs with what ifs.

The funeral would be hard, but she would get through it. The emotions would be genuine, the tears she would cry would be real. Her stomach turns over inside her belly when she thinks about it. She would move out of the flat, straight away, saying that it had too many bad memories, she'd burn the bedding and his cuddly animals. She'd move away from here, back to Newcastle, and she'd rent a place and get a primary school teaching job, she'd find a younger boyfriend and sleep with him, they'd go abroad during the summer holidays. She'd be tanned and free and tall and so beautiful. She would never have to wake up in the night for him calling, never have to rub his back for him to fall asleep, there'd be no more puke or shit to clean, and no more of his stupid face every day, looking up at her. She drops her cigarette into the plant pot outside and closes the door.

She puts her head in her hands.

It is all so very wrong, even for her to think this. She's a nice person, a kind person too, and she loves her son. She would never do anything to hurt him and yet, there is evil dragging at her in the darkness, and, in the cupboard under the sink in the kitchen, there is the aerosol with the facemask that Dennis gave her.

She moves away from the back door, turns off the kitchen light and walks through into the living room. There he is, in his chair watching a cartoon on the big screen in front of him, the back of his mouth gurgling as he enjoys himself.

She'll have to wear gloves. She has some marigolds under the sink as well. She will have to get rid of the evidence, and not in the rubbish bin either, somewhere else. Liz takes a deep breath as she stands there looking at the back of her son's head in his wheelchair. She has not thought it through enough, she should wait, at least another night, but then, how many nights will it take? If she does not get this job done and soon, then she may never have the courage to do it.

How is she going to step into the future? How can she live the rest of her life like this?

There's a tap on the front door. It's a bit late for visitors. She walks down the hall, turns the latch, then pulls the heavy door open. Any other night and Liz may have sensed the evil already, but sorrow and bitterness coarse through her this evening, as if her veins are selfish and cruel under her skin. There's a figure dressed in a balaclava. He's a little shorter than her and framed by the streetlight outside. She is not quick enough to close the door. The man barges in, shoves her backwards with hands in gloves, and slams the door behind him. She stumbles at the force and crashes against the bottom of the stairs a few yards away, falling onto her side. The man steps through and past her into the living room where the 50-inch screen TV blares out a cartoon to Joel. His boots are heavy. Liz's senses blur and her brain takes a fraction of a second to calculate what is happening. The balaclava. The men who came to the taxi office a week or so previous, the look of concern on Our Dave's face and the promise that this would not happen again.

And, there's a man with a balaclava and leather gloves in the living room. In the same room as Joel. Her Joel.

Liz uses the wall to get to her feet and her eyes swim as she staggers around the doorframe to the front room. He's there to cause as much damage as he can, the man pulls the flat screen TV off the wall and hurls it into the corner where it cracks in half, he pulls down a bookcase and stomps his big boot through the low coffee table next to Liz's armchair. Joel

142

begins to yell and the man turns on him, the whites of his eyes bright against the darkness of the black woolen balaclava as he stares at the disabled lad howling in his tall, motorized wheelchair. He grabs the wheelchair arms and leans in towards Joel – the man is a thug and he's been paid to act as one, so he will terrorise the boy as well. Joel is a flurry of tears as the man shakes his chair, he rattles the joystick controls and the machine shudders as the wheels spin in the wrong direction against each other. Liz staggers around the door to see the whole wheelchair contraption fall onto its side and Joel's little body tumble out onto the smooth laminate floor with a thud. She blinks up at the man in the balaclava standing opposite her, she could let this happen, she could run upstairs to the bathroom and lock the door, but something keeps her rooted to the spot, like anger has awoken in her stomach.

Liz is not a violent person. She doesn't shout. She loses arguments with friends so as not to upset them and won't factually correct someone for fear of making them look stupid. All this time she has pretended that she did not want Joel around and that her life would be better with him out of the way. She feels rage in her as she steps in towards the man with the balaclava. She does not know what she is going to do, only that she cannot let this happen. He's a little shorter than she is, but stronger, he's also done this kind of thing before and, ten minutes previous, sitting in the back of the black BMW that had been driven from Manchester this afternoon, he snorted two fat lines of low-grade cocaine from the leather seat. It makes the job go better and gives him a wilder quality.

Liz dashes for him and he grabs her by the shoulders and flings her across the room at the far wall where she knocks two paintings from their hooks as she thumps into the pale marigold plasterboard. The man with the balaclava moves towards her again, turns her to face him and puts leather gloves around her neck. He doesn't know anyone in this town, and he's just following orders like any good soldier does. He's been told to do whatever he wants to frighten and hurt the people inside this flat, and that's what he'll do. He pins Liz's neck against the wall and presses his chest up to her. He's not going to rape her – it's not his thing, and he's not going to kill her either because he's under strict orders not to. He looks into her face with her teeth barred under her short black bob hairstyle, his hands grip her neck and there's a strange pleasure in watching her struggle to breathe, as her hands claw and pull at his arms and her eyes bulge. The man in the balaclava must be careful not to get carried away with this. The cocaine is already wearing off, and the longer he spends inside the flat the more danger he is in. He needs to finish this off. He can hear the disabled lad shouting beside him at his feet.

He releases his grip and watches her slide down the wall as she gasps to take in deep breaths of air. All he has to do now, is make it out of the flat and back to the parked black BMW down the next street and this part is done. Liz eyes him from against the wall, one of her hands is at her bruised throat and her lad squeals on the floor where he has come out of his wheelchair. The man in the balaclava sees her eyes flash in anger, and she roars as her legs power her forward towards him. One of her hands forms a claw at his eyes. He has lost his momentum. As he looked down on Liz with her face turning red, he had already taken himself out of the fight because he considered that he had won, and, once you lose the rage and bluster and anger, only a very good fighter knows how to get back there.

Liz's fingernails claw the eyeholes of his balaclava and he is not quick enough to move his head, she pulls the woolen mask down over his eyes so he is blind. She rages against him and pushes his chest so he staggers and trips over Joel's wheelchair on its side. He falls. She is on top of him, a mess of whirring strikes with her boney fingers as she shrieks at him, he brings his arms up to cover his face. He's already been here too long, the request was to frighten and injure the people inside the flat, not to fight with them. He senses that's she's tiring on top of him and waits for the strikes to stop, then sweeps her hands out the way and swings a deft punch up into her jaw, Liz collapses backwards off him and he gets to his feet, adjusting the balaclava so he can see what's happening. He has bloodied her mouth and nose. Joel yells where he lays.

144

The man in the balaclava steps back out the room, turns down the hall in the darkness, fiddles with the Yale lock at the end and opens the door. He slams it shut as he goes.

Our Dave closes the front door of Liz's flat on Marlborough Ave gently behind him as he leaves. He came as soon as she called him. She is a mess but he cannot stay with her while this man may still be around. He's angry. Our Dave is not a hothead, and even back in the seventies nothing was done in anger. He never enjoyed the danger of the life he was in, but he was never afraid of it either. It was all justified. It's dark and deserted at this time of night, his feet tap on the stone as he walks down the little path looking one way and then the other down the street.

This night is far from over.

Whoever Charles Boyce has unleashed onto these streets will not be finished yet, not by a long way. Our Dave has other friends that they will visit, and he must get to them before Boyce's thugs do.

The matt black BMW waits round the corner from Dilva's street on Chants Ave. It's eleven o'clock. Monday night. The driver taps his fingers on the steering wheel while the man in the back gets ready. He's snorting more lines from the leather seat in the semi darkness of the streetlight with unnecessarily loud sniffs, like it's part of what they've been hired to do.

They have three addresses. They've been hired to perform a service, much like someone who cleans an oven or maintains a garage door, they turn up, do what's been requested and then leave. This could be Runcorn near Liverpool or Fir Vale Sheffield, they could be somewhere south of Newcastle. The streets and the people are always the same. These two don't know each other. The driver provides the car and gets rid of it and the porter is the one who carries out the actual duties. You might say one job is easier than the other, depending on what you think is easy, but, both roles have their fair share of ups and downs. Granted, the porter has to put the frighteners on folk and, if he's unlucky he could come up against some sort of local hard man character, but once he's in the car, he's done his bit and the drive home is taken care of. If they're followed, they split up. The driver also has a pistol on the front seat in case things get weird. Things do get strange in this line of work, and it's not as straightforward as fixing washing machines but, once you've done a few jobs, you get to watch out for certain things. They get paid the same too, sometimes there's more than one porter but not tonight. The driver taps on the wheel and checks the mirror front and behind, it's good to be mindful of where you are, even if you could be anywhere.

"You ready?" he asks the man in the backseat. He gives another sniff and grunts a yeah. "Not so slow this time," he says, "we've got one more visit after this one, then it's done."

"I'm doing the best I can." He's confrontational already and the driver looks across at the bag on the front seat with the pistol in it. He doesn't know who the porter is and doesn't give a toss either.

"You've got the screenshot of the house?"

"I've seen it." Get the wrong place and you've done the wrong job. Kill someone and you've killed yourself. Get injured, it's your own fault. The driver would say good luck, but he's had that sort of talk drilled out of him.

The porter in the backseat gets out, closes the car door gently and walks away from the BMW, down Westbourne Ave out of sight. He'll replace the balaclava when he gets nearer. If either of them get caught they genuinely don't know who their accomplice was and, they honestly don't know who employed them either. On the passenger seat of the car, under the pistol, is a bag full of twenty-pound notes which they will split.

The porter steps along the narrow street and to the houses at the end with long front gardens. At the top of the path, he puts on the balaclava. The drugs course through his veins, he grits his teeth and loosens his shoulders as he approaches Dilva's house. He is not going to mess about this time.

It takes about ten minutes and the porter returns so quietly that the driver doesn't notice him till he taps on the back window. In the darkness, he unlocks the car and the porter gets in. There's a funny smell about him, sweet and sweaty somehow, but the driver will not ask about what has happened in the last ten minutes – he doesn't care anyway. He starts the engine, the car purrs into action and they pull off into the street. They have one more address. He looks into the rearview mirror and sees that the porter hasn't taken his balaclava off and he's sitting in the opposite seat from before.

"You don't have to keep that on," he says to the man in the backseat. The porter just shrugs his shoulders. The driver looks at him again through the mirror, there's something different about him, maybe he's taken a kicking but he doesn't have time to care as he follows the satnav on his mobile screen in the dock next to the wheel.

"It makes me nervous," he says to the back seat, "and it doesn't look good if there are any coppers about." Again, the man in the back seat just shrugs his shoulders. The driver didn't think much of him anyway, he thinks less of him now.

He follows the satnav down Park Avenue. It's a big and wide street flanked by trees with huge Victorian terraces on each side. They pass a decorative roundabout with white figurines illuminated by the headlights. The driver takes another look at the porter in the back, he's not sitting up straight – something has happened to him alright. They've got one last address and after that, they can get back on the M62 and be away from here. In less than an hour, they'll be all done. He parks the BMW at the side of the road, opposite the address they have been told to hit. He turns off the engine. The streetlights are darkened by the trees. This is Our Dave's Street. The lights are off. The driver looks across at the door and there's a man coming out. He's tall with a beard, older but still with some spring in his step.

"That's him," says the driver over his shoulder. The porter sitting behind him in the seat takes a deep breath but does not reply. Our Dave closes his front door and walks down a few steps to his Ford Galaxy parked up on the road. "Are you going to bloody do something?" he asks the porter again. The man in the back seat does not respond. They do not want to do anything in plain sight after all. They watch Our Dave get into his car and start the engine.

"We'll just have to follow him." The driver is getting tired of his own voice. "You're not bleeding all over those seats are you?" he asks. The man in the balaclava in the darkness of the back seat does not respond, again.

Our Dave pulls out and drives away down Victoria Ave. The driver follows. It's deserted at this time of night. They turn left and cross past Pearson Park in the darkness of Monday evening, then drive down to the end of Princes Ave and onto Queens Road, towards Sculcoates Lane. The houses change around them, they move past these big terraces with high ceilings to smaller rattier houses, run down pubs and across Beverley Road with chip wrappers and pizza boxes blowing along the gutters. Just as he gets past the Woodshop on the corner of Sculcoates, right before the quiet industrial estate, Our Dave hits the accelerator on his grey, non-descript Ford Galaxy. The car moves off, touching fifty as he turns the corner past the ready-mix concrete factory and, as he nears the roundabout at the bottom of Air Street next to the poorhouse graveyard, he has to use the handbrake to make the turning because he is travelling at such speed. The BMW following responds, easily, accelerating with a low purring engine, the driver barely touches the pedal to move the beast forwards. At the bottom of Air Street, he too has to hit the brakes to make the turn, and he speeds up as he follows Our Dave down Wincolmlee. In the past, this part of the city would have been busy with industry, ships, boats and people. These days, on a Monday, you'll be lucky to see another car, especially at this time of night.

By the time he has passed Fountain Road, Our Dave is doing seventy. The BMW keeps the pace without issue, the driver steady on the wheel. He won't follow him for too much longer, and then he can tell whoever asks that he gave a reasonable chase to catch him but couldn't. All they are meant to do is put the frighteners on these people anyway, whoever they are. Our Dave's Ford rattles along Wincolmlee and at an open slide iron gate, he brakes and turns in. The driver doesn't know this city and for all he is aware, this could be just another road to go down. He brakes hard and turns the sleek, black BMW through the opening, then screeches to a halt when he sees that he is in a rundown car park on the side of the river. Our Dave's car is parked in front.

He's been set up for this.

The driver goes for the weapon he has in the bag on the passenger seat but as he reaches over, a heavy fist clobbers him on the back of his head. He bounces off the dashboard and the man in the backseat leans forward to hit him again. The driver's head swims as the man belts him one more time with a measured and experienced blow. He senses the car door opening and is yanked out onto the gravel. His hands are pulled behind his back and his wrists bound by a cable tie, all very professional. A rope goes around his neck and pulls tight. He feels the pinch at his throat. This is the nature of the game, sure it's easy money but there is always a chance that something like this can happen to you. The driver isn't stupid, but he feels so, as hands lift him into the trunk of his own black car then fit two pieces of duct tape across his mouth and slam the door shut above him.

Ryan takes off the balaclava. He and Our Dave stand well away from the BMW so the driver won't be able to hear.

"Thanks for the tip off," he says to Our Dave in front of him. It's not unlikely that these two know each other, not in a town as small as this.

"It was Dilva I tipped off," he says.

"She told me." As the real porter approached Dilva's house about half an hour ago, just as he got to the path, Ryan hit him round the head with a motorbike spanner. He took his jacket and balaclava and then took his place in the back of the car.

"What's going on?" asks Ryan. He has heard rumours about Our Dave, just rumours of course from lads who drink in the Avenues Pub. Now he knows they're true.

"Every so often some clever sod comes to try and do me over, Ryan. It's nothing to worry about." The tall man smiles.

"I'm not worried," he answers.

"You'll be paid for your time," says Our Dave, "and for

keeping your mouth shut." Ryan looks around him at the yard, there are rusted up car bodies and stacks of tyres under a single floodlight.

"Happy to help. What will happen to the car and the driver?" Ryan asks.

"There's a junk boat that comes by most mornings, we'll get it on that. I should think the car will fetch a fair price. I just hope they check the boot before they sell it. He didn't see you, did he?"

"Not at all, but he does know who you are."

"He knew that before he arrived in Hull."

"I'd check the front seat," says Ryan. "He was reaching for something in it."

Our Dave goes to the passenger seat door, opens up and pulls out the grey sports bag. It's heavy. He sets it on the floor and undoes the zip. There's a long black pistol inside and rolls of twenty-pound notes in rubber bands. He grabs one of these as he closes the bag back up. Ryan stands a little way off. Now he knows about Our Dave, he reasons he should stay out of his way.

"Here's the first payment," says Our Dave as he passes Ryan one of the rolled-up bundles. Ryan takes it and spirits it into his pocket without looking.

"Thanks, Our Dave," he says.

"Now, would you like a lift home?" Ryan nods.

Our Dave makes Liz a cup of tea. He dropped Ryan off and came back here after he stopped at home to collect a few things. He's brought over another TV that he said he had spare, and it sits as a replacement on the wall. Our Dave wants things to be back to normal as soon as possible. The same cartoon blares out for Joel who is back in his chair and the lad makes gurgling noises as he watches, even though he should be in bed at this time. The side of his face is red and a little bruised, but he is okay.

Our Dave sets the peppermint tea down in front of Liz as he sits at the thin dining table opposite her. Her eyes are red and her nose swollen from where she was struck. The neck is

150

not so bruised because the man was trying to scare her only.

"I deserved it, Our Dave," she says. The man looks down into his watery peppermint tea with the teabag still in it and does not say anything. The first job, if you are going to help anyone, is to listen to what they have to say, listen and not judge and not give advice.

"How do you work that out?"

"It's karma."

"What have you done?" Our Dave wonders why Liz could think she deserved such an attack.

"I wanted him dead, Our Dave."

"Who?"

"Joel." Dave does not judge, first he has to listen.

"I wanted him gone," she says. There's a faraway quality about the way she speaks with none of the passion or the warmth that she usually has. "I thought if it was just me again then I'd be happy, and I'd be free as well. I'd be free to do and go where I wanted. I'd be free to have a life." She does not look herself.

"You wouldn't be the first mother to have thought that, Liz," he says.

"I thought it and I wanted it, so you see, that's why I deserved this." Our Dave lifts the floral mug and takes a sip on the tea. In his younger days, he would have blamed himself for this event because it is he who deals with the likes of Charles Boyce, Leatherhead and the Doyles of Manchester; not so these days, the responsibility for this action rests on Charles Boyce's shoulders and Our Dave will see to it that he is compensated for that. In the meantime, he has already called Bev, to tell her and Chloe to lock the doors. He thinks about his own semi with the windows drawn and the lights off. This will not be the end of it for Charles Boyce. Our Dave licks his lips, he doesn't much like the peppermint. The act of violence on Liz will be retaliation for young Janes Boyce going to sea.

"Can you be punished for thoughts?" he asks.

"No, but you can punish yourself. As well, the world has a way of serving up justice, one way or another."

"Did you ever hurt the lad?" She shakes her head. "You

151

haven't done anything wrong, Liz, even if you wanted to, you didn't. Go ahead and beat yourself up for it, but it won't do you any good."

"It's not meant to do me any good, Our Dave, it's my punishment. I wanted to be free."

"Lots of women, lots of parents, feel like that."

"Did you?"

"I didn't look after kids like you do. I was out. I just came for the fun bit."

"Answer my question. Did you ever wish you could have your life back?"

"I did then, aye, at times, but not now."

"Your son grew up. Joel is never going to grow up." He takes another big gulp on his peppermint tea. It's bitter to his mouth. He may not know how it feels to be Liz, but he can sense her despair.

"Kids come to define you in the end. When they're gone, you forget how it was to be yourself."

"You've been reading too many women's magazines, Our Dave." He has lived through many things that Liz has not but he would never share these with her, or anyone else. What has gone on, any heartbreak Our Dave has known is his own and nobody else's. There are many horrors that he will not admit to himself, not even now.

"It's my fault that you got visited, Liz. I didn't think it would get to this, but it has. There are people I know who want to get at me and they'll do this by getting at you."

"Bev says you're mixed up in some sort of business."

"I am."

"What will you do?"

"Respond," he answers. Liz takes a deep breath and feels along her neck where the man held her. She remembers, fleetingly, the look of scorn in his eyes behind the balaclava.

"Will you send people to do what he did?"

"I don't have any people, Liz. It's just me. It's only ever been me."

"That's fairly typical of men your age. You do everything alone. You are alone. You talk about Hazel all the time, but

152

it's not like any of us have ever met her." Liz is not being cruel. After the attack and with this big gentle man sitting at her table drinking tea, and with Joel happy watching his cartoons, she feels safe enough to say what she wants.

"I could accuse you of that, Liz," he says. "If you were struggling with Joel here, you only had to let me know, or Bev and we'd help. You know we would."

"How could you help?"

"We could take him out, take you out, babysit, you could talk to us or we'd find someone to talk to you."

"I need a favour," she asks. Liz feels clarity to her thinking.

"Of course," says Our Dave.

"There's a big aerosol in the cupboard under the sink. It's white with no writing on it and has a facemask that fits over your nose connected to the top. I need you to get rid of it for me. Don't let anyone see it or find it. Can you do that for me, Dave?" She looks at him with earnest eyes, for once that is gone from her house, it will be her and Joel together, forever, stuck like glue.

"I can get rid of it. Should I ask what it is?"

"It's what Dennis killed himself with."

"The miserable bloke in the wheelchair?" asks Our Dave.

"Yes. He left me it to use on Joel." Our Dave can see now that Liz was a little further along than just thinking about what she might do – she had the means.

"When this is all over, Liz, we'll talk." He does not want to say the violence won't happen again because, that is what he said last time, and it did happen again. "I'm here if you need me, Liz, if you and Joel need me." She nods. That's what everyone says, and nobody means it.

The attack has answered her question. She had wondered how she was going to step into the future, and the future is here with the little boy sat in his highchair watching cartoons – that is her future.

"It's under the sink, Our Dave, you can't miss it."

It's the least he can do.

CHAPTER EIGHTEEN
Bev

Bev messages Lars a lot. He had been busy that night with a problem at the factory, that's why he didn't call her back. He is all forgiven. She sends him pictures of her day. A new dress she bought, the dinner she cooked for Chloe, a new plant she got for the garden, the sunset over the Humber Bridge, her neighbour's new kitten. Lars sends her photos too, yachts on the canal out of Groningen, the sunset from his window, his cat, Misha, the meal he ordered in the Chinese restaurant, a picture of his smiling, white-haired mother. It has become a kind of addiction to her, each time her phone buzzes she feels a shiver of excitement down her legs.

Lars is not rude but flirtatious. He sends her pictures of his bare chest with his beard showing and his bright white teeth smiling, he asks her questions about her day, he remembers what she has told him. It's not just the messages, after last night, Bev called him. He was on his way home from the factory and they chatted as he drove. He called her back an hour or so later, and Bev laid on her bed while they talked about everything from here to the sun and back again. His English is good with a slight accent, he does not understand all of Bev's slang, but she loves the way he speaks. He pronounces all his words and does not trip over them or garble them. They have talked about relationships too. Lars was married and has two older teenage sons who are off studying. He has had girlfriends before but nothing serious. Bev is level with him. She has had boyfriends too but there has been no meaning to the fumbling and kissing. The relationship is going as well as it can go considering they have only chatted a few times and live in different countries.

Chloe scowls at her mother when she sees her grinning at her phone screen and she stomps up and down the stairs when she hears her giggling on a call. She asks her mother questions about him, his previous relationships and his financial stability, his employment and his health. Chloe is the voice of reason that chips away at the dream, she has heard of men who entrap women, message them for years and end up stealing their life savings. Though Lars has not asked Bev for any money, Chloe is sure that he will. The more she hears about Lars and the more photos she sees, the more she is convinced that it is not true. Like her father, Chloe is a realist. It's not that her mother does not deserve someone special, it's just that Lars is six foot two, well-built and handsome, he is not rich but he is not an alcoholic, or a drug addict, so she's told and he does have a job. Chloe is not sure, and she would not admit it to her mother, but, she gets the feeling that Bev may be punching above her weight.

It's just after eight in the office of Avenue Cars. It's Tuesday. Liz's face is bruised, that's what getting smacked in the jaw does; and she's wearing a kind of neck scarf to cover the marks from the night before. Dilva has made her a cup of peppermint tea and sits next to her as they both scroll their mobile phones. Liz is not defeated, but the spark just behind her eyes is dimmed for the time being. Our Dave is in the galley kitchen doing the washing up. Hazel trained him well.

Bev enters through the back door, she has already heard what happened from Our Dave the night previous. He looks up at her but doesn't say hello as he washes the cups in the sink. He's wearing yellow marigold gloves.

"We won't take any more of this, Our Dave," she whispers. "Liz text me earlier, I don't know why she's come to work at all. I'm not sure I would have."

"You came back to work just fine when it happened to you," he says.

"That's because I killed a bloke." Dave carries on washing the mugs. "I mean, if this happens again, we'll all be out. I'd rather not have a job than be dead, and so would the other girls. Whatever is happening, we don't need to be part of it."

"Agreed," says Our Dave. "After tonight, it will all be back to normal."

"You said that kind of thing before. Do you even know what you're mixed up in?"

"I'm not sure I do anymore, Bev. I used to. Seems like I

went to sleep one day and the world changed and all the rules with it when I woke up."

"It's called getting old," she answers.

"Maybe. I need you to do me a favour after you've made your drop offs this morning."

"Will I get shot?" she's joking, but Our Dave looks at her with a serious and dark expression.

"I don't think so." He is telling the truth but the fact there is a slight possibility Bev could get shot is unnerving.

"I've got a daughter, Our Dave."

"You won't get shot," he adds, as if she missed the irony, but Bev does not make these kind of mistakes. "You'll just have to drop off a bag with someone on Hessle Road."

"What's in the bag?" There's no point lying.

"A gun and some money."

"Can't you do it?"

"They know me round there."

"What if I get stopped by the police? What if that copper DI Lyndsey shows his ugly face?"

"He won't."

"What if he does?"

"Say you don't know what it is."

"You're taking the piss, Dave. I've got a daughter and I've got a record. If I get caught doing anything wrong, then I'll get a face full of shite." Our Dave takes off his marigold gloves and sets them neatly on the side of the sink.

"If we're going to get through all this, I need your help."

"Why should I?"

"I helped you, and I'll help you again." This is true. "I just need the bag dropping off with someone and then we can wash our hands of it all. I've got one more job to do and this will all be over. Things can go back to the way they should be, quiet and boring and steady."

"What's happened to young James Boyce?"

"He's still on the trawler, as far as I know."

"Nothing's going to happen to him though, is it?"

"No." Our Dave frowns. As far as he's concerned the lad is just a civilian, like Bev here.

"So you'll drop the bag?"

"I'd rather shit in one of my hands and clap to be honest, Our Dave." Bev has been waiting to say this line. She heard it from one of the rough kids she drives to school. "What's in it for me, if I do it?" she asks.

"What do you want?"

"A holiday."

"For you and Chloe?"

"No, just for me, and while I'm gone, you'll look after her." Bev is thinking about Holland.

"Where you want to go?"

"I need a return to Amsterdam." Bev is going to get what she wants. He's a little confused at her choice.

"Bev. I wouldn't ask if I didn't need your help."

"Where is it?"

"It's the grey sports bag by the door." She nods.

"Where am I taking it?"

"It's Hawthorne Ave. A car park just before the Dairycoates Inn. There's someone who needs what's in the bag more than I do. I've told her to meet you there."

"How's that going to help the situation?"

"I don't know, but it feels right."

"Giving someone a gun?" asks Bev. Our Dave takes the tea towel that hangs on one of the drawer handles and begins to dry a mug with it. He's honest for once:

"I don't have anyone else to talk about this to, Bev. I just know that my heart is not usually wrong." She looks into his blue eyes and sees the man who has employed her all these years, the man who fitted her kitchen, the man who services her boiler and changes the oil on her car. There is more to him than just a friendly handyman or the old fella who has two allotments behind Newland Avenue.

"I want that ticket, Our Dave," she says. "Amsterdam. A return."

"Drop the bag off, and it's yours."

It's just after half nine and Bev has picked up and dropped off the sweet nine-year-old lass that she takes to school across

157

town. Although she never says a word to Bev, the story is that the girl stabbed her primary teacher in the shoulder with a pair of scissors, and that's why she can't go to normal school anymore. Bev likes her and hopes the story is true and that the teacher she stabbed won't think it's okay to take the piss out of other students in the future.

She has that bag Our Dave asked her to take down to Hessle Road. It's like a bomb under the front seat. She knows it can't go off but while it's there, she feels vulnerable. She waits at the traffic lights on Anlaby Road and drums her fingers on the leather of the wheel. The car in front is familiar somehow. It's a light blue Mondeo. The driver's door opens while the lights are still on red. She sees the curly hair of DI Lyndsey as he gets out. Her heart drops. It had to be him, didn't it. He gives Bev a smile and a wave and then he points to the bus stop a few yards in front.

"Would you pull in for a minute?" he shouts. Bev's mouth is suddenly dry and her heart starts. She must comply with him, if she drives off, he'll know for sure there's something wrong. She gives him a false, toothy smile that she hopes he doesn't think is nervous. DI Lyndsey gets back in his car, and when the lights turn green, he pulls into the bus stop and she parks behind. He gets out and walks over to the passenger side of the white Mercedes. Bev presses the button to wind down the window and he smirks at her. Today he's wearing a grey suit with a green shirt and a black tie not done up tight enough to his neck.

"Mind if I get in?" he asks.

"I'm busy," says Bev.

"It'll only take a minute," he answers as he opens the car door and gets in. Just under where he sits, tucked in, is the grey sports bag that Bev is so worried about. He smiles at her again, and it's false. DI Lyndsey enjoys talking to her because he can see that she's unnerved.

"We can't park here in a bus stop," says Bev.

"This is police business, we can stop where we like."

"What is it then? Have you been following me?"

"I have. I didn't want to talk to you with that young lass in

158

the car so I waited till you dropped her off. Then pulled in front."

"What is it you want?"

"Just wondered if you'd heard anything."

"About what?"

"I dunno, you tell me." He has an earnest look on his face now his smile is gone but DI Lyndsey doesn't have the experience to speak to people and get the answers he wants. Instead, he sounds like something from a Sunday night TV drama.

"I haven't heard anything. It's all been normal." Bev does not want to mention the man who attacked Liz the night previous, the same one who Ryan clobbered round the head and left in a bush. DI Lyndsey will probably know all this anyway. Bev thinks about the bag under the seat and wonders what would happen to her if he found it – she'd be taken in and she'd have to take the blame too. She gives DI Lyndsey a smile because she is in danger.

"I heard that Our Dave has been in all sorts of trouble."

"You know more than I do, then," says Bev.

"The net's closing in on him, and when he gets caught, the people who worked with him will get caught as well. If you want to look after yourself and that daughter of yours the best thing you can do is cooperate." She has to hold her nerve.

"I am cooperating. I told you, I don't know anything about Our Dave. He's been a good boss to me."

"Look, both you and I know that there's something not quite right. If you tell me what he's up to, then when he does get pinched, it'll be a lot easier on you."

"He just runs a taxi business, officer. I'm just one of his drivers." The curly haired plain clothed policeman shakes his head as if she's not telling him the truth.

"Dave is going to get what's coming to him. You don't have to be mixed up in any of it, if you don't want to be."

"I'm not mixed up in it."

"You would be though. I'm sure I'd find something." Bev feels her anger rising. If it weren't for that grey sports bag under where he sits, she'd ask him to get out the car. DI

Lyndsey can sense Bev's unease somehow. "I could keep you out of it, you know, if I wanted to. If you'd help me out."

"What do you mean?"

"Well, you're an attractive lady. I'm sure we could come to some sort of arrangement." There's no smile on this man's face now. His curly hair is greasy and Bev can see the line of grime on the collar of his green shirt around his neck, she can smell onions on his breath from whatever he's eaten. He is propositioning her. She is not sure what to do for a moment, her heart tells her to slap him round the face, but her brain races ahead and thinks about the pistol in the bag under his feet.

"I'm sure we can work something out," she says. He grins.

"I thought you might say that." He's arrogant and it makes him uglier even.

"Let me get finished and I can give you a call," she says. Her heart is beating in her chest. She just wants him out the car and she'll deal with his advances later. She can tell him to piss off once she's got rid of the gun.

"I'll leave you my card, shall I?"

"Sure." Bev flashes that false smile once more. DI Lyndsey takes out his wallet and pulls out another of his cards. He passes it to Bev and she takes it between her fingers.

"I'll be off then," he says. He reaches his hand down to her knee and gives it a little squeeze. It makes Bev's stomach turn over.

"I'm looking forward to seeing you," he says. She finds it hard not to scowl. "You've made the right choice." DI Lyndsey gets out the car and looks back in through the open passenger door window. "I get finished about six," he says. She nods, and watches him walk back to his blue Ford Mondeo and get in.

Bev takes a series of deep breaths as she starts the car. She has to get rid of this bag.

It's ten minutes later, on Hawthorn Ave, the road leading to the Dairycoates Pub. Every time Bev drives along here, it seems that the train barriers are down and she has to wait for the train to rattle by before she can get on her way. Today is no different. She taps the big wheel in anticipation. The bag under the front seat has made her nervous. She checks the mirrors to see if DI Lyndsey has followed her but there is no sign of him and she has driven around the block a few times to make sure he is not there. She texts Lars while she waits and he sends one back. She smiles. She wonders if he is real, just for a second, because, like Chloe, she knows he is too good to be true and that their relationship or whatever it is will take a nasty turn. For now, she's happy to pretend that he is real and does want her, and that one day, she really will go to Holland and see him and they will be in love and hold hands as they walk down the river in the pictures he sends her. She thinks of DI Lyndsey with his dirty shirt and onion breath.

After the barriers go up, she drives halfway down towards the Dairycoates Inn and turns into a deserted car park at an industrial unit. There's a small woman with red hair waiting in the corner, she has a lady's bicycle with a wicker basket on the front. Bev pulls in next to her and gets out.

"Are you Kasia?" she asks. Leatherhead's Kasia nods her head but does not smile. Bev goes to the passenger side, opens up and takes out the sports bag. She walks over to the woman and sets it on the floor. "This is from Our Dave," she says. Kasia picks it up and puts it in the basket, then pulls the zip down and looks inside. She sees the pistol and the money but her face does not change.

"What does he want for it?" asks the Polish girl.

"He says it's a gift and that you'll know what to do with it." Again, the red-haired woman's face does not alter. She looks back at Bev.

"Tell him I said thank you," says Kasia. Bev takes a deep breath through flared nostrils.

"You do know what's in there, don't you?"

"Yes," comes the answer.

"What are you going to do with it?"

"Use it."

"What for?"

"To shoot someone." Bev swallows. The Polish girl is

161

calm, neat and small. The basket on her bike has a line of fake flowers around the rim. She has a summer dress that finishes below her knees and sensible sandals.

"I hope it's someone who deserves it." Bev is not prepared for this level of supposed honesty, so she reasons it must be a kind of joke.

"They do deserve it," says Kasia. "Dave knows that as well."

"You didn't get it from me, if anyone asks." Kasia looks at her with flat and level eyes. Bev gets back in the driver's side of the big Mercedes and starts the engine. She looks through the windscreen at the red-haired Polish girl as she gets on her bike with the grey bag in the front basket. She doesn't look like she could pick the gun up, let alone use it and Bev gives her a smile but Kasia does not smile back.

Bev reverses and drives out the car park onto Hawthorne Ave. She looks through her rear-view mirror to see the red-haired girl on her bike going the other way towards the Dairycoates Inn.

She scares Bev.

CHAPTER NINETEEN
Dilva

Aziz says he's not afraid of dying. Dilva doesn't think that's true. He is getting worse, so he can't get dressed in the morning and his lungs rasp in his thin body. There's anxiety in him when he cannot get his breath as he sits in his armchair, and the drugs from the nebulizer aren't working as well as they should. His eyes glaze sometimes and he cannot remember words, he's losing what little weight he had and his once black moustache is thinning and his hair is falling out. Dilva has seen people die before, not as slowly as this, she's seen the eyes dim as the body begins to accept what is happening to it. She does not know what they will do when he goes.

It's Tuesday, early evening. Mohammed tells them he has joined the football team at school and Layla says she has a boyfriend. They are already pulling away from the world that Dilva understands. She has made them chicken and rice, again, because it's all Aziz will eat even though he cannot make it to the table in the kitchen.

"I need your help," Dilva says to both of them. Mohammed looks up with a wrinkled nose.

"How?"

"I need you to translate. There's a nurse visiting to look at Aziz, and she wants to talk to us."

"What have we got to make with that?" asks Layla. She is losing her Kurdish as quickly as she is getting better at English.

"I don't know if I'll understand her, but between all of us we should be able to work it out." The girl nods at the woman who is her mother in every way.

"He's going to die, isn't he?" Dilva frowns. She should never underestimate a child, and there's no point in lying to them, her grandmother taught her that.

"Yes, I think he is." She grabs Mohammed's hand in hers and takes Layla's in the other. "He will need us to be strong for him, he'll need us to make light of it, like he does. That's how it doesn't frighten him." Dilva feels her eyes welling up. In asking them to stand firm she is losing some of her strength.

She feels Layla grip her hand.

"It's not good to make a joke out of it, mother," she says. "It's not good for Aziz to do that."

"He has to. It's all he's got left and that's just how he is."

"Will he die and never come back?" asks Mohammed. He examines Dilva's face as he asks.

"If he dies, he'll be gone but we'll always have what he left us with. We'll have his humour and his spirit too and it'll help us and comfort us." The children both know that Aziz is ill and in pain, they live in the same house. They hear Dilva giving him a bath and watch him cough so that his whole-body rattles with agony.

"He told me you were a soldier, mother," says Layla.

"I was… I am a soldier."

"He says you're a fighter."

"We're all of us fighters, in one way or another, you too." She grips both of their hands tight. There's a knock at the frosted glass of the front door. It will be the nurse.

The medical woman from the hospice is fat and wears a dark blue uniform, it's a tabard and trousers and she has black, sensible shoes. She smells of flowers and has blonde curly hair that is dyed and a sweet and calm smile. She examines Aziz with the rest of them in the room, Dilva next to him and the two kids sitting on the floor in front of the gas fire that is not on. The nurse is patient with him, she listens to his chest and checks his pulse, looks at his fingernails and in his eyes, his ears too. At points, she asks the children to translate for her and they tell him to take a deep breath or cough. Aziz is a good patient, like he's a good man, he does everything he can to make it easier and he has that same good humour that Dilva spoke of.

The nurse sits down in one of the armchairs opposite and writes notes in a logbook, she fills in numbers and looks at her watch to write down the time. When she's done, she returns all her equipment back into a little bag and then puts her hands on her lap and looks all serious.

"He's very ill," she says. Dilva nods. They knew this. You

don't need to be a nurse to work that out. "I think he'd be better if he came to stay at the hospice." Dilva shoots a glance at Layla and the little girl translates.

"What's a hospice?" asks Dilva.

"It's where we can keep him comfortable. He's not going to get better. We have everything there for him, we can manage his pain too." Layla translates.

"I'd rather die here, with people I know," says Aziz. Layla translates this.

"I understand," says the nurse, "but you'll be in a lot more pain here. Your family can come and stay with you, while you're there. You won't be alone."

"I need to think about it," says Aziz.

"Take all the time you need, but, you haven't got a lot of time left." The nurse leaves a card with a number on it. Dilva is to call this if he gets worse, not the hospital, it's gone past that now. She sees the nurse to the door and watches her waddle down the path to where her car is parked on the street.

In the front room, Dilva sits down next to Aziz. He is leaning on his knees with his elbows, and his rolled-up shirt sleeves show his bony arms.

"I'd rather die here," says Aziz.

"I know, but it will be easier on you there. They can give you the drugs you'll need."

"I'd rather die at home, I'd rather be back in Kurdistan. I'd rather be back in the village." When Aziz grew up in the eighties, the villages in the mountains would have been traditional. They'd raise goats and chickens. There'd be big families and smiles all round, brothers and sisters and the kind of community that Aziz thinks does not exist in the UK. Nowadays there are wide streets in the same villages and the kids play video games hooked up to the internet and there are four by four trucks parked in the drives. Dilva can see the light flickering on and off in his head. She has read that his brain will start to slow down when he can't get enough oxygen in his blood.

"I never did tell you where I'm from, did I?" asks Aziz.

"You don't need to," she says.

165

"Would you let me tell you, Dilva? I need to tell someone, even if it's just the corners of the room." The children have disappeared upstairs already, not because they are rude, but the seriousness of the conversation scares them.

"You can tell me," says Dilva. She does not know if she will be able to stay strong in the face of whatever his story is. He has always skirted over his past and avoided it, like it was something not valid, as if it were a mistake that he lived through and does not need to be talked about.

"You know, nobody cares about stories," he says, "unless they're in them, or they know someone in them."

"I care about your stories," she says.

"I've never told you any." Dilva closes her eyes. "I'm sorry, but I don't know who else I'll tell. There'll be no one who speaks our way where I'm going, and I don't mean the hospital. I just need a minute of your time. I can't go under without telling someone."

"You're not going under," she says, but she knows that he is, and quick with it too. His kind brown eyes blink up at her from where he leans.

"I had a son. A big one. He was six foot at sixteen and so smart and clever, brave too. I had two daughters and the small one was twelve and the older one was fourteen. Their mum was a big woman, she was, but wicked, in a good way. She could take it as well as give it. I liked that. We lived in my dad's house in the village until he died and then he left it to me. It was a big place with a bit of land and a tractor that was ancient even when the old man bought it. I was in my forties, and that was life for me, so I thought. That's where I thought I'd be, on the side of that mountain with the sky clear and the winter cold, you know how it is, Dilva." She nods. She does know the vivid blue sky and the crisp, cold snow up to your knees. She knows the smell of the fresh air and the punishing heat in the summer. Aziz continues:

"I thought that was where I'd stay and that would be all that I'd be. You know the trouble we've had in our country, but it missed us, somehow. I never went to school. My dad said I didn't need to and he was right. I drove his tractor and

166

we had cows. Life was simple." Aziz looks at her from far away. Dilva squeezes his hand gently.

"Tell me, old man," she says.

"Do you remember when America attacked Iraq?" Dilva shakes her head lightly. Of course, she knows about it, but the events are fuzzy and lost in time. Aziz coughs.

"It was like a bomb in a lake far away, it took a while for the ripple to get as far as us, and the Americans were keen to protect us anyway. We thought, like always that whatever happens at the bottom of the mountains was nothing to do with us, and that life would go on the same. We were foolish to think like that. Life, like water, is always moving and flowing, and changing. Soldiers came from across the border – they didn't care about who we were, it was to send a message to the Iraqi government." He leans forward and his body shivers as he coughs, as if he can't quite get the phlegm out of his lungs and he grips Dilva's hand tight with the struggle. Between his gasps he hears the shouts outside his house in the village all those years ago, looks out of a window to see the Iranian soldiers kicking down the door of a neighbour. He hears the gunfire and there are soldiers in his house, and more gunfire in the darkness and his big son yelling and the rat-ta-ta of a weapon. The door to his room opens and a machine gun judders in the soldier's hands as he sprays the space inside, the bullets shatter the picture on the far wall and Aziz falls with his wife on top, as all the warmth dribbles out of her onto him. The coughing fit lasts a while, Dilva rubs his back until it subsides.

"That's enough, you can tell me the rest another time." He shakes his head.

"While I'm in the mood." Aziz manages to get his breathing under control and he loses focus. For a moment he is back in his village in the morning, moving his wife's heavy body off him on their bed and seeing his hands red with her blood. Outside there's the smell of cooking and burning, and smoke is billowing from the houses in the distance, the cattle have been shot in the field. His eyes stream then as they stream now.

"All of them gone," he whispers but he cannot explain the horror, nor does he want to let Dilva hear it because she has been good to him and to burden her with more suffering would be cruel. She's a woman who knows what happens. She will work it out.

"You have a new family now," she whispers.

"There I was, 45 years old and no family and no village either." His eyes are wide as he looks back into the past of his days that he has not spoken of before to Dilva. He has never thought to because Aziz feels that the past does not matter, he has only to wipe away the tears from his face and it is all gone or buried more like.

"I became a Kolbar then, just to make money." Dilva knows these men, they smuggle goods on their back through the snowy mountains of Kurdistan and across the border into Iran. Kolbar literally means 'one who carries by his back' and some fall or get shot by border patrols. They bring in radios, flat screen TVs, toasters, cigarettes, and they go back with peaches, homemade alcohol, goats, even guns sometimes. It is a hard road.

"You were one of them?" Dilva shakes her head. "You'll have to tell Mohammed. You must have a million stories."

"Not really," he rasps. "That's why my knees are so bad. Too many days of walking up a mountain in the snow with one of those square packs strapped to my back, and then walking back down, which is worse. I was like a donkey. When I had enough money, I went north and I paid the smugglers to get me to Europe." His eyes are red and the light from them dims in and out.

"You met me and the children on the road."

"Yes. Thank you for listening to me, Dilva," says Aziz. She has not heard his story really. She knows the facts but not the feelings, he will keep these hidden within him. They hug and she can hear his breathing rasp as they do.

Dilva leans on the back door of her little house and lights up one of Aziz's cigarettes. She takes a toke and the smoke hurts her eyes. The garden is very different since Ryan has cleared it. The smashed up green house and climbing frame are gone along with the bags of rubbish, the long grass has been cut tight to the floor, the path has been jet washed. It's a place for someone to be. In the far corner there's a big and heavy blue pot with a wide fern plant, Dilva hears slow footsteps coming round the corner and Ryan appears with another of the same kind of pot in his big arms. He gives her a nod as he struggles past and to the opposite corner where he sets it down. He smiles back at Dilva as he approaches.

"I didn't know you smoked." She looks at the cigarette and shrugs her shoulders because it's easier than attempting to say something in English. It makes her seem aloof, which she isn't.

"Thank you for the garden," she says.

"I enjoyed doing it." Like anyone, Ryan enjoys hard work.

"I don't have money to pay." He grins.

"I know. It's a favour."

"There is no dinner today," she says. "Aziz is very sick."

"Your husband?"

"He's not my husband," she has told him this before and Ryan heard it but was not sure if she made a mistake with her language. He nods.

"And the children are not yours either?"

"Mohammed is my brother. Layla is my cousin. You know this. Where is your wife, Mr Ryan?" she asks. Dilva has another unprofessional toke on her cigarette and does not take the smoke back.

"There isn't one," he answers. With anyone else he would have given a spiel about this girl and that girl, and how he left her and she left him, but he knows she will not understand. He's got nothing but the truth. "I've never met anyone I liked." This is a new fact that even Ryan did not know. Now he has done the garden, he has no legitimate reason for coming back to visit her, and this troubles him. He does not know what he can offer but he wants to see her again, and not in an unsavory way, but just so he can be around her. It's a foreign, sweet and yet lost feeling inside him. He looks back at the garden.

"You could do with a new fence," he says. Dilva frowns.

169

She has been pursued by men before when she was younger but there's a puppy dog tenderness to this big man who doesn't quite seem comfortable in his own body.

"What do you want from me?" she asks. Her grandmother taught her to be direct if you need answers.

"I don't know," he says. Ryan has never really been honest before. It's a liberating feeling. She's not afraid of him, he does not intimidate her and it makes him feel like a normal person for once.

"Aziz is going to die," says Dilva. "The nurse will take him somewhere. She said he won't be in pain." Dilva dabs the end of the cigarette on the wall to put it out. It makes her feel sick.

"If you need anything," says Ryan, "I'm just next door." This is not the kind of thing that Ryan would say. He's a different person when she's near him. She looks up with her brown eyes and her high cheek bones. She's afraid. They are a million miles apart these two. Ryan, big boned and rough schooled, northern English with a quick, angry wit to cover how he really feels, bad teenage tattoos on his upper arms and a life in the army that gives him unpleasant dreams and heart palpitations sometimes. Dilva, a Kurd from the mountains, designed to care and to fight for the people she loves, and not afraid to show it either. She's never been to a nightclub or taken MDMA, she's never sat at the back of a classroom shouting obscenities at a teacher or had a pint in an alehouse. Ryan has never spent time with his grandmother, or grandfather, he's never sat in the big kitchen of his mother's house with all the family as they eat dinner. Both of them have had a rifle in their hands, both of them have had to do things they did not expect and it has affected them. They are both lost.

"I need to ask you something," says Ryan. "The gun that you took from me – did you know it was a fake when you pulled the trigger in my face?" She takes in breath through her nose. She shakes her head. "Did you think you would kill me?" his question is genuine. There is no malice here, for if anyone pulled a gun on Ryan, he would try to do the same.

"I wanted to kill you," she says. "You brought a gun into

my house and near my children." He nods. This is what he thought, and what he hoped too.

"I would look after you, if I could," he says as he swallows. This is unsure ground for Ryan. He is in territory now, bordering on the mawkish, it is overly emotional behaviour that would see you ridiculed among other men of his kind, as if feelings have no place in the world at all. He cannot help himself. It comes spilling out of him like blood pouring through an open cut, raw and hot and so very dangerous because it will leave him vulnerable.

"I think I love you," he says like a teenager, flush with passion. She looks down at his big army boots and then back up to his face. She does not know what this means at all.

"I have to get back to Aziz," she answers. He nods and steps back as he understands his mistake. Dilva reaches out and grabs the top of his arm, grips him tight through his jacket so he can feel her fingers. There's electricity in her touch.

"Thank you," she says and before she knows what she is doing, feelings she did not know she had are forming. Perhaps it is the mixture of emotions that she feels inside her, the worry for Aziz coughing in the front room, and the attention from this big, rugged man. "You will need to give me time, Mr Ryan. Do you understand?" He nods.

"I understand," he answers.

His heart does a double skip in his big chest.

CHAPTER TWENTY
Our Dave

There's a fine sky above the allotment behind Newland Avenue. Our Dave has come here early. It's five. They used to leave the swing gates at the entrance unlocked years ago, but in the 90s, smackheads started to steal chickens and break into sheds so they added a big padlock.

Our Dave stands in the darkness of his own shed with just a camping lightbulb hanging down from the rafters. The little building has a corrugated iron roof and no windows, and, under a sheet of heavy metal, dug far down into a hole, wrapped in a bit of carpet, is a double barreled 12-gauge shotgun. Our Dave does not know where it came from originally but he acquired it in 1981 from a man who says he found it in Dane Park Road fishing pond off the North Hull Estate. Of course, this is not where he would have got it, but it suited Our Dave at the time and he bought it. He's wearing surgical gloves as he digs – it stops his hands getting dirty and makes sure he doesn't leave any of his details all over the place. It takes him a good few minutes to dig far enough down through the earth, and finally he pulls out something big in a plastic bag.

He unwraps the item carefully, takes it out of the old bit of carpet and there's a greasy rag across the stock and tied neatly across the barrels. This was how Our Dave left it, so that it would not rust. It's not that he expected to ever have to use it again, but just that it's good to keep things working, he has been taught to look after things. In the darkness of his shed, he removes the rag and inspects the chambers, takes out the plugs of cotton wool soaked in oil from each and examines the mechanism from the trigger. It's an old gun, not an antique but probably from the forties or fifties. Our Dave holds it up to his eyes and looks down the sights at the door to his shed. It brings back memories and things that he did that he would rather forget, but that's how Our Dave got here.

He's brought his green fishing rod case, the long one with the strap that you can put over your shoulder. It's been a while since he's been fishing but he kept the bag in his garage just in case he ever needed to transfer the gun anywhere. The weapon fits snuggly inside. Our Dave puts the metal sheet back over the hole and covers it over with earth as it had been half an hour before. He doesn't like to dig up the past, no one does, and there are things buried that he would rather not think about. They aren't the things you'd expect. It isn't so bad to shoot a man who deserves it. The real ball ache is cleaning up afterwards if you have to.

Outside, Our Dave padlocks his shed door. The allotment is deserted at this time on most days and he walks to his car that he's driven up the track, opens the boot and puts the fishing bag inside. The sun is a bright orange over the school building that stands guard over the allotments. They closed it in 2006 and developers have been meaning to make the Victorian building into flats. They'll probably knock it down in the end. It's watched over Our Dave for his whole life.

He reverses down the track and out the big iron gates which he left open and into Raglan Street. Then, he spins the car round and is off into the city, in his boot, the fishing bag with the shotgun weighs heavy on his mind. He's not sure how this will play out.

It's still a few hours away from rush hour and so the streets are thin of traffic. Our Dave drives out of town, he makes the journey over the railway track and past the houses tightly packed together with small front yards. He travels west, where the gardens get bigger along with the houses until he is as far as Kirkella Golf club on Pacman Lane. He is going to visit Charles Boyce. Rather than pulling up outside, he eases the car onto the drive and parks facing the brown front door with the two bay trees outside in pots. Our Dave has done his research, he knows that James's father, Charles, is due in London today, because he's been tipped off, and he knows the well-dressed man will drive to the station in Brough to catch the early train. He also knows the misses has moved out, to her sister's house in Lincolnshire. Our Dave turns off the engine, gets out and stands behind the open driver's door. As if he's planned it,

Charles Boyce steps out into the six o'clock air. He's wearing a crisp pale grey suit with an open collared black shirt. His expression does not alter when he sees Our Dave but his heart skips a beat somewhere in his chest. He closes the door behind him but does not take his eyes off Our Dave.

"James's not here," he says. They are both aware he is out in the North Sea somewhere.

"I know. I thought I'd give you a lift."

"I'm not paying for it," says Charles Boyce. Our Dave gives a light shrug of his shoulders as if this is the last thing on his mind.

"Hop in," says Our Dave. Charles Boyce could refuse to get in the car of course, but it would make him look weak in the face of his adversary. He does not want to look weak, that's what his father used to accuse him of being. He walks round to the back of Our Dave's car, opens the rear door and slides his briefcase onto the backseat, then, he gets in and pulls the seatbelt over his shoulder till it clicks into place. It's not as swanky as Charles Boyce's own car, but he'll humour the man.

"You know, if anything happens to me," says Boyce from the back seat, "there are men who know where you live. There'll be lads on your Hazel. It wouldn't be very nice for anything to happen to a woman of that age, you know how rough and eager lads can get." The threat is unnecessarily descriptive which robs it of some power. Our Dave shrugs his shoulders again at the man in the back seat. Something is going to happen to Charles Boyce. If he knew anything about the line of business he has entered into, he would not have accepted the lift.

"What time is your train?"

"Half six," comes the reply. Our Dave fits a blue surgical mask around his face and nose, then hooks the string around his ears. He starts the engine.

"Covid is over, you know, Dave," says Charles Boyce. "You don't need to wear those anymore."

"It's company policy," he answers. Boyce scoffs. The car purrs into action and our Dave reverses gently out the drive and onto the street taking care that the revs of the engine don't wake the neighbours. They make off down Pacman Lane and out of the posh suburb to the fields. A few weeks ago, Bev drove a man out this way, and he tried to kill her, so Our Dave heard.

Charles Boyce is calm in the back. He looks out the windows at the fields streaming past them, the green of the East Riding and crows taking to the wing from far off trees. He thinks that other people do the dirty work, that they add the numbers and make the coffee, wash the floors and hoover the stairs, sail to catch fish on trawlers in the ocean, and so, he thinks that Our Dave will not do the dirty work either. This is the wrong attitude because there's no job that Our Dave won't do if it needs to be done. He'll drain a heating system or a boiler, he'll carry an old sofa to the tip or scrub potatoes. He'll shoot a man too if that's what's required.

"I got in touch with my boy," says Boyce. There's a smug tone to his voice. "Turns out the skipper knows a friend of mine who used to work for my father. He let me chat to him too. He's doing fine on board. It might even be good for his attitude."

"It'll make a man of him," says Our Dave as he looks through the rear-view mirror at his passenger.

"You don't imagine this is going to turn out well for you, do you, Dave? Whatever game it is you're playing." This is one of those rhetorical questions. Charles Boyce can't quite pull them off with enough menace. "I told you to close down your business and you refused, so you left me with no other choice to inform associates I had over in Manchester." This is a common tactic for Boyce, to make his choice seem like it was actually caused by you. He did it to his first wife. He does it to James. Our Dave keeps the car at a steady speed on the country road.

"We saw the Manchester lads last night," says Our Dave, his voice is a little muffled through the mask, but clear enough. "It's all sorted and they've gone back." He makes it seem like there was a problem with a car exhaust pipe or a leaky drain that was of no consequence and was easily fixed. Charles Boyce looks at the man driving when he hears this. He was

175

assured that hard men would be visiting Our Dave and his taxi drivers. Men who were well paid to do things unpleasant in nature. He finds it a little unnerving that this older man seems to just shrug it off so easily.

They drive across the undulating chalk hills of the Wolds, fields stretch on either side of them, with Swanland up the hill to the right, and rolling green pastures to the north. Our Dave holds the car steady as they stream through a thin forest and down the hill on a narrow and fast country road. There's a faint smell of something in the back, a kind of surgical whiff that irritates Charles Boyce's nose; his hand goes to the button to open the window. It clicks as he presses it, but the glass does not slide down.

"There's something wrong with the windows back here," says Boyce.

"We've had to disable them," answers Our Dave from the front. "The kids just mess about with them."

"I'm not exactly a teenager, Dave. Just what is it you want? What was the point of picking me up? What do you have to say?"

The car begins to slow.

"What's going on?" asks Charles in his pinched voice.

"I'm not sure." They have come to the bottom of the hill and Our Dave pulls the car into a deserted track off the main road, there's a rough gravel car park. It's empty. Our Dave stops in the corner.

"I've got a train to catch, Dave," says Charles Boyce. He's candid. "It's not as if anything you're going to do now will stop the inevitable. You can either stand aside, or you'll be knocked to the ground and you'll stand aside anyway. It's your choice." There he goes again with that blame thing. Our Dave turns and looks over his shoulder while he gives him a smile.

"I just have to get something out the boot," he says. Charles Boyce cocks his head. Our Dave gets out of the car and his shoes crunch on the wet gravel as he steps to the back, opens the boot and returns. In the time it takes him to do this, Charles Boyce has opened his briefcase and removed something from it, so, when Our Dave gets back into the front

176

seat, things have changed somewhat. Leaning forward, Charles Boyce holds a matt black pistol on his knee, the barrel pointing at Our Dave. He grins.

"Try anything out here, and I'll blow your brains all over the windscreen." Our Dave keeps his movements slow when he sees what his passenger has in his well-manicured hand on his knee. He's had guns pointed at him before. He puts the box of surgical gloves that he got from the boot on the front seat, then shows both his hands to prove there's nothing in them. "What did you go to the boot for?" asks Boyce. Our Dave starts the engine.

"I've got a shotgun in the back, I was going to take your head off. I lost my nerve." Boyce smirks at this. It's clearly a joke.

"You made the right choice, old man. I can promise you that I won't lose my nerve." Boyce has only ever fired a shotgun once, on a stag do in Ireland back in the noughties – that's the extent of his ballistics knowledge.

"Are you going to shoot me?" asks Our Dave.

"I'd rather not," answers Boyce. "I do have a train to catch and I don't want to get blood on this suit, it's probably worth more than your car." The man with a bald head and surgical mask nods his head. He looks defeated. "Just drive," says Boyce as he puts the pistol back in his suitcase.

He backs the car up and sets off on the road again. They are silent these two, as if Our Dave has played his hand and come up short. The Ford Galaxy picks up speed. Charles Boyce tries the window again. There's something irritating his throat.

"You need to get these windows fixed." Our Dave looks in the rear-view mirror.

"The kids will just mess about with them," comes the reply. Charles Boyce looks out of the window that does not open.

"Why did you pick me up then, Dave, if you haven't got the guts to get rid of me?" Boyce thinks he is learning the working-class way of joking, going along with what Dave told him, even though he knows it can't be true.

"I need your help," says Our Dave. The man in the back

scoffs. "I'm shutting down the business, and I need a buyer for the taxi office. It's the least you can do." Charles Boyce wishes he hadn't shown the gun. He was wrong to bring it out. The man at the wheel seems older than he did a few minutes before with his mask tight to his mouth and nose.

"How much do you want?"

"Fifty grand. Enough for me and Hazel to get away, somewhere warm, and set up again." It's a very reasonable sum. Boyce could sell the building for more than triple that. He takes a deep breath.

"I think that sounds fair, Our Dave." His tone is softer now he realises why the man has made the trip, and why he is driving him to the station. Boyce suddenly feels sorry for him, but he would never show any humility. He thinks on the lessons his father taught him. "I'll give you forty," he says. Our Dave does not respond for a moment as he concentrates on the road, his hands grip the wheel.

"That sounds good," he says. Boyce has him.

At Brough station, Our Dave pulls up just beside the platform and turns off the engine. There's no train yet, but a line of well-dressed business types wait holding briefcases with laptop bags hooked over their shoulders.

"So that's it then, Dave," says Boyce.

"That's what?"

"You've lost," he answers. Charles Boyce beams. "You'll shut down the business? The imports and everything?"

"I already have," he says. His voice is grey.

"You've made a smart choice. You see people like me, Dave, we were born to win. We play the game better, we're smarter, braver, quicker and we get the upper hand every time we play. That's why people like me are rich, and men like you are poor. I'm responsible for my success, just like you're responsible for your failure." Our Dave does not say anything. "I'm a fair man, Dave, I'll be good to my word for that taxi office."

A train slows to the little station. Boyce gets out and reaches back for the briefcase and opens the car door, it feels good to breathe fresh air.

178

"You look after yourself, Dave," he adds. "I'll be in touch." Charles Boyce closes the door and taps up the few steps to the train platform, he's just in time to slip between the sliding doors after the last passenger has got on. He finds a window seat and looks through the glass at Our Dave, sitting in his taxi with a grey face. Charles Boyce gives him a little wave and a half grin out the side of his mouth. He feels, after all this time, that he is finally his father's son, overflowing with guile, wit and barefaced cheek that the world cannot contain. He is a winner, and he has won this one on his own, with his own hands. He takes a deep and proud breath as the train pulls off.

Our Dave waits till the train is out of sight, then opens up all the windows. He removes some surgical gloves from the box he brought from the boot and snaps one over his hand. He must be careful how he plays this part. Our Dave fishes under the passenger seat and pulls out the aerosol can that Liz told him to get rid of from her house. He takes the duct tape off the nozzle. Like any good gardener, you don't throw anything away, you'll always find a use for it. He wonders if it was enough. Maybe it was too much. He gets out and takes off his mask, putting the can into a black plastic bag.

Our Dave drives back down to the posh suburbs, across the green fields with the blue morning sky above. He goes down, past the church and the exclusive golf club to the house where he picked Charles Boyce up an hour earlier. He doesn't park in the drive this time. Our Dave knows that the camera above the garage does not work because Charles Boyce's son James told him his father didn't bother to turn the CCTV on. Our Dave gets out, closes the door and goes to the boot where he removes the fishing bag. He swings it over his shoulder and walks up the drive.

James Boyce is away on a fishing boat. Charles Boyce is on a train to London. The CCTV is off. He goes to the green bin, flips the lid and then deposits the fishing bag inside. It takes him less than a few seconds, and, in under a minute, he is cruising down the road back to the city. The shotgun has a bit of history, and any copper who's worth his pay will link it to

179

shootings from the seventies and eighties. Maybe they'll link it to Boyce's father. Maybe they'll link it to Leatherhead.

Charles Boyce felt uneasy during the journey. He washed his face in the little toilet with the tepid water while the train rattled over the tracks below him.

He didn't feel sick, but uneasy.

At 9.15, when he's crossing the road outside King's Cross Station, Charles Boyce collapses, face first into the concrete of the street. London is not as unfriendly as you might think. Passersby try to help. An ambulance is called. A kind young woman stays with him, his eyes flutter as he lays there, as his chest draws in great gasps of air.

He's dead by the time the ambulance arrives.

The police find a matt black pistol in his briefcase.

CHAPTER TWENTY-ONE
Bev

Bev is still on the phone. It's been two hours and it's late. It must be half ten. Chloe can hear her through the wall of her bedroom, giggling and laughing like she's a teenager. It's the man from Holland that she talks about all the time. Lars. This is how her mum is. Chloe has seen her fixate on men in the past, and it never ends well. She believes everything they tell her and, despite the fact that she is the most streetwise woman Chloe has ever known, when it comes to men, she is as stupid as a broom handle. Chloe thumps on the bedroom wall with the fat part of her fist.

"I've got work in the morning," she yells. Her mother has work too. There's the sound of footsteps coming across the landing from her mother's room, and Bev opens the door on her daughter.

"I've finished talking to him now," she says with her phone in her hand. "Don't you want me to be happy?" she asks. Chloe sits up in bed.

"Of course, I do," she answers, "but you've not even met that fella."

"I talk to him every day."

"So what, he could be telling you anything."

"Do you think I'm stupid?"

"No, but I think, when it comes to men you're easily led." Bev considers this. Her daughter's eyes are smooth and intelligent and there is a part of Bev that knows she is right.

"I think he's real, Chloe. I think what we have is real." This is Bev breaking cover, it's as honest as she will allow herself to be.

"I hope so," says Chloe. She means this.

There's a loud knock on the front door from downstairs and, instinctively, Bev pulls her dressing gown tighter around her and redoes her belt. Chloe gets out of bed.

"Who will that be?" she asks.

"I don't know," says Bev, "but Our Dave told me not to answer the door to anyone last night."

"Does that apply to tonight as well?" Bev frowns.

"I guess it does." The banging comes again, this time more insistent hammering on the glass of the front door. There's also shouting. Bev goes to the top of the landing and Chloe follows. The person bangs again and they hear him shout from outside:

"Police! Open up." Bev makes her way down the stairs when she hears this, but Chloe touches her on the shoulder in caution after the first step. Bev looks back to her daughter. She's right to worry. The voice comes again from outside the front door, and this time, Bev recognises the tone, it doesn't have much gravel in it. It's the curly haired copper who stopped her in the car the other morning. It's DI Lyndsey.

Bev walks down to the bottom step and stands at the door. She can see the shadow of the man outside against the orange streetlight.

"What do you want?" she calls through the frosted glass.

"Police business, can you let me in?"

"It's late."

"Can you unlock this door?" He is insistent. The handle rattles as he tries to turn it from outside. The voice of DI Lyndsey makes her nervous. Bev pulls her mobile phone from her dressing gown pocket and goes to her inbox with her thumb, she finds Our Dave's last message and taps that. In the box she writes, 'Need help with my boiler'. He will know what that means. Last winter Our Dave fitted a new boiler for her, and so, there won't be anything wrong with it. He'll know this is a call for help.

"I'm not opening the door," she calls.

"If you don't open up, I'll get the lads in the van here to smash it through. It makes no odds to me. Now get this door open." Bev hesitates. Chloe appears on the stairs above and she turns to her daughter.

"Go upstairs and close your door, don't come out for anything," she whispers. Chloe looks flustered. She runs back to her room. The door handle rattles again and the man on the other side tries his weight against it with his shoulder.

She'll have to open up. He'll wake the neighbours and

whatever it is - she'll deal with him, she's had worse. Bev turns the silver key in the lock and opens the door. There's DI Lyndsey, with his face red under the curly hair and a cocky look in his eyes. The other morning, Bev had a bag with a gun in it under her passenger seat, and so she was nice to him. Now, there's nothing for her to hide so she can be straight.

"What do you want?" she asks. She can see, instantly that his eyes are not quite focused and there's the faint smell of booze on his breath and onions, again. She looks past him to the street and there's no police van. He must be here on his own.

"You didn't call me," he says. So, this is not police business.

"I was never going to call you," she answers.

"I thought you said you would."

"I just wanted you to piss off. I was at work." DI Lyndsey examines the blonde hair and her pink towelling dressing gown. His lips are wet. He's been thinking about her. He leans forwards and whispers through his teeth.

"You know, I could have this place searched. You wouldn't believe what we'd find."

"Don't threaten me." Bev is calm.

"Just let me come in for a bit. Show me some of what you said you'd show me before, then I'll be on my way."

"On your way, dickhead," says Bev. She spits the words. Now she's sure there's no back up and that he's operating outside his real duties, she's not so worried. He holds his finger pointing up to her face. He doesn't shout, but there's menace to his voice.

"I know people," he says.

"You do realise, I've got this on video," says Bev. She hasn't. "There's a camera up there recording everything you say."

"There's no camera, love. I've checked this house out a few times. I'd have seen it, I'm a copper." Bev goes to close the door and DI Lyndsey puts his foot in the way by stepping onto the welcome mat.

"Get out of my house," says Bev through gritted teeth.

"I told you what I want," he whispers as he pushes against the door with her leaning on it. DI Lyndsey is not a big man, but he is stronger than Bev. The door slowly opens against his weight.

Bev has been in situations like this before. There was the night at Hull Cheese when she was forced into a corner by some bull like bloke, and she smashed that pint glass over his head. There have been times she's been afraid in the taxi, she was scared when the man in a suit tried to abduct her, she was scared when her father attacked her, she's scared now. This is a copper, however, and whatever you might think about the steady honesty of a British policeman, this is a man who is pushing his way in, and there is something he wants that makes him powerful and reckless. He'll be protected whatever he does because the force looks after their own. Bev knows how to be afraid, and part of her wishes she had just accepted what was going to happen already. It might have been the safest thing to do.

He shoves his way in, and steps onto the thick hall carpet with his cheap and slightly battered shoes, closing the door behind him gently. From his suit pocket he pulls a small bottle of mace spray and holds it loose in his right hand with his finger over the spray nozzle. This has gone too far already. DI Lyndsey is not a natural thug, he doesn't have the strength or the anger for it, but he has cruelty, and entitlement. Bev stands with her back pressed against her long hall mirror, looking at his ugly face in the dim glow from the spotlight above his head. He hasn't touched her yet.

"I'd rather you enjoy it," says DI Lyndsey. "I'm not a monster. I'm not going to hurt you but I will spray this all over your face if I have to," his voice is a raspy whisper. "Have you ever been hit with pepper spray before? It hurts like hell. Of course, it'd be a different experience for me, what with you screaming and that, but I'm sure I'd cope. Tender would be better, though, for both of us." Bev's nostrils flare in a mixture of hatred and fear.

DI Lyndsey moves forward so he is nearer to her. She can smell his breath, the faint stink of sweat under the cheap aftershave, she can see his shirt collar open and his grin as he approaches. She is a tough woman, but there is only so far she can go, only so many times she can stand up for herself and other people. She killed someone a few weeks back and she knows this will come out sooner or later. This man's threats are real, because that's the kind of thing that happens to a working woman from a poor northern city who doesn't have a university education and is middle aged and is single. It is at times like this, that Bev feels the weight of it all on her shoulders, like all she can do is succumb to what is expected of her.

He reaches out his hand and the long, sticky fingers clasp around her exposed throat, not with any force, but in an attempt to make this between them erotic.

"You'll enjoy it," he whispers, and then he moves forwards so his lips are on hers and his grip tightens very slightly on her neck as he pulls her towards him. Her legs shiver and her stomach turns over. She is frozen. She is not allowed to be anything but a slag or a battle-axe. It is time to give up.

Bev blinks and she is far away in time.

It is 2010. She walks through the door of her mother's terraced house on Lee Street off Holderness Road in East Hull. It's murder to find a parking space. She calls out "Mam" up the stairs and into the house as she walks into the little front room, there's the chemical smell of lavender air freshener. Now Bev's father is dead, her mother lives alone here, at peace with her radio and knitting and the gaggle of old lasses she talks to from up and down the street. Something is wrong. The thin old woman is slumped in her highchair, with her permed hair tight and her head forward and at an angle. Bev shouts at her again, goes down to her and grips her shoulders as she rocks her frail body back gently. One of the old woman's eyebrows twitches in response and Bev yells her name once more as she shakes her. She has a heart problem does Bev's mum and has been on pills for years. Bev shouts down at her but she cannot hear her own voice somehow, the old woman's face seems to drain of all the blood to leave it pale and grey cloud white. Bev puts her hand on her mam's chest and begins to pump at the heart like she's seen on telly adverts. Three short bursts then a rest. She feels the watery, paper-thin skin on her mother's breast as she touches it. On the second round of three pumps there's a wet crack as one of her mother's ribs breaks under her palm. Tears stream down Bev's face. She is at it half an hour before she gives up and steps back in the front room looking down on her mother's dead body.

It's time to give up. You can't change things. You have to give in. Like this DI Lyndsey who is about to force himself onto her. She has to let it happen.

There's another voice somewhere in Bev. It's this city. It's the cheap comments that she shouts at lippy kids on street corners, the quick remarks for rude customers, it's getting up and looking in the mirror at your wrinkled face and putting your make up on anyway. There's no point fighting against it, but you will. What else is there to do? She is broken, lonely, and old, but it is impossible for Bev to go under without a fight.

She is back on Lynton Ave with the curly haired copper kissing her. She bites down on his lip hard – like it's a piece of gammon steak. He yells. She grits her teeth and as he pulls away she yanks her head to the side, taking a bit of his bottom lip with her. She pushes him back and grabs at the little picture frame that sits on the windowsill behind her. It's a picture of her and Chloe in a posh Leeds restaurant with steaks in front of them and evening dresses on. She smacks him round the head with it and the cheap wood breaks on his forehead. He staggers back against the opposite wall and his eyes roll in his head under the curly hair.

Chloe appears at the top of the stairs with her phone in her hand.

"I'm calling the coppers," she yells.

"Don't," commands Bev. She is about to clobber him again when the front door opens. A head pops round the glass. It's Our Dave.

"Just in time," she says. Of course, there is even sarcasm here. She has a line of DI Lyndsey's blood from her mouth like she's a vampire.

"I got your message," he says. DI Lyndsey has now collapsed against the wall in the little hall, there's blood over his chin. Bev steps forward and stamps on the hand with the pepper stray in it. He yells overly loud.

"Looks like you didn't need me," says Our Dave as he steps in.

"I don't need you," she answers.

"Well, I'll deal with him from here then, Bev."

"As long as you two are out my house, I don't give a toss. You owe me for the picture frame as well, Dave."

He opens the front door wider, grabs DI Lyndsey by the collar, and turns him out down the steps. The copper falls onto the path, his hands go out to stop him and he's pathetic as he tumbles. Our Dave walks after him, grabs him by the jacket and hauls him up to his feet. Bev closes her door and there's the sound of the key turning in the lock. Once again, even though Our Dave promised it was all over, he was wrong.

"You're dead, Dave," DI Lyndsey whimpers, he's too shocked to come up with anything else. He's been assured by the Doyle Family that he'll be looked after, and that he has free reign to do whatever he wants in this city. Our Dave pushes him down the drive where DI Lyndsey stumbles and falls again.

There's a car cruising slowly down Lynton Ave. It's a matt black BMW, very much the same as the one that Our Dave had to deal with a few nights before. The new tyres pull up a few yards away, and DI Lyndsey gets to his feet. He sees the car as well and he grins as he looks up at the man who has just pushed and pulled him down the drive and into the road. He knows these blacked-out windows.

"You're done for now, old man," he says. This is the same kind of car that picks him up on Sunday afternoons, where he chats to his handler. A door opens and a man dressed in a navy funnel coat gets out of the passenger side. His face is rugged under short hair. He looks like a bouncer, only better dressed in dealer boots and drainpipe trousers. DI Lyndsey beams at him but the man does not smile back. He has a strong Manc accent when he speaks.

"Would you get in the car, son," he says to DI Lyndsey. "We'll give you a lift."

"Where to?" he asks. The smile drops from his face and his eyes widen. It's a stupid question.

"The Doyle Family have lost interest, officer," says Our Dave from behind. "I think they're pulling out of Hull."

"You're talking shite, Dave," he says.

"They've lost one of their key players, as of this morning, Charles Boyce. They found him in London, dead. He was carrying a pistol in his briefcase and I've heard they're searching his house right now. I'm surprised you're not there. I was looking forward to telling you, but it looks like these lads want to tell you as well." The man in the navy funnel coat asks again in his Manc accent. He tries to sound polite even though he's rough:

"We'll give you a lift, officer," he repeats. DI Lyndsey looks lost suddenly.

"I don't want a lift," he calls. He's got a slight slur from the drink. Another man steps from the BMW, he's dressed in a bomber jacket and a black beanie and with the same stern face. DI Lyndsey is suddenly childlike as he glances up to Our Dave, and his eyes are wide with fear. Perhaps he knew this would happen.

Our Dave did warn him.

"You're not going to let them do this to me, are you?" he asks. There's no reply from Our Dave. The first man moves forward and grabs DI Lyndsey by the shoulder while the second opens the back door of the car. The curly haired copper stumbles as he's pulled and the man stops him from tumbling over. It's not hard to get him in the car. He's not a fighter. The second thug with a beanie nods at Our Dave as he gets into the front seat. They are the same kind of hired muscle who might once have been in the forces and who don't know what Our Dave did to the same sort of men just a night previous. He nods back.

Bev is in the kitchen. The door is locked. Our Dave taps on it with his car keys and she answers when she sees that it's him. He follows her through to the kitchen. There's a wineglass with some sort of clear spirit on the table that she picks up and sips.

"I'm out, Our Dave," she says.

"What do you mean?"

"I'm quitting."

"It's all over. There'll be no more trouble now." Bev has had men lie to her before.

"That's what my ex-fella said, and my ex-husband, I don't think there has ever been a man in my life who hasn't said that things were going to get better. Well, I've had enough. I'm not coming back."

"Take a week off, I'll get someone to cover you."

"I won't be back, Our Dave. I'm not doing it. It's a taxi office. I shouldn't be threatened by coppers, I shouldn't have to deliver sports bags with guns in them, I shouldn't be attacked at work. Do you understand?" Our Dave swallows. This humbles him. He does not want to let anyone down.

"I'm sorry," he whispers. "I'll make it up to you."

"Men have said that to me before, Our Dave. I won't change my mind. I'm finished at the taxi office." Her voice is monotone." She picks up the glass and is about to take a mouthful but sets it down. She's had enough of it all, and that includes the drinking.

"You'll feel better in the morning," says Our Dave.

"I won't be at work."

"Just text me if you're not coming in tomorrow. Sleep on it, at least. That's all I ask." Bev examines Our Dave with her blue eyes, the black eyeliner has faded but she's still pretty.

"I'd like you to leave," she says.

CHAPTER TWENTY-TWO
Daz

It's just after half six in the morning. Our Dave has been to the allotment to make sure things are as they should be. It's late summer and the sun is warm but orange, even at this time in the morning. He opens up the back door of Avenue Cars with his wide bunch of keys, steps through the galley kitchen and into the back office. It's deserted. There's the smell of mold and cheap air freshener, perfume and coffee.

It's not the same taxi company he bought in the nineties. Back then it stank of fags and takeaway pizza, men's sweaty feet and yesterday's ale, belched out through fat stomachs.

He's not the same man who bought the place either. He's older of course, and wiser, as the saying goes, but he notices more detail than he ever did and he's quieter too. He's more worried about getting things right, especially for the people he cares for.

He has not slept well.

Our Dave used to drink, back in the days when he had nothing to be sober for but work, but not anymore. He'd rather buy you a drink instead. This business with Boyce has left a bad taste in his mouth. Once upon a time he would have drunk it all away, like he did other jobs the Leatherhead made him do.

The sun streams through the front shutters he has just opened and Chanterlands Avenue is asleep in the early morning. There's a different quality of light at this time of day and a peacefulness that only early risers will appreciate. Our Dave looks through the post that arrived yesterday and then comes back into the office looking at the brown letters and pizza shop menus. As he enters, he senses something - there's another person here. Hidden in the darkest corner, and as still as a fox, there's a figure that he has not noticed until now. Our Dave won't make any sudden movements, so he doesn't pause what he's doing, but his memory goes to the snub-nosed pistol that is still in the drawer in the galley kitchen under the microwave – the one that fell out of an attacker's pocket, the one he has kept there for emergencies until this has all blown over. He puts the letters down on the table and opens the laptop. Dave pretends to log in but a foul aroma of cigarette smoke touches his nostrils and he looks up. Coming towards him in slow steps is the ragged figure of Daz, the heroin addict who works for Leatherhead. They spoke a week or so back – he delivered Our Dave a message.

"I broke in last night," says Daz. "I climbed on the flat roof and forced the window open. I wish I'd thought of it before." Our Dave considers the skag head with his grubby tracksuit and his hands in his pockets as he melts out of the darkness.

"What can I do for you, Daz? Have you come to give me another message?" he asks.

"I have. It's like a final eviction." Daz's eyes blaze and Our Dave can see that he is no longer the lad who once fixed a cam belt on a VW camper at Richmond Street garage. There's something running through his veins, perhaps a combination of smack and high strength lager, maybe some spice.

"How long have you been here?"

"I got in about an hour ago."

"I see," says Our Dave. He can smell spirits from Daz as the man stands in front of him. "So, what's your message?" Daz grins and shows off his black teeth, squints his eyes and removes a dull looking hammer from his tracksuit pocket.

"This is your message," he answers. Our Dave does not move from the office chair he sits in. He's not afraid, more disappointed. He invested in Daz. He bought him cups of tea in Chants Ave Café, pints in the pub along the way, gave him time and listened to him explain his problems, all in the hope that Daz would become useful to himself and useful to the world, and maybe, useful to Our Dave. He got him the job at Richmond Street Garage, lent him money till payday, gave him a coat in the winter, and lots more.

"Are you going to do me in with that?" he asks.

"I am," answers Daz. Our Dave sighs.

"Are you sure you're capable? I mean, I might be in my sixties, Daz, but you're a mess. I'm impressed that you can stand up straight, let alone do me in with a hammer." The man attempts a nasty smile, again, and shows his blackened teeth.

"You think I'm an idiot, Dave, you always did. You thought you could use me like you use everyone else down this street. I'm not here for you to take the piss out of."

"I never wanted to take the piss out of you, Daz. I wanted to help you, that's what I wanted all along. That's how I started. I know there's an honest part of you in there somewhere, but there's also the gear running through your brain cells. Take a minute. Have a cig. Calm down and we'll have a chat, like we used to."

"I'll get ten grand for doing this," he says. "Leatherhead has promised me ten grand and the chance to deal for her."

"You'll get nicked for doing this. Daz, you can't even see straight, and you couldn't deal, you'd be dead in a week from taking too much of the shite you'd be meant to sell." Daz steps forward and he's shaky.

"You can't fix everyone, Our Dave. You can't fix this street and you can't fix me, you can't fix yourself because you can't fix what's happened in the past either. Leatherhead told me about you and what you've done – the people that suffered at your hands."

Dave's face creases. He feels remorse.

Many a fool has spoken wise words. What's this all for anyway? It's just a game to Our Dave, perhaps to see if he could get away with it, but the money gave him power to be someone more than he would otherwise have been. He could afford to pay the rent on his mam's council house, he could take Hazel on holiday to Spain, he could buy a round of drinks for his friends, then he could buy his brother a car and pay for Christmas. He was someone. That's what this life has been about – it was never the money. His brain comes back to thin and dirty Daz standing in front of him with a nail hammer in one of his hands. Our Dave will defend himself.

"You better get on with it then," he says.

Daz reaches his left hand into his pocket and yanks out a yellow plastic gun with a blue tipped barrel. This is a standard issue police taser and Daz was given it by Leatherhead yesterday morning. She instructed him on how to use it and

192

explained that the settings were on maximum so that Our Dave would receive the full amount of charge. Leatherhead also explained that a man Our Dave's size would not be incapacitated for long, and so Daz ought to get to work with the hammer quicker rather than later. Leatherhead cautioned Daz also on Our Dave's past and his reputation for violence himself in the late seventies and early eighties, should he not give the old man the full extent of the hammer's benefit, Daz could be in danger himself.

Our Dave has a look of concern when he sees the yellow plastic with the blue tipped barrel. He knows what it is straight away. Before he can stand up, Daz has pulled the trigger and two prongs fire from the barrel of the plastic taser, streaming across the six-foot gap between the two men. The first needle strikes Our Dave in his chest through his checked shirt while the other hits him in his solar plexus. The electric charge surges into Our Dave's body straight away and his muscles contract in a tight movement that makes him grit his teeth and yell out in pain and shock. Daz steps in with the hammer in his right hand raised above his head, his rotten teeth are barred and his eyes are raw with menace.

A single gunshot roars out into the early morning of Chants Ave. The crows on the trees in the cemetery take to the sky all at once. It must be a car misfiring.

Bev stands in the doorway to the office of Avenue Cars with the silver snub nosed pistol in her hands. Her face is smooth and steady, her nostrils flared. Opposite and slumped against the wall is Daz. His chest has been blown open by the gunshot wound and his eyes are wide. Our Dave sweeps away the little prongs that are embedded in his chest and stands up. He looks first to the body dying against the wall and then to Bev in the doorway.

"I came back to drop the car off. It's in your name. I heard him talking. I remembered the gun in the drawer under the microwave." Her voice sounds apologetic. She steps forward as she lowers the weapon, her eyes are confused at what she's done and her brain races forward as to what will happen to her. There is a wide splat of blood on the wall behind where

Daz is slumped and his head is at a funny angle.

"Take a deep breath," says Our Dave to her. "Just breathe. This is all going to be fine, you'll see. I know what to do."

Our Dave does know what to do.

He's done it before.

Anne Leatherhead is having her hair dyed. She's complained about the roots showing through for a few weeks and because Kasia does everything else around the pub and the business, she also helps to do her hair. Leatherhead has opted for a very dark auburn. She sits in a chair with her head leaning over the sink and towels over her shoulders. Kasia has already applied the dye and they have left it for half an hour while she had a cup of tea and Kasia swept up.

"It looks much better on the box, it always does," says the old woman into the sink. A drip of the dye runs down her forehead and splats onto the white porcelain below her. She and Kasia have done this many times. She can hear the Polish girl behind her getting ready with the shower head from the bath. Leatherhead is too old and unsteady on her feet to get into the shower to do this on her own; she's actually too lazy and too fat.

"And I don't want no streaks like you did last time. I want a smooth colour, like the picture on the box." Leatherhead grumbles at Kasia, like she usually does. The red headed woman takes the pistol from her apron pocket and holds it pointing downward with her finger over the trigger. Her face is impassive as she wraps a towel over and around the barrel, she hopes to deaden any of the sound the shots will make. Kasia approaches the old woman with her head over the sink.

"Are you ready?" she asks.

"Just get on with it," answers Leatherhead. Kasia holds the barrel of the gun just below the back of the old woman's head and squeezes the trigger three times, one after another, to make sure the job gets done. The shots are muffled.

Blood and hair dye splatter the sink.

It's not like she didn't have it coming.

CHAPTER TWENTY-THREE
Dilva

Dilva found Aziz an hour earlier, laid back in his armchair with his mouth wide open, the TV on silent but the screen flickering with pictures from the Kurdish news channel. His skin was pale and cool, his eyes closed, there were long pauses between his breaths and his stomach moved less than his chest. She called the number on the card the nurse left but nobody answered, so she called an ambulance. Dilva answered the questions as best she could, but the woman on the other end was short with Dilva when she said she didn't understand so many times.

That was twenty minutes ago. She waits for the ambulance and settles next to him, kneeling on the floor holding his hand in hers, and with her head on the armrest looking up at him. She does not wake the children.

Dilva has seen people die before.

Not as peacefully as this.

At least here, Aziz is with the only family he has left, even if they are not really his family at all, and even if he cannot feel Dilva's warm hand holding his or see her big brown eyes looking up at him. She wishes she had talked to him more, not about the day-to-day things they discussed, but about his life back in their country, about his wife and his son and his daughters who are long gone. He kept his sadness well hidden, just as she has tried to keep her horrors inside her. She wishes also that she had told him of what she saw and what happened to her; perhaps he's the only one who would understand it. When he is gone, she will not know which way is up and which way is down.

It's five in the morning and there are silent blue lights down Westbourne Ave. In the calm of the early morning the flashing of the ambulance is noiselessly eerie, parked up outside Dilva's house. The paramedics are swift and kind, they are a fat man with a beard and a middle-aged woman with curly hair and a high voice. It does not take them long to work out that Aziz needs to be in hospital and that time is short. Dilva tries to explain about his condition and about the visit from the hospice a few days before. The fat man has tattoos up his arms and gentle eyes as he listens to her explain. The woman readies a green medivac chair that they will use to transport Aziz to the back of the ambulance.

"We'll have to take him in," says the woman.

"I have children upstairs," she says. "I can't go."

"He'll be in safe hands,"

"He will be alone," she answers. "It's better if he dies here."

"I don't think he'll die, love. He's breathing badly but he's got a pulse. If we take him to the hospital there's every chance for him. He can't stay here."

"I need to be with him," says Dilva.

"You can ring up later in the morning." The kind middle aged woman with curly hair is earnest. She does this job because she can make a difference in the world with it, Dilva can see that she is not lying. There's the sound of the front door opening and the clump of boots as someone walks down the hall then turns into the front room.

"I came as soon as I saw the lights," It's Ryan. Dilva looks up at the man from next door who she tried to kill a few weeks ago. She does not know what to say to him.

The paramedics gently lift Aziz onto the green chair, keeping him covered with his blanket. His head flops backwards. They turn the chair and the fat man goes carefully as he pulls him out of the living room and down the hall to the door. Dilva does not know what to do.

"I must be with him," she repeats.

"I'll stay here," says Ryan. "I'll get the kids ready for school."

"They will know what to do," says Dilva up at him. Her face is pale.

"It'll be okay," he says, not knowing if it will be or not. This is Ryan. He does not know quite what he is doing or why he is doing it. His stomach feels it's the right thing to do. His life is changing before his eyes. This woman is the catalyst for it and he's not afraid, perhaps for the first time in years.

When they have lifted Aziz into the ambulance, Dilva hangs back at her front door with Ryan standing inside.

"Keep them safe," she says. He nods and she feels what she did not think she could ever do again – trust. It gives her courage.

"Call me when you can," he says down to her. She nods, and then reaches up to embrace him, her arms go around his back and she hugs him tight to show that she is grateful. Ryan watches her get into the ambulance and sees it drive off before he closes the door.

"Is he your partner," asks the curly haired lady in the ambulance.

"Yes," she says.

CHAPTER TWENTY-FOUR
Loose ends

Our Dave has parked the Ford Galaxy in the car park overlooking the lonely river Humber. It's windswept and deserted on a grey and overcast day like today. He walks up to the pub with his hands in his jacket pockets and his collars up against the light drizzle. Reaching to the other side of the river above him, is the mighty Humber Bridge. It's midafternoon. They call this the Country Park, it's empty today but there's a forest that can at times be full of dog walkers and weekend runners. The pub is soulless and afraid, overlooking the huge, flat dirty river in front. It's a good place to meet folk from out of town - the motorway is close. Our Dave has asked Robbo Doyle to meet him in the far car park behind the pub because it's quiet.

Our Dave walks past the old windmill painted black and goes round to the rear of the pub, past the smell of grease from the kitchens and the bins, he walks further along the side of the wide river and there, parked facing away from the water is a long black Lexus. The back windows are tinted and the car has a sleek, tapered design, it looks new.

As Our Dave approaches, a man gets out the back. He's not quite what you'd expect. He's small and with a mod haircut, a pointed nose, tight black jeans and a leather jacket. This is young Robbo Doyle putting on aviator sunglasses as he gets out, even though it's overcast.

"Alright," he says in greeting. "I take it you're Our Dave." His accent is thick and nasal, pure Manc with a ring of honesty to it as well. He reminds Our Dave of his granddad, Doyle senior straight away. There are other men in the car, but it's clear that rockstar Doyle here will do the talking.

"That's me." Our Dave holds out his hand and they shake. The younger man's grip is firm.

"I've got something for you," he says and he beckons Our Dave to the boot of the sleek Lexus. It could be something nasty, Mancs might be all friendly but they can be rotten just as quick. Our Dave figures that if they are going to shoot him, there's not a lot he can do about it. The smaller man opens up the boot and there, with a bit of grey gaffer tape across his mouth, is curly haired DI Lyndsey with his hands are tied. His eyes are wide and frightened. "What do you want us to do with him?" asks Doyle.

"He works for you, doesn't he?"

"He did, but he was shite. This is your town, so he's your problem." Doyle can see that Our Dave is not sure what to do so he closes the boot. The two men turn and look out across the Humber. Far to the other side are the green hills of Lincolnshire, before that is the grey dirty water and a lifeless buoy bobs halfway out. The bridge stretches to the other side and the two big towers make it look industrial and ugly.

"I thought you'd be a bit more like your associate, Charles Boyce." Doyle scoffs at this.

"I may have inherited a business from my dad and his granddad, Our Dave, but I'm still a working-class lad. You can't do what I do if you're not willing to get your hands dirty."

"You liked him well enough to help him. Those were your lads who visited town, we're they?"

"He paid for them. I was just the middleman. It was just business."

"It's not always business though, is it? You need relationships. You need to trust people and know who you're dealing with." Doyle nods and takes off his aviator glasses. He has piggy, intelligent eyes.

"That's what my granddad used to say."

"I knew him, from way back," says Our Dave.

"I gathered. I knew him as well."

"Probably not like I did."

"Probably not." Robbo is more his grandfather than Our Dave could have imagined. He's got the humour and the spirit of the man.

"Did he ever tell you about this place?" asks Our Dave. "Did he tell you about Hull?" Doyle looks over the muddy water, past the ugly bridge to the petrol plant in the far distance on the other side.

"He said it was best left alone. There wasn't much worth

coming for. The best thing you can do here is leave." Our Dave has heard worse.

"He was a good lad, your granddad, a very good lad." Our Dave does not have to lie here. They were friends.

"How did you know him?"

"There are only so many people in the north of England who are prepared to shoot someone in the back of the head. Your granddad could do it, and so could I. Sorry to hear about your dad, by the way."

"Don't be. It was time he shuffled on. The world's changing."

"It's always changing. I never meant to get into this game, Robbo. I was like your granddad, just a kid off the street who saw how to make a few quid. It wasn't so I could buy myself anything, there's nothing I want. It was so my mum could pay her rent, so she could buy herself a new dress, so I could buy the lads in the pub a drink. That's what it's about now, too."

"You shouldn't be in business, Our Dave, with an attitude like that. How have you survived?"

"I don't know. It's just what I do and I can't let anyone down, not ever. Your granddad left me alone and I left him alone too."

They look at each other. Doyle nods.

"I guess that's how I'll play it as well," says Robbo Doyle. Our Dave holds out one of his big hands. They shake.

"Do you want this bent copper?" Our Dave wrinkles his nose.

"Go on then," he answers like it's another pint on a Sunday afternoon. Doyle opens the boot once more, he and Our Dave fish curly haired DI Lyndsey out the back and stand him on the gravel of the car park on his shaky legs. Doyle goes to the back door of the Lexus leaving Our Dave holding up the copper.

"If you need anything, give me a call, won't you?" says Our Dave, like he's a next-door neighbour and this man might one day need a hand with lifting a heavy sofa.

"I will," says Doyle. He gets into the car. The engine starts up and it drives away leaving Our Dave holding DI Lyndsey by the arm. There's a light drizzle. Our Dave goes to take the gaffer tape from DI Lyndsey's mouth and stops. He remembers how much the man goes on.

"Are you going to be a good lad, officer?" he asks. DI Lyndsey nods. "There's no need for us to be enemies. We can help each other. That's what we do in this town. That's how we get by, do you understand?" DI Lyndsey nods again. Our Dave can see he'll need a little training to get right, but he's got plenty of time.

"I'll buy you a pint. There's a new landlady at the Dairycoates Inn. I think you should meet her."

Bev is nervous as she waits. She sits on an iron bench in the arrivals lounge of the airport with her hand resting on a black trolley bag. Her features are smooth and her blue eyes are beautiful with dark eyeliner. She's had her hair done and it's sleek blonde to her shoulders. Bev caught the plane from Leeds-Bradford airport in the early morning with the ticket Our Dave bought her, and the flight took an hour and fifteen minutes to get to Amsterdam. She felt like she could vomit. Bev has taken advice from Chloe about what to do, there should be no drinking prior to meeting him, the perfume she wears should be young and fresh, she should smile and make eye contact and not swear so much. Lars knows her and she knows him, even if they have never met. Bev confessed her fears to her daughter, what if he's fat, what if he doesn't look like his pictures, what if he doesn't turn up, and Chloe, as wise and calm as any eighteen-year-old explained that meeting him was the only course of action to take and the only way she could find out the truth. Bev is not sure she wants the truth.

The last message she had from him was 15 minutes ago saying that he would be late. She dare not text back and, sitting in the arrivals area, she can feel eyes upon her. There's the male cleaner emptying the bin from the corner of the lounge, the man in a sharp suit waiting a few benches away. They will not do anything, but their eyes are on her, she is a good-looking woman, alone, waiting for someone.

The minutes drag on.

She looks at her phone and then slips it back in her handbag. What else did she expect? She is a poor lass from a run-down northern town. She has a string of failed relationships behind her. She is in her early fifties. What did she think would happen with a man she met online in another country? Chloe was right. So, chin up.

Bev stands. She will go to the office, change her ticket and get the first plane back. She'll be in Hull in a few hours. Perhaps this time she will learn not to dream, or rather, not let them become her master.

At the airline desk she presents her ticket to the lady. Lars had said he was looking forward to meeting her. He did not seem overly excited, but he was keen to pick her up from the airport. More than anything, Bev is embarrassed. There's that rash of emotion that runs up her neck and across her jawline and into her cheeks, a reminder that there are winners and losers in this world, and she is one of the losers.

There's a light cough behind her. "Are you leaving already?" It's a man's voice. "Bev? Is that you?" Before she turns, she gives a smile from the corner of her mouth. Whatever happens from here on in, he is real, and Bev was not wrong – for once.

She swivels on her heel.

He is six foot perhaps, neck length wavy blonde hair, a white smile and a stubble. It's the same Lars from the photos. Not quite as attractive, but real. It's true.

"The traffic was bad," he says.

Bev smiles.

Printed in Great Britain
by Amazon

41282879R00118